JOY

KERRY BOOK SERIES BOOK 4

CAROL CANNON

"Consider it pure joy, my brothers and sisters,
Whenever you face trails of many kinds,
Because you know that the testing
of your faith produces perseverance."
James 1: 2-3 (NIV)

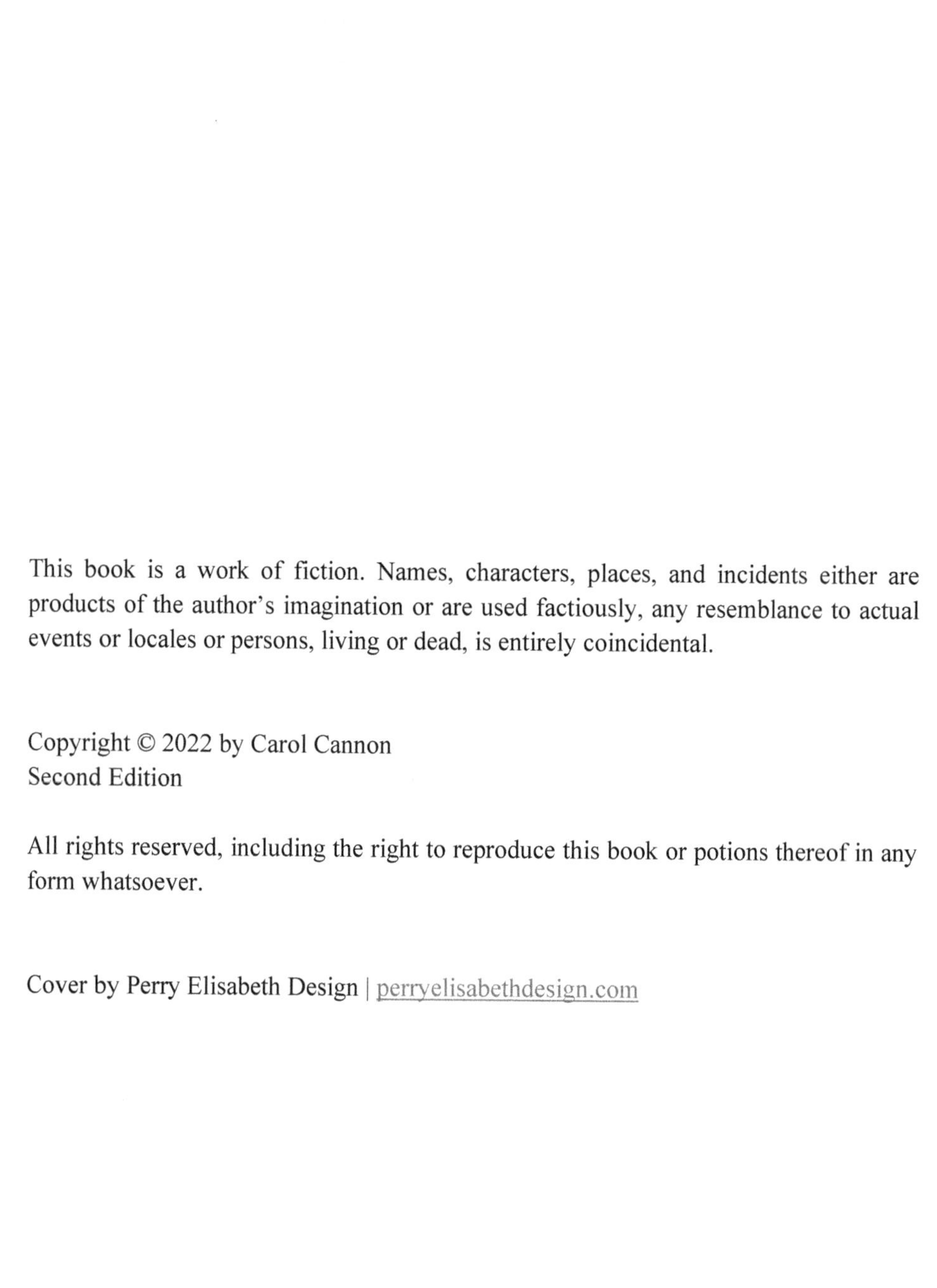

Cover by Perry Elisabeth Design | perryelisabethdesign.com

I dedicate this book to my girlfriends,
those old and those new,
those near and those far,
you know who you are!

List of Characters by Family				
Fearsome Foursome	Layne Bryson Clairmont Weaver	Nona Jane Foxx-Harris	Dixie Rae Randolph Bradley	Betty Jo (Elizabeth Jolene) Chapman Breedlow
Husband	Mark	Bill (William) (Divorced)	Alex (Alexander)	Don (Donald)
Child	Nathan Heather (wife) Grayson (son)	Grace Adrian Bannerman (husband)	Hailey Josh Merrill (husband) Kaiden (daughter) Alexa (daughter) Rae (daughter)	Ethan Chloe (wife) Kelli (daughter) Matthew (son) Chase (son)
Child	Blair Zeke Coby (husband) Rachel (daughter), Madison (daughter)		Jason	Lily Matt Morton (divorced) Kendall (daughter)
Child	Aaron Jenny (fiancé)			

Chapter One

Betty Jo checked her watch for what seemed like the tenth time in an hour wondering if her shift on the pediatric wing would ever end. She'd realized too late that it had been a mistake to accept this job. She should have turned it down, but Marci, the charge nurse, had begged her for her help. She hated to let Marci down. Since she'd retired from her nursing position at the hospital over five years ago, she'd been called two or three times a week to fill in when a nurse couldn't make her shift, or the hospital needed extra hands. Usually, she enjoyed working at the hospital, especially in the Pediatric Wing, but today was different. Her mind was consumed with all she needed to get done at home before her son Ethan and his family arrived.

Betty Jo's son Ethan was a lieutenant colonel in the United States Air Force and until a few days ago had been stationed at the Pentagon. He had lived in the Washington, DC, area with his wife, Chloe, and their three children, Kelli, Matthew, and Chase, for almost five years. The job he'd held at the Pentagon had been highly classified, so neither Betty Jo nor her husband Don knew exactly what his duties were. They did know that he enjoyed his job. A few months ago he'd received orders to report to the Naval Submarine Base at Kings Bay, Georgia, to head up a confidential collaboration project between the Air Force and Navy.

Betty Jo knew Ethan was excited about the possibility of a promotion that might come along with the move. What excited her the most was the possibility of seeing her grandchildren more than twice a year now his family was moving to Georgia. Both she and Don wanted to be a part of their grandchildren's growing-up years. Neither her parents nor Don's had lived close to them as Ethan and his sister Lily were growing up. She'd always felt sad that her children had missed out on that special bond between grandchild and grandparent. She felt she had that bond with Lily's daughter Kendall and wished to have it with Ethan's children. There was one obstacle that could keep her from getting her wish—Chloe, Ethan's wife.

"Betty Jo?"

At the sound of her name, Betty Jo was brought out of her reverie. Looking up from her position at the nurses' station, she saw Marci standing on the other side. "Oh, my goodness, Marci. I was so lost in thought that I didn't even notice you were standing there."

Coming around the nurses' station to stand next to Betty Jo, Marci patted her on the back, "No problem. I just came to thank you for helping me out today and to let you know that the evening shift nurses are here to take over."

Betty Jo turned to gather her purse and sweater from the shelf behind her. "You're so welcome, Marci. I was glad I could help out."

As she hurried down the hall, she called back, "I'm sorry to rush off, but I need to get home. My son and his family are coming to stay for a few days. I have some things to finish up before they get here."

Leaving the hospital, Betty Jo paused to put on her sweater. It was a beautiful October day with a slight chill in the air. As she walked to her car, she breathed in the fresh air while taking in the splendor of the changing leaves on the trees surrounding the parking lot. Once Betty Jo was settled in her car and on her way home, her thoughts turned to the problems she had with Chloe. She wondered why it was that the two of them had never seemed to click. She'd met Chloe for the first time at Ethan's graduation from Virginia Military Institute. She and Don had been so proud of their son graduating with honors and were looking forward to meeting his new girlfriend, who was the sister of one of his roommates. Betty Jo could tell by the way he'd talked about her during their weekly phone calls things were getting serious between the two of them. She made the decision before she ever met her that if Chloe was special to Ethan, then Chloe would be special to her.

Betty Jo had to admit that when she'd caught sight of Chloe and Ethan as they rounded the corner of the restaurant where they were meeting, she hadn't been prepared for the tall, thin girl on her son's arm. Chloe was not at all like she'd pictured her. When Ethan told her about his girlfriend, she'd imagined a girl. This was not a girl. This was a woman with a shapely figure and midnight-black hair that flowed over her shoulders and contrasted with her porcelain skin. Her eyelashes looked like velvet surrounding her azure-blue eyes. She was wearing a simple, sleeveless, black shift dress with a pearl necklace and earrings to match. Betty Jo couldn't remember when she'd seen a more beautiful woman.

Ethan had made the introductions. "Mom, Dad, I'd like you to meet Chloe Bristol."

Betty Jo remembered how Chloe, with great formality, had reached out her hand toward Betty Jo. "It's a pleasure to meet you, Mrs. Breedlow."

Betty Jo was at first confused by Chloe's heavy Boston accent. She assumed she'd have a Southern accent since she was from Virginia. Her confusion caused her to hesitate an awkward moment too long, which left Chloe's out-stretched hand dangling empty in front of her. Flustered, she finally took Chloe's hand in hers, pumping it up and down, over and over as if it were the first time she'd ever shaken anyone's hand. "The same here. I mean, I'm glad to meet you too, but you sure aren't what I expected." As soon as she said the words she wanted to take them back.

Chloe raised an eyebrow as she pulled her hand away. "Oh, really? What, exactly, were you expecting?"

Her question caught Betty Jo off guard. She began to babble. "I guess a. . . Southern girl and you don't sound Southern at all, you know with your accent and all and you're definitely not a girl. I mean you're obviously a girl, well a female, but you're more of a woman. . . a rather beautiful woman at that." Recalling how she'd sounded like a country bumpkin who didn't know how to act in polite society still made her blush with embarrassment.

Chloe had stared at her for a few seconds, then she'd smiled stiffly. "Why. . . thank you. . .I think."

Don quickly opened the door to the restaurant. "I think it'd be a good idea if we all went inside instead of standing out here on the sidewalk."

They had a reservation, so were seated without delay. As soon as they settled in their seats, a waiter was there to take their drink orders. Don insisted on ordering champagne to celebrate Ethan's graduation. Betty Jo recalled her surprise when Chloe ordered a double vodka martini, but she kept quiet when she really wanted to ask her why she needed an alcoholic beverage to go along with an alcoholic beverage. Instead, she began making what she thought of as polite conversation. "I understand both of your parents are doctors, Chloe."

"Yes, they are."

Betty Jo waited for Chloe to offer more details, but when she didn't, she followed up with another question. "Are they general practitioners, or do they specialize?"

Chloe took a long drink from her martini before answering. "Of course, Mrs. Breedlow, they specialize. My father is an orthopedic surgeon and my mother is an ophthalmologist." After taking another drink, she added, "I understand you're a nurse."

Even though Chloe didn't say the word "just," Betty Jo heard it in her tone. She took a deep breath before she smiled and answered, "Yes, I am."

"And a darn good one at that," Don added as he'd reached over to give her hand a squeeze. "Now, let's order before we all starve to death."

It seemed that their first encounter had set the tone for her relationship with her daughter-in-law. Maybe it was the way she'd reacted to Chloe's appearance and accent or how she'd held onto her hand too long that had given Chloe the wrong impression. Maybe she hadn't measured up to what Chloe had expected either. Now, her great hope was that since they would be living closer to one another, she and Chloe could get to know one another better and possibly become friends. Don warned her about putting such high expectations on their relationship improving simply because they would be living in the same state, but she couldn't seem to stop herself. After all, anything was possible.

As Betty Jo pulled into her driveway, her thoughts returned to her list of all she needed to get done before Ethan and his family arrived. Grabbing her things, she hurried out of the car and into the house. She kicked off her shoes and dropped her purse on the counter as she entered the kitchen. She stopped in her tracks as she took in the scene before her. Their breakfast dishes from this morning were still on the table exactly where she'd left them. Added to the dishes was a stack of mail with the opened newspaper spread out across the table. The frying pan with congealed bacon grease was sitting on the stove top. As she was rushing to get ready for work that morning, Don had promised to clean up the kitchen for her. She'd trusted that he would. It was evident that her trust in his promise had been misplaced. She looked over at the clock on the stove to see that it was almost five o'clock. Ethan had said last night when they'd talked that they would be there around five thirty. The last thing she wanted was for Chloe's stay with them to start off in a dirty kitchen.

Anger began to build up inside her as she gathered dishes from the table. She called out to her husband, "Donald Breedlow!"

There was no answer. Unless he had suddenly gone deaf, there was no way he hadn't heard her call his name. As she put the dishes in the dishwasher, she called out once more, "Don, you'd better get in here to help me right now!"

Still no answer. She fought down the panic she was beginning to have deep in the pit of her stomach. When Don didn't answer her immediately, her thoughts changed from anger to worrying she might find him passed out in a diabetic coma. It was a recurring concern of hers ever since Don had been diagnosed with Type 1 diabetes. She quickly searched through the house. When she didn't find him in the house, she realized that there was a strong possibility that Don might be outside in his greenhouse or workshop. Now that she thought about it, he might not even be home. She'd been so preoccupied with her mental list of chores she needed to get done before Ethan's family arrived that she hadn't even looked to see if his truck was there when she pulled in the driveway. She walked to the kitchen window that looked out on their driveway. Don's blue 1959 Chevy Apache pickup truck he'd restored was parked in its usual place, but his new Ford F-150 was gone.

None of this was making sense to Betty Jo. It wasn't like Don to not clean up the mess in the kitchen and then leave home knowing that Ethan would be arriving soon. She reached for her purse and took out her cell phone, swiped the screen, and called him. At first, she was confused when she heard the University of Georgia fight song, Don's ringtone, coming from the table. But after moving several pages of the newspaper aside, she found his phone buried beneath. As the realization came to her that Don had left home without his phone, fear replaced the concern she'd been feeling. She was scrolling to her daughter Lily's number in her phone when she noticed a piece of paper with Don's handwriting on top of the stack of mail.

Ethan called. Won't be coming today. Going to spend a couple of days in Atlanta before heading our way. Kendall and I have taken the canoe down to the river for the day. Sorry about the mess. Will clean up when we get back.
Love, Don

With a heavy sigh, Betty Jo plopped her tired body down on the closest chair. She wasn't surprised that Don and Kendall, their twelve-year-old granddaughter. were together. Ever since Don had been diagnosed, he'd made it a point to take Kendall with him on whatever adventure he'd cooked up for the day. The two of them had become inseparable. However, she was surprised that he hadn't left a voice or text message on her phone instead of leaving her a note sitting precariously on a stack of mail. After all, there was a good chance she might never have seen it.

She recalled how she'd been consumed with thoughts of Chloe after she got off work. Had she even checked for messages? She looked down at the phone in her hand and found she did in fact have both a text message and voice mail from Don. How could she have been so preoccupied she hadn't even thought about checking for messages? She read the text and listened to the message. Both reiterated what she'd read in his note. She was relieved to know that Don was fine, but disappointed she wouldn't be seeing her son and grandchildren for a few more days.

Hoping to shake off her disappointment, she decided the best thing she could do with her time was to tackle the household chores she still needed to finish up before Ethan's family arrived. For the next two hours, Betty Jo worked to check items off her list. She was finishing mopping the kitchen floor when she heard Don's truck and trailer pull in the driveway. She hurried out the back door hoping to stop Don and Kendall from walking through her clean house with whatever mess they were sure to bring in with them from the river. She didn't know how they did it, but when the two of them got together they seemed to come home covered from head to toe in either dirt or mud.

Betty Jo shook her head as she watched her husband and granddaughter get out of the truck and walk back to the canoe. It was obvious from the way Kendall's long hair was matted down with leaves and dirt that she had fallen out of the canoe, probably more than once, and landed in the muddy river.

With her hands on her hips, Betty Jo called out to them. "What have the two of you gotten yourselves into this time?"

They looked up at her at the same time, then looked back at one another and began to laugh. Betty Jo waited for them to get their laughter under control so they could answer her question.

Still laughing, Kendall began her explanation. "Oh, Gigi, it turns out that this canoe just isn't as stable as Pops' boat. Every time I got a fish on the line and stood up to reel it in, I ended up swimming with the fish!"

Smiling, Betty Jo walked up beside her granddaughter. "Kendall, from the way you look, you must have spent more time in the river than in the canoe."

"Near about, but she managed to hold onto her rod and wrangle several fish in as soon as she got back in it." With a look of pride on his face, Don held up a string of fish as proof.

Putting her hands back on her hips, Betty Jo turned her attention to her husband. "So why is it you look like you spent some time in the river along with Kendall?"

"How do you think she got back in the canoe? Someone had to give her a push." He looked over at Kendall and the two of them laughed again.

Betty Jo gave each of them her stern, no nonsense look. "Well, you two laughing hyenas are not allowed to walk in my clean house like that!"

"I promise we'll hose off all traces of the river if you'll just bring us a couple of towels," Don said.

Betty Jo turned and began walking toward the house while Don and Kendall headed to the backyard to get the garden hose. She called back, "And don't think you're going to clean those fish at my spotless kitchen sink either." When she was safely in the house away from the two of them, she closed the door behind her and let out the laughter she'd held inside since she first saw her husband and granddaughter get out of the truck.

While Don and Kendall cleaned up, Betty Jo patted out hamburgers and cut up potatoes for supper. She'd already put the marinated steaks she bought the other day from Harris Grocery in the freezer to keep until Ethan's family decided they'd had enough of Atlanta and headed down to Kerry. Lily would be there soon expecting to have supper with her brother, niece, and nephews. Betty Jo realized that she probably should have called Lily to let her know the change in plans. She hoped Lily wouldn't be too upset she wouldn't be having supper with her brother.

"Is this better, Gigi?" Kendall stretched her arms out wide as she walked in the kitchen with her hair still wet from her garden hose shower. She'd already changed into clean clothes. Since Kendall spent many nights with her grandparents, she had extra clothes for times like this.

"Much better!" Betty Jo reached out to give her a hug. "You smell much better too!"

"What about me?" Don asked as he came up behind them.

"You? You need to take those hamburgers out to the grill."

"Hamburgers? I thought we were having steak."

The three of them turned to see Lily standing in the doorway.

Betty Jo released Kendall, who ran straight into her mother's arms and immediately began telling her about her day. "Mom, I had the best day with Pops. I kept falling out of the canoe every time I tried to catch a fish, and Pops had to keep getting out and pushing me back in, but I never lost a fish, not one. It was so much fun!"

Lily looked over Kendall's head to see her father smiling and her mother frowning. "I'll bet it was."

"Well, I'd better get these hamburgers on the grill." Don grabbed the plate of hamburgers and headed out the door.

"I'll help you, Pops." Kendall rushed out to join her grandfather.

Turning to her mother, Lily asked, "So, what happened with the supper plans? Where's Ethan?"

"They've decided to stay in Atlanta for a few days to see the sights before coming this way."

"Hmmm. That's interesting. I just talked to Ethan last night. He told me the kids could hardly wait to see us and he'd be here today." Lily picked up one of the raw potato slices and began to munch on it. "This has to be one of Chloe's brilliant ideas."

Betty Jo knew Lily had never been a fan of Chloe's. Chloe had made several hurtful comments to Lily when Lily had divorced Matt. Lily had also mentioned she didn't like the way Chloe treated Betty Jo and wanted to say something to Ethan about it, but Betty Jo had asked her not to for fear it could cause problems between Lily and Ethan.

Without looking at Lily, she hoped to divert the conversation away from Chloe. "You have to admit there are so many great places to visit in Atlanta. I'm sure Ethan wants to take the kids to the Georgia Aquarium and the Coca Cola Museum."

Lily chuckled as she gave her mother's shoulders a squeeze. "Okay, Mom, we'll go with that for now."

Betty Jo fried the potatoes while Lily fixed a salad. When Don and Kendall brought the hamburgers in from the grill, they sat down to supper without saying another word about Chloe or why Ethan's family was spending a few extra days in Atlanta instead of coming home to Kerry. Lily and Kendall hurried off as soon as they finished with supper. They'd offered to help Betty Jo clean up, but she'd sent them on their way. While Betty Jo cleared away the dishes, Don took care of putting away the canoe and fishing tackle. She was getting the kitchen back in order when he came walking in the back door.

Don put his arms around her as she stood at the kitchen sink. "I know you're disappointed that the grands aren't here with us tonight."

Drying her hands on the kitchen towel, she turned toward him. "I am, but I understand there's a lot more to do in Atlanta than here in Kerry."

He took a step back so he could get a good look at her face. "Now, you and I both know that isn't why they're staying in Atlanta instead of coming on down to Kerry."

"I know, but it helps me to think it could be the reason." Looking up at him, she added with a sigh, "We both know the real reason is Chloe. She doesn't want to be here with me and is keeping our grandchildren away as long as she can and by any means possible."

"I know." Don pulled Betty Jo in close. "We'll just have to make sure that when they do get here, they have more fun than they ever could have anywhere else."

Betty Jo wiped a tear from the corner of her eye.

"We can at least try."

<h1 style="text-align:center">Chapter Two</h1>

Betty Jo woke up to a rainy, dreary day. She'd tossed and turned most of the night and finally fell into a deep sleep around three. As usual, Don had gotten up early to go fishing with Mark at Lake Seminole. Most mornings he made so much noise getting ready she'd finally give up and get up herself. She was thankful he'd let her sleep in this morning. She had the strong urge to pull the covers up over her head and go back to sleep, but then remembered today was Tuesday—her favorite day of the week. The Skinny Dippers met on Tuesday.

Betty Jo and her three best friends, Layne, Nona, and Dixie—the Fearsome Foursome, as Layne's husband Mark called them—had been going through one of their "Get-In-Shape" phases when they first joined the Skinny Dippers weight loss program. That had been a little over nine years ago. They met once a week on the second floor of the Dream Bean Coffee Shop. They would weigh in, listen to a motivational message from their leader—whoever it might be at the time, then they'd head downstairs to the coffee shop where they'd each order one of the delicious muffins or chocolate donuts the Dream Bean was famous for and catch up on one another's lives. She hadn't planned on making the meeting this week because she was supposed to have had her grandchildren with her, but since those plans had changed so unexpectedly, she decided she would go.

She quickly showered, dressed, and was in her car on her way to the meeting when her phone rang. Looking at her car display, she saw it was Ethan calling. Maybe they'd changed their minds about staying in Atlanta and were heading to Kerry.

She cleared her throat in an attempt to keep the excitement she was feeling from her voice. "Well, hello, Ethan."

"Hi, Mom."

"What's up?"

"We're getting ready to head out to the aquarium for the day, and I just wanted to touch base with you to make sure you're okay with our change in plans."

"No problem," she lied. "I'm heading out as well. I've got so much going on today, so your change in plans really worked out for all of us."

"That's a relief. I was worried you'd be upset with us."

"No, it's all good."

"We should be there tomorrow evening sometime."

"That's great. I'll have supper for y'all when you get here."

"Don't go to any trouble. We can pick up something before we get there."

"It's no trouble at all."

"Sounds great, Mom. We'll see you then. Gotta go. Love you."

"Love you too."

She ended the call. The effort she'd put into that whole conversation to sound upbeat and positive left her drained. As she searched for a parking place, she considered her earlier plan of spending the day in bed. She was about to head home when a place opened up. She debated for a second, but finally decided to pull in. She knew deep in her heart what she needed now were her friends, not more sleep. She grabbed her umbrella, opened it, and headed to the back door of the coffeeshop. The rain was coming down harder than when she'd left home. As she reached out to push open the door, she ran smack into Nona, who was pulling in the door to leave.

"Oh, Nona, I'm sorry! I didn't even see you. Are you okay?"

Nona chuckled. "I didn't see you either. I'm fine. Are you okay?"

"I'm fine, but I'm getting wet. Are you leaving already?"

"I was, but now you're here, I'll stay. I haven't seen the others yet. Let's go in."

Nona shook the water from her umbrella. "Can you believe this rain?"

"No, but we sure needed it. Don's garden is about to dry up and blow away."

"I thought you weren't coming to the meeting today?"

"Change of plans. I'll tell you about it later." Betty Jo checked her watch. "We're late. I think we've missed the weigh-in."

"Well, as long as we don't miss the motivational speech."

They both laughed.

Nona turned to Betty Jo as a thought came to her. "You know what?"

"What?"

"I think we'd be a disruption going into the meeting late. Why don't we skip it all together and go straight into the Dream Bean?"

"Sounds like a good plan to me. I sure wouldn't want to be a distraction."

They left their dripping umbrellas by the door then hurried in to the coffeeshop.

Betty Jo and Nona took their usual places at their usual booth. They ordered coffee and then Betty Jo saw Layne and Dixie entering the shop. Nona waved them over.

Layne slid in the booth across from Betty Jo. "I'm surprised to see you here. I thought you'd be spending the day with your grandchildren."

"I thought I would too, but they decided to stay in Atlanta for a few days to see the sights."

Raising an eyebrow, Dixie took her seat next to Layne. "Oh, 'they' did, did 'they'?"

Layne leaned over the table. "We all know who the 'they' is that made the decision."

Betty Jo shrugged. "There's nothing I can do about it. She's the one in control."

"I can think of a few things I'd like to do," Nona said under her breath.

"I can too, but I don't think it'd help our relationship if I did them or let you loose on her."

They all laughed.

A smiling Anna Claire, their favorite waitress, came to their table with a pot of coffee to top-off Betty Jo's and Nona's cups. "Good morning to y'all. What can I get for you on this less than beautiful morning?"

Dixie gave her a warm smile. "And a good morning to you, Anna Claire. You can bring us our usual order. Thanks, dear."

"Y'all are my easiest customers," Anna Claire said with a laugh as she hurried back to the kitchen to put in their orders.

Betty Jo was appreciative of her friends' support, but she didn't want to talk about Chloe. Hoping to change the subject, she turned to Layne. "How are things going with the wedding plans?"

Layne's son Aaron was engaged to marry Jenny, a nurse he'd met when his father was in the hospital after a terrible accident. Their plan was to get married in Bowers, Indiana, Jenny's hometown, but Betty Jo hadn't heard if they'd set a date yet.

Layne hesitated before answering. "To tell you the truth, I'm not sure how they're going. Aaron and Jenny don't talk about it much. Every time I ask them if they've set a date, they just look at one another, smile, and say, 'Not yet, but we will.' I may just strangle both of them if they give me that answer one more time."

"Do you think there's a chance they might be having second thoughts about getting married?" Nona asked.

Without even taking a moment to consider the possibility, Layne shook her head. "No, I think they like things the way they are and aren't in any hurry to get married."

Dixie slapped a hand down on the table. "We need to think of something we could do that will ignite a fire in the two of them!"

Layne put her hand over Dixie's and gave it a squeeze. "I wish I knew what that was."

Dixie gave her a sly smile. "I'm going to do some thinking on that."

"Speaking of fire." Betty Jo turned her attention to Nona. "I hope the fire between you and Monty hasn't fizzled out."

Nona had been dating Michael Montgomery—"Monty" as he was known to his friends—since he'd represented her when her husband of over forty years filed for divorce.

Nona blushed as she looked down at the table. "No, I have to say that fire's burning pretty hot and bright."

Betty Jo leaned over to give her a little hug. "That makes me so happy."

"Me too!" chimed in Dixie.

"Me three!" Layne added. "You deserve some 'hot and bright' in your life."

They all smiled as Anna Claire walked up with their order and placed it on the table. "Enjoy, y'all!"

They bowed their heads and Layne said grace. "Dear Lord, we ask that you bless this food. We thank you for our friendship and may it grow ever stronger. Amen."

"Now, tell us how Mr. James is doing in his new place?" Betty Jo used her napkin to wipe the table where the chocolate had dripped from her warm donut.

Mr. James was Nona's father who had been diagnosed with Alzheimer's. Nona had moved in with him to help when he'd first been diagnosed, but his disease had progressed to the point where she could no longer take care of him at home. Two weeks ago, she and her brother Riley had moved their father to Homewood, a facility that specialized in caring for Alzheimer's patients. Betty Jo was sure it hadn't been an easy transition for any of them.

"Daddy has settled in and seems to be happy there. Actually, I think he's doing much better than I am." She took a sip of her coffee before continuing. "I called Grace to see if she wanted to help Riley and me move her granddad into his new place. You know, see where he was moving and all. She didn't take my call. I left her a message, but I haven't heard back from her."

Grace was Nona's only child, who took her Dad's side in the divorce and had refused to have anything to do with her mother for over three years.

Betty Jo noticed a tear slide down Nona's cheek before she quickly brushed it away. She gave her a sympathetic smile. "You did what you had to do, Nona, but I'm sure it's been tough for you."

Unable to speak, Nona simply nodded her head.

"I've got some good news," Dixie announced.

Layne leaned in closer to her. "Well, don't keep us in suspense."

Dixie beamed with pride. "Jason is doing so well with his rehabilitation that they're going to let him come home this weekend for a visit. This will be the first time he's been allowed to leave the NextStep Center since he committed himself."

Dixie and her husband Alex had been through a rough time with their son Jason, who had made some poor choices and almost died due to his drug addiction. He'd been through detox and was now at a rehabilitation center working to get his life back on track.

"That is good news, Dixie." Layne placed her hand over Dixie's.

Nona patted Dixie's other hand. "I know you'll be so happy to have him home again."

"Alex has warned me that I shouldn't make a big deal about it. I'm trying to stay low-key and not get too excited, but, as y'all know, that's hard for me to do."

Nona withdrew her hand. "I think Alex is right, Dixie. Jason needs calm and stability in his life now."

"I really am going to try my best. I've been praying nonstop that it will be a good weekend for all of us."

Betty Jo looked at Dixie with concern. "I'm just worried how Jason's going to react, since this will be the first time he's been back to the house since he almost died there of an overdose."

"Me too. It's one of my greatest concerns. That's why Alex and Josh totally renovated his room and bathroom. Hopefully, that will keep him from being haunted by any bad memories he might associate with those rooms."

Betty Jo smiled. "We'll all be praying for this to be a great weekend for your whole family."

Layne and Nona nodded in agreement.

Chapter Three

After leaving the Dream Bean, Nona went straight to Homewood to see her father. He'd requested a couple of books from his library that she wanted to take to him. She'd also gathered up a few things from the house that she wanted to put in his room in hopes they would make it feel less institutional. When she got to his room, her father was reclining in his chair and reading the *Atlanta Journal-Constitution*. She was thankful that he was still able to read. Dr. Davis had warned them that in most cases Alzheimer patients find it difficult to focus on the words when they tried to read. He said that often they would keep reading the same sentence over and over, unable to remember what they'd just read. Thankfully, that had not been the case with her father. She most often found him just like he was now– reclined and reading a newspaper or book.

Trying not to disturb her father, Nona placed the bags with the items she'd brought from home on the counter and began emptying their contents. When she'd finished, she walked over to his recliner. Standing in front of him, she spoke softly, hoping she wouldn't startle him. "Hi, Daddy."

Mr. James lowered his newspaper just enough so he could see over the top of it and stared at her with a questioning look. She waited and watched as recognition slowly come into her father's eyes and a smile spread across his face. Putting down his newspaper, he opened his arms to her. "Well, if it isn't my Nona."

Overlooking the fact that her father hadn't called her "my Nona" since she was in college, Nona went into his arms and gave him a hug and a quick kiss on his cheek. She was thrilled he'd recognized her at all. This was the first time he'd known who she was without her having to tell him since he'd moved to Homewood.

Nona pointed to the newspaper he continued to hold in his hand. "So, what's going on in the world these days, Daddy?"

"The same things that have been going on since the beginning of time–dirty politics, unrest, and pandemonium." Laying the newspaper aside and putting his recliner into the upright position, he turned his full attention on Nona. "What I'm most interested in is what is going on with my daughter these days."

Nona sat down in the chair next to her father's recliner. "I'm happy to report things are going well with your daughter these days, Daddy."

"Really?" he asked taking off his glasses and giving her a stern look. "If I recall correctly, your Constitutional Law Class with Doctor Peterson was kicking your behind last time we talked."

Nona almost laughed out loud. It'd been almost fifty years since she'd sat in Doctor Peterson's Constitutional Law Class, but her father was right. It had kicked her behind. Once again, she was amazed that he could remember a detail from so long ago and yet not remember what had happened recently. She hated what Alzheimer's had done to her father.

She patted his arm reassuringly. "I think I've got that class whipped, Daddy."

"Glad to hear it." With that, Mr. James picked up his paper and reclined his chair. Nona knew that was the signal their conversation had ended. Her father had often ended their conversations this way throughout her life. She continued to sit beside him watching him for a few more minutes before getting up and quietly leaving him to his newspaper and recliner.

As Nona got into her car, she checked the time. It was straight up noon. She decided since everyone would be heading out to lunch, this would be a good time to go to her Foxx and Foxx Law Firm office to check messages and answer emails. She'd turned most of her cases over to Nathan, her law partner, who was also Layne's oldest son. Since he handled much of the business, she didn't work on the day of her Skinny Dippers meeting. However, since she'd taken some time off to get her father settled into his new place, she gotten behind on a couple of her cases. She'd always prided herself in being ahead of the game and despised how she felt when she fell behind.

Her plan hadn't worked out as she'd hoped. The first person she saw as she walked through the door was her secretary Lily, Betty Jo's daughter. Lily had been hired by Nona's father when he was the senior partner in the firm. Nona had taken Lily as her secretary when he'd retired.

When Lily caught sight of Nona, she quickly stood. "Ms. Foxx. I'm surprised to see you here today"

"Well, truthfully, Lily, I'm just as surprised to see you here. I thought for sure I could sneak in here while everyone was out to lunch."

Lily held up a paper bag. "Sorry about that," she said with an apologetic smile. "I'm brown bagging it today."

"Why don't you just go back to whatever you were doing and pretend I'm not here? I need to catch up on my messages and email."

Nona headed to her office but suddenly turned around and added, "Please don't let anyone else know I'm here."

"Mum's the word!"

Nona walked in her office and closed the door behind her. She'd been in her office for about an hour and a half when she heard a soft tap on her door. Irritated by the interruption, she looked up from her desk. "Come in."

Lily pushed open the door. "I'm sorry to disturb you, but I just got a call from Mom that has me concerned."

Nona took off her glasses, giving Lily her full attention. "What is it?"

Lily hesitated. "I'm not exactly sure, but she said she needed me to come to her house as soon as I can get there. It's something about Ethan, but she wouldn't tell me what's going on."

"She told us this morning that Ethan and his family were going to spend a few days in Atlanta. Maybe they're coming down here earlier than she thought, and she wants you to help her get things ready."

"Maybe," Lily said shaking her head, "but Mom sounded upset, not happy. She'd be happy if they were coming here early."

"I'm sure every thing's okay, but you need to go on over there."

"Thanks," Lily said as she turned to leave.

"Lily?"

Lily turned around to look at Nona. "Yes?"

"Would you please let me know what you find out?"

Lily nodded. "I will."

As Nona watched her leave, she said a silent prayer for Betty Jo and her family.

After leaving the Dream Bean, Layne drove to Whitlock Assisted Living to check on her mother. Her mother had lived there for over six years since her father had passed away. She checked on her mother everyday either with a visit or a phone call. She used to visit in the afternoons, but since turning ninety-three her mother had started taking long afternoon naps. She changed her visits to the morning so she wouldn't interfere with naptime. Layne enjoyed her visits with her mother, but it hadn't always been that way.

Everyone called her mother Miss Louise. She was liked by most, but always seemed to have problems with Miss Tucker, who lived across the hall. Her mother was what many people would call a character. She had a great sense of humor and could entertain people with her stories, but she also had an opinion about everything and everyone, which she shared with anyone who would listen. Some people wanted to blame that on her age, but she'd always been that way. Layne's father used to say she had no filter. "If your mother thinks it, she says it!" He often had to come behind her to offer apologies and explanations to their friends and acquaintances. When he passed away, that job had fallen to Layne. She tried to do what her father had always done, but then one day she realized people were much more tolerant and forgiving of her mother's comments now she was in her nineties. She thought of it as one of the perks of living longer than most people.

Layne found her mother sitting in front of the muted television working the almost completed thousand-piece puzzle she'd brought her last week of London's Big Ben. A few years ago her mother had taken up the hobby of putting together puzzles. She was surprisingly good at fitting the tiny pieces together. The more complicated it was, the better she liked it. She said it kept her mind sharp. Layne had bought her a puzzle board so she could keep everything in one place. It fit neatly on the small table she pulled up next to her chair.

Before taking the chair next to her mother's Layne leaned over to give her mother a kiss on the cheek. "Hey, Mama."

Without acknowledging Layne's presence, she fumed, "I can't find the clock face. I've looked everywhere. It's the most important piece of this puzzle. Without it, the puzzle doesn't make sense."

Leaning over toward Layne, she took off her glasses and dropped her voice to a whisper. "I just know that miserable ol' Miss Tucker came over here while I was out and stole that piece just to drive me crazy!"

Layne cleared her throat to suppress a laugh. "Now, Mama, I can't imagine Miss Tucker would do something like that. Let me see if I can find it."

"Go ahead and look all you want. I'm telling you, it's not here!"

Layne began to search the area around her mother's chair for the missing puzzle piece. She was about to give up and admit her mother was right about Miss Tucker when she spotted the lone piece. Somehow it had gotten to the corner of the room. After retrieving it, she held it up. "Here it is, Mama."

"Well, I'll be! How did it get way over there?"

"Who knows, but what was lost has been found."

Layne handed the piece to her mother then sat back to watch as she completed the puzzle.

Her mother beamed with pride. "Ta Da!"

"Congratulations, Mama! It's beautiful."

"Thanks to you. I don't know what I'd do without you."

"Neither do I, Mama." Layne chuckled.

As Layne drove home after visiting with her mother, she was

consumed with thoughts about Aaron and Jenny. It didn't make sense to her they hadn't set a firm date to get married. If they were expecting everyone to travel all the way up to Bowers, Indiana, they needed to be making some decisions. Mark had warned her to stay out of it, but it was getting harder and harder for her to keep silent. She loved Jenny and couldn't think of a better match for Aaron. She could hardly wait for Jenny to become a part of their family, but it was obvious they weren't in any big hurry to make that happen.

Layne remembered how excited she'd been to marry Mark. They'd made practical plans to graduate, get jobs, work a couple of years in order to save enough money to buy a nice house, then get married. Things changed in a hurry when Mark was called to serve his country. They could have done the sensible thing and waited to marry until after he got out of the Army, but with the threat of his being sent off to war in Vietnam, they decided not to wait. They'd married only three days after graduating. Layne still considered it one of their best decisions.

Maybe that was the problem Jenny and Aaron were having about setting a date. There was no sense of urgency. Now that she thought about it, she was the only one feeling they needed to hurry up and get married. Maybe Jenny and Aaron were the ones being sensible. After all, they both had good jobs, were saving money to buy a nice house, and when they reached their goal, they'd get married. Until that very minute, Layne hadn't realized Jenny and Aaron were working the same plan she and Mark had intended to follow all those years ago.

Layne took a deep breath hoping it would help to calm her down and clear her head. She needed to take a break from thinking about that. Her worrying about it wasn't going to help anyone. Mark was right. She needed to stay out of it. She suddenly felt a weight had been lifted from her shoulders.

Layne was on her way upstairs to her bedroom to change her clothes when she heard the back door to the kitchen open. She couldn't imagine who it would be at this time of day. All three of her children were at work and Mark was off fishing with Don and Alex. She called out, "Hello?"

"Hello," Mark called back.

"Mark?"

Layne panicked. Something had to be wrong if Mark was home this early. When he'd left that morning, he'd told her not to expect him back home until late that night. She hurried back down the stairs and ran straight into Mark who was coming around the corner. He grabbed her just as she began to fall backwards.

"Good grief, Layne! Where are you going in such a hurry?"

She took a step back. "I'm just wondering what you're doing home so soon."

"Don got a call from Betty Jo asking him to come home. It has something to do with Ethan, but she didn't tell him what it was. She said she'd explain everything when he got home."

His answer caught Layne by surprise. "That's interesting. Just this morning, Betty Jo was telling us that Ethan and his family were going to stay in Atlanta for a few days."

"I guess their plans changed."

"Maybe so."

Betty Jo calling Don to come home worried Layne. Sensing something might be wrong, she said a silent prayer for Betty Jo and her family.

Dixie was relieved to see the UPS truck when she pulled into her driveway. Her decorator Sharon had ordered the comforter with coordinating curtains for Jason's bedroom. She'd worried they wouldn't arrive before his weekend visit, but now she could put the final touches on his bedroom renovation. She hurried out of her car and up to the truck.

Dixie called out in a sing-song voice as she approached the opened side door of the UPS truck. "Oh, Jackson, I can't tell you how happy I am to see you here today."

The UPS truck driver turned toward Dixie with a smile on his face. He was holding two large boxes in his arms. "Well, thank you, Mrs. Bradley. I don't usually get such a warm greeting when I make deliveries."

Dixie returned his smile. "I'm sure you make many people happy with your deliveries, but you're usually in and out so fast they don't get a chance to say it. I'm the lucky one today. I caught you in the act and was able to express my gratitude." Patting his arm, she added, "How about you carry those boxes on in to my house?"

"Yes, ma'am, I'd be glad to." Dixie opened the door and held it for him as he set the two boxes down on the kitchen island. "See you next time," he said as he turned to leave.

"Have a good day," she called after him, closing the door.

Dixie got the scissors out of the drawer by the sink and walked over to the boxes. She carefully opened the top box. The thick navy blue and white comforter sprang out of the box. She was thrilled to see the colors in the nautical design looked bolder and more vivid than they had in the picture from the catalog. She couldn't wait to see the coordinating curtains. She quickly opened the box and gasped as she pulled back the tissue paper to find a box filled with bright fuchsia curtains that were anything but coordinating.

Lifting one curtain panel from the box, she cried out, "ARGHHH!"

Dixie threw the panel back in the box, reached for her phone, and dialed Sharon's number. Sharon had been one of their daughter's best friends since high school. She was one of the top realtors in Kerry, but did interior decorating jobs on the side when business was slow. Dixie couldn't imagine she'd ordered fuchsia curtains on purpose. She just hoped it was a mistake that could be fixed before Friday.

"Hello."

"Good grief, Sharon, they're fuchsia!"

"Ms. Dixie? What's fuchsia?"

"The curtains are fuchsia! I opened the box with the comforter, which is absolutely gorgeous, by the way. Then I opened the other box and found these awful, horrid fuchsia curtains inside. Please tell me you didn't intend to order fuchsia curtains to go along with the nautical theme of Jason's room."

Dixie waited, allowing Sharon a minute to process the bad news.

"I promise you I did not order fuchsia curtains for Jason's room."

"Well, that's a relief, but what are we going to do now to get his room ready by Friday?"

"It's all going to be okay, Ms. Dixie. It'll just take a few phone calls. I assure you, the room will be ready when Jason gets there."

Dixie sighed. "I'm going to trust you'll have it all done by this Friday,

Sharon."

"You can trust me," Sharon said reassuringly.

Dixie ended the call feeling a little better about the situation, but not totally convinced Sharon could get it all together by Friday.

She'd just picked up the comforter box to take back to Jason's bedroom, when she heard what sounded like Alex's truck pulling in the driveway. He'd left early that morning to go fishing with Don and Mark. She didn't expect him home until late that night. Concerned, she put down the box and met Alex at the door.

"I didn't expect to see you this early. Is everything all right?"

Alex shook his head. "I'm not sure what's going on. We'd just settled in and were catching fish when Don got a call from Betty Jo telling him he needed to come home. So we pulled up anchor and came home."

"It must be something important for Betty Jo to interrupt your fishing trip. Do you have any idea what's going on?"

Alex shrugged. "All I know is it has something to do with Ethan."

"Ethan?"

"That's all I know, Dixie." Alex kissed the top of her head as he walked past her heading down the hall to his room. "I need to take a shower."

With disturbing thoughts racing through her head about what could be going on with Ethan, Dixie once again picked up the box. As she slowly walked back to Jason's room, she silently said a prayer for Betty Jo and her family.

Betty Jo had stayed longer with her friends at the Dream Bean than she'd planned. She was anxious to get home. There were a few more things she wanted to finish up before Chloe got there. She usually didn't stress out this much when her daughter-in-law was coming for a visit, but for some reason she had the feeling it was important that everything be the best it could be for this visit.

She was holding on to a secret hope that Chloe wouldn't be staying with them for very long. All she needed to do was convince Ethan to take

Chloe to St. Mary's to look for a place to live and leave the children with her and Don. She could imagine what fun it would be to reconnect with her three grandchildren without Chloe breathing down her neck all the time. She was deep in a daydream about the places she'd take them when she pulled in the driveway and slammed on her brakes, stopping short of hitting a parked car. She sat there with her heart pounding from the near accident when she noticed three towheaded children hurrying out of the house. She stared at them for a minute before she recognized her three precious grandchildren—Kelli, Matthew, and Chase—running toward her.

Betty Jo could hear their excited squeals of "Gigi" as they came closer. She opened the car door just in time to wrap them in her arms. "Oh, my goodness! I can't believe y'all are here!"

"We're going to live here!" four-year-old Chase announced.

Six-year-old Kelli corrected her little brother in the all-knowing voice of a big sister. "We're not going to live right here."

Chase stood back and stomped his foot as he declared, "Well, I am!"

Kelli rolled her eyes as she shook her head. "You can't tell him anything."

Betty Jo laughed out loud as she pulled them closer. "I've missed y'all so very much."

"Gigi, Daddy got an important phone call," five-year-old Matthew whispered in her ear.

"He did, did he?"

"Uh huh," Kelli said nodding. "That's why we left Atlanta this morning to come here instead of going to the Georgia Aquarium like Daddy promised."

With love filling her heart, Betty Jo looked at her grandchildren. "I'm sorry you didn't get to go to the aquarium, but I'm sure glad y'all are here now. Let's go in the house and find out what that important phone call was all about."

Taking Chase's and Matthew's hands in hers with Kelli following close behind, they headed to the house. Before they got to the door, it opened. Ethan stepped out and embraced his mother.

"Mom! It's so good to see you."

Releasing her grandchildren's hands, she hugged him back. "I'm glad to see you too, but a little surprised."

"I know you are. Let's go inside to talk. I'll tell you what I can."

The five of them walked in the house together. No sooner had they walked in the house than all three of the children began to beg to go in the backyard to play on the elaborate wooden play set Don had built for their daddy to play on when he was their age.

"It's fine with me, if it's okay with your Daddy."

All six eyes turned anxiously to their father.

Ethan put his hand to his chin, taking a minute to think about it, then smiled down at them. "Of course you can, but make sure you follow the rules we've talked about."

The three of them were out the door before he'd even finished his warning.

Betty Jo looked around, expecting to see Chloe. "Where's Chloe?"

"She's upstairs lying down." Ethan shook his head and sighed. "She's pretty upset."

"You're telling me she's so upset she has to lie down just because she didn't get to go to the aquarium?" Betty Jo asked with more irritation in her voice than she'd intended.

"No, it's not that." Ethan shook his head. "That's what I need to talk to you about. Why don't we sit down? I have something I need to tell you."

Ethan took a seat in his father's recliner. Betty Jo could tell by the tone of his voice that his news was serious. She wished Don were here but knew it would be hours before he'd be home. She sat down on the edge of the chair next to him, nervously waiting to hear what he had to say.

"What is it, Ethan?"

Ethan looked directly at her. "I won't be going to St. Mary's as planned, at least not right now. I got a call right after I talked to you this morning from the Pentagon alerting me, I've been issued new orders."

The first thought that popped into Betty Jo's mind was that he was being sent back to work at the Pentagon. Disappointment flooded through her as her dream of her grandchildren living closer to her faded away.

"I'm being sent forward TDY on special assignment."

She stared at her son in disbelief. Those were not the words she had expected to hear. "TDY? I know I've heard you use that term before, but I've forgotten what it means."

"TDY stands for a Temporary Duty Assignment."

Betty Jo nodded. "The temporary part sounds good to me. So, that means you'll only be gone a few days, right?"

Ethan hesitated. "Well, it most likely will be for more than a few days. A TDY can be anywhere from thirty days to six months, but we can hope that I won't be gone for long."

She looked at her son with concern. "Okay, we'll hope and pray it won't be for as long as six months. Now, tell me about the other part."

Ethan looked baffled. "What other part?"

"The 'special assignment' part."

"That's harder to explain, Mom." Ethan took a deep breath before continuing. "I'm not sure what the special assignment part is yet. I haven't been informed where I'm going or why. I do know this TDY is at the highest security level. I can only tell you I've been ordered to report to Kings Bay Naval Base by zero seven hundred tomorrow morning and from there will be transported to Langley Air Force Base."

"So, your TDY is Langley?"

Ethan lowered his head. "No. I will be transported from Langley to my TDY special assignment." He looked up at his mother. "Mom, that's all I can tell you."

Betty Jo's hands flew to her mouth as she realized the full meaning of what he was telling her. "Do you mean you could be sent overseas? Into a combat area?"

Instead of disappointment, Betty Jo was now filled with fear. If Ethan was being sent somewhere on special assignment at the "highest security level" it most likely meant he was being sent into a hostile area on a mission that was most likely dangerous. She pushed back the tears that threatened to fill her eyes. Ethan didn't want or need her tears right now. He needed her to be strong. She put a hand on his knee and gave it a squeeze to show her support.

Ethan reached over and took his mother's hand in his. "I'm sorry to spring this on you, Mom, but I thought it was best to tell you the news as soon as possible."

Betty Jo held onto his hand. "I'm glad you told me. It's just that it took me by surprise. It wasn't anything I was expecting."

Still holding onto his hand, she stood up. "Well, I think we've got some decisions to make before you have to skedaddle on out of here."

"Skedaddle?" Ethan chuckled. "Really, Mom? It's been a long time since I've heard anyone use that word."

"Truthfully, I can't tell you when I've ever said that word." Betty Jo joined in with his laughter.

The two of them stood in the middle of the living room with Ethan still holding onto his mother's hand, laughing uncontrollably, when out of the corner of her eye, Betty Jo noticed Chloe enter the room. With her hands on her hips Chloe asked, "What can be so funny at a time like this?"

Ethan immediately released his mother's hand and went to Chloe. "I'm sorry, I know there's nothing funny about what's happening here."

Betty Jo wiped the tears of laughter from her face. "I'm sorry too, Chloe. You're right, there's nothing funny about this situation."

Turning away from Ethan and Chloe, Betty Jo headed to the kitchen to get her cell phone out of her purse. "I need to call your Dad and Lily. I think this is a time to gather our whole family together."

When she reached the kitchen table, she sat down, lowered her head, and began to cry.

Chapter Four

Don, Betty Jo, Ethan, Chloe, and Lily were gathered at the kitchen table. Kendall had taken her three younger cousins outside to play. Betty Jo was still trying to wrap her head around the fact Ethan had to be at Kings Bay Naval Base by seven tomorrow morning for his flight to Langley Air Force Base where he would leave to go wherever it was they were sending him. "I can't believe they're sending you off without giving you much time to prepare."

"That's military life for you, Mom."

"You may be right about that, Ethan, but it just doesn't seem right for them do this to a man and his family."

Ethan took Chloe's hand in his. "Let's not dwell on the unfairness of the situation for now. We've got some tough decisions to make for our family."

"Do you have any idea how long you'll be gone?" Lily asked.

Ethan shook his head. "No way to know."

Stating the obvious, Don said, "It seems to me that your biggest concern is where Chloe and the kids will live while you're away."

Betty Jo had been thinking about their options since Ethan broke the news to her about his deployment. She knew what she had to do, but she also knew it wouldn't be easy for her or Chloe. However, she was sure it would be the best thing for the children. "Well, I think Chloe and the kids should stay here with us."

Chloe, who had been silently sitting with her head down, looked up in surprise. "That's a generous offer, but I think Ethan and I need to discuss this privately before we make our decision."

Smiling, Lily leaned in close to Chloe. "I know Kendall will be thrilled to have her little cousins here. Just think, Chloe, you'll have a babysitter anytime you want."

Don added. "We've got plenty of room here for everyone. You and the kids can have the run of the whole upstairs."

Betty Jo silently chastised herself for not realizing this was a decision Ethan and Chloe needed to make as husband and wife without any pressure from his family. "Of course, you should discuss this without us putting in our two cents." She looked to Don and Lily. "Why don't we leave these two alone? Let's go outside to check on the kids."

As Betty Jo stood outside watching her grandchildren playing, she couldn't keep her mind from going back in the house with Ethan and Chloe. She was sure Chloe would try her hardest to convince Ethan that staying with his parents while he was gone would be the worst place for her and the children. What she wasn't sure about was if Ethan could come up with a convincing argument as to why staying with his parents was the right decision. The sound of Ethan's voice broke into her thoughts.

"Mom, Dad, Lily. Would you please come back in the house? We've made a decision."

When Betty Jo walked back in the kitchen she sat down on the edge of the chair. Her heart went out to Chloe. She knew Ethan's leaving Chloe alone with three young children to handle on her own was going to be hard no matter where she decided to go. Betty Jo wanted Chloe to know if she stayed with them, she'd try to make things as easy as possible for her and the children while Ethan was gone. "I hope you'll stay with us, Chloe. We love you and will be here for you and the kids. We'll help out any way we can."

Chloe gave Betty Jo a smile. "We're going to take you up on your offer. I'm sure the children will be thrilled."

Betty Jo sat in stunned silence. She wondered if she'd heard correctly. "You're really going to stay with us?"

Ethan chuckled. "Yes, Mom, they're staying with you."

Lily clapped her hands. "I know I'm thrilled. I'm so happy you're going to stay."

Ethan stood up and took out his cell phone. "I'll call the movers and reroute them to Kerry."

Don headed out the door behind him. "It won't be a problem at all to have your furniture and other things stored until Ethan gets back. I can arrange for a storage building."

That left Betty Jo, Chloe, and Lily sitting at the table. The three of them looked at one another. "Well, what should we do?" Lily asked.

Betty Jo smiled. "Let's tell the children."

Before they could get up from the table, Kendall, Kelli, Matthew, and Chase came rushing through the back door. Breathlessly, Kelli asked, "Can we have an ice cream bar?"

Smiling, Betty Jo faced the children. "You sure can. Kendall can show you where they are."

Rolling her eyes, Chloe sighed loudly. "Now that your Gigi has given you permission to have an ice cream bar, you'll need to take them outside." She stood up and walked over to the children "But before you go, I have some big news."

Matthew's smile faded from his face. "Oh, no, not more big news."

"This is good big news, Matthew. We're going to stay here with Gigi and Pops while Daddy's gone," Chloe announced.

The room was suddenly filled with squeals and screams of delight. Betty Jo hoped and prayed they could all hold on to that excitement until Ethan returned.

Ethan came walking in the back door just as the kids were heading out with their ice cream bars in hand. He chuckled as he held the door open for them. "Now there go some excited youngins!"

Chloe met Ethan at the door. "And why wouldn't they be? I just told them that we're going to be staying here with their Gigi and Pops."

Ethan smiled as he kissed her cheek. "Well, it's all arranged. The movers should be here sometime Thursday or early Friday." He sounded relieved. "I was worried they were en route to St. Mary's with our stuff. Turns out they haven't even left."

Betty Jo patted Ethan on the back. "That is good news, Son. I'm sure your dad will take care of storing your things. In the meantime, we need to get busy with settling Chloe and the kids upstairs and getting you ready to leave early tomorrow morning."

"Before we start, I need to talk to you about something."

Betty Jo looked at him expectantly, waiting for him to continue.

"Privately."

Betty Jo gave her son a curious look as she went outside through the door he held open for her. She couldn't imagine what he needed to tell her that he couldn't say in front of Chloe and Lily. She sat down on the side porch step and patted the spot next to her for him to sit down. He remained standing.

"Mom, I can't thank you enough for letting Chloe and the kids stay here with you and Dad while I'm gone. That's taken a huge weight off my shoulders."

"You don't have to thank me. That's what family does for one another."

Betty Jo could tell there was something else on his mind he was having a hard time saying to her. She watched as Ethan used the toe of his shoe to dig out a stray rock that had found its way into the yard.

"I'm concerned about you getting along with Chloe while I'm gone."

Betty Jo stiffened, readying herself for what she feared was coming next.

"You sometimes overstep your boundaries with the kids, Mom. You need to remember that Chloe is their mother."

Ethan stopped kicking at the stone and looked over at her. "You have to let her make the decisions when it comes to the kids. I know it's hard for you to let someone else be in charge, but when it comes to the kids, you have to take a back seat or else Chloe might just pack up the kids and leave."

This was the first time Betty Jo could remember Ethan acknowledging there were problems between her and his wife. In her heart of hearts, she'd always hoped he saw Chloe as the one who caused the problems they'd had over the years. Many retorts to what he'd just said flew through her mind. It was hard for her not to defend herself and put the blame on Chloe. With great effort, she held her thoughts back. Taking a deep breath, she pushed the words away that might force her son to choose sides. She wouldn't do that to him or to herself. She closed her eyes and silently prayed, *Dear Lord, give me strength.*

Betty Jo opened her eyes and stood up. "I promise I'll try my best."

"I'm sure your best will be more than enough." Ethan reached out to embrace his mother.

Betty Jo returned his hug then stepped back and clapped her hands together. "We better get back inside. We've got a lot to do and not much time left to do it in."

They found Lily and Chloe seated at the kitchen table with glasses of iced tea. They stopped talking when they saw Betty Jo and Ethan. Lily looked at them. "Well, it's about time the two of you got back in here. I thought maybe y'all had left us."

"We were beginning to get worried," Chloe agreed.

When Betty Jo looked over at Chloe, she felt an understanding of trust pass between them. "Nope, we're still here and ready to get y'all moved in."

Lily turned to Chloe and Ethan. "I'll tell you what. I'll take the kids home with me. That way you'll have less to deal with while you're getting settled in."

"Oh, Lily, that would really be a big help." Standing, Chloe gave her a hug.

Lily hugged her back, then picked up her purse and walked out of the door calling to the children.

"Wait!" Ethan yelled as he hurried out behind Lily. "You'll need their car seats!"

Chloe looked at Betty Jo and shook her head. "I was so thrilled she was taking the kids that I totally forgot about their car seats. As usual, Ethan remembered. What in the world am I going to do without him here to remember all of those little things I forget?"

Betty Jo reached out and took her hand. "I know it's going to be hard, Chloe, but I'll be right here to help. Maybe between the two of us, we can handle those little things."

As Chloe gave her hand a squeeze, Betty Jo had to bite down on her tongue to keep from adding, *if you'll let me.*

Ethan, Chloe, and Betty Jo were on their third trip of unpacking Ethan's car and small trailer when Don drove up. The three of them, thankful for a break, watched as he got out of his truck.

Don walked over to the group. "What are y'all up to?"

Betty Jo's voice dripped with sarcasm. "Can't you tell? We're building a sand castle."

Ignoring her comment, he turned to Ethan. "I got you a whole storage building for your things. The best part is it's free."

Ethan stared at his father in disbelief. "Free? Where? How?"

"It's one of Alex Bradley's that he happens to have empty right now. He said we could use it until he needs it, which won't be for at least six months."

Ethan clapped his father on the shoulder. "That's hard to believe. Way to go, Dad!"

Don put his hand on Ethan's shoulder and looked him in the eyes. "I'm counting on your being back in those six months."

Ethan returned his father's look. "I am too, Dad."

Betty Jo fought back tears as she watched the exchange between her husband and son. She didn't want to think about how long he might be gone. She walked over to the pair. "That's great news, but we still have a bunch to unload and take upstairs. Talk time is over."

Don spread out his arms. "Just tell me what I need to do. I'm here to help."

"How about you and Ethan finish with unpacking the car and trailer while Chloe and I work upstairs to get things put away and set up so everyone will have a clear path to get to their bed tonight?"

"Sounds like a plan," Don agreed as he took a box out of the back of the trailer.

Betty Jo and Chloe headed upstairs. "It's good we have three bedrooms and a bath upstairs for y'all to use. I just wish we had one more bedroom. I hope the boys won't mind sharing."

"They'll be fine with it. In fact, I bet they're going to love it. There are many mornings I go into Matthew's room and find Chase sleeping next to him."

Betty Jo smiled at the image of her two precious grandsons curled up together.

When they reached the top of the stairs, Chloe hesitated, which made Betty Jo think that she might be unsure about where to begin. She didn't want to overstep her boundary but was aware they needed to get busy if they were going to have things ready by bedtime. She offered a suggestion. "Would it be okay with you if I worked in the kid's rooms to put things away while you worked in your room to get it set up?"

"I like that plan." Chloe turned toward her room.

The two of them went to work unpacking suitcases and boxes. As she put the children's things away, Betty Jo tried to push down her excitement of having Kelli, Matthew, and Chase right here with her every day. She'd get to hug and kiss them each morning and again each night as they went to bed. She made a mental note to herself to get the children's books from the attic she had saved from Ethan and Lily's childhood She hoped they would love them as much as Kendall had when she'd read them to her.

Don brought a box into what would be Kelli's room and set it down on the floor. "Well, that's the last of the boxes. What do you want me to do now?"

Betty Jo stopped folding the clothes she was putting away in the dresser to look at him. "I think Chloe and I have this under control."

"Then if you don't need us for now Ethan and I can go turn in the trailer so he won't be charged for another night."

"Okay with me." Betty Jo went back to folding clothes.

Betty Jo rested her tired back against the wall and thought to herself, *I hope I wasn't supposed to check with Chloe before giving them the okay. I'm not going to make it through the next few months if I have to check with Chloe about every little thing.*

By seven that evening, the trailer had been returned, the bedrooms were ready, Lily was back with the children, and everyone was hungry.

There was no way Betty Jo was going to have the time nor the energy to fix supper. She decided, without consulting anyone, to order pizza from Joe's Pizza. If Chloe wanted something else for her family that night, she could fix it. When the three large pizzas– a pepperoni, a cheese, and a supreme—along with a double order of hot wings and bread sticks were delivered, she noticed no one was upset with her for deciding on her own. In fact, it appeared to her all were happily enjoying this decision she'd made all by herself.

After the pizza had been eaten and the table cleared, the children begged to go outside with Pops to check on the plants in his greenhouse. They thought of his greenhouse as an enchanted place with its lush green plants and the sweet fragrance of the flowers. Chase and Matthew took Pops' hand and Kendall held on to Kelli's as they trekked outside.

Betty Jo couldn't help but smile as she watched Don with all their grandchildren. She felt blessed to have her entire family here with her. She pushed away the negative thought it might be a long time before she would have another evening like this. She had them all here for now, and that was enough. She turned back to the kitchen sink and began rinsing the dishes to put them in the dishwasher.

"Let me help you with that, Mom," Lily offered.

"No, I've got this. It's such a beautiful evening. It'd be shame to waste it here in the kitchen. Why don't you, your brother, and Chloe go on out to the front porch and visit? I'll be out as soon as I finish up with this."

"You're sure?" Lily asked.

"I'm sure."

The truth of the matter was she wasn't sure of anything right now. Her whole world had been turned upside down in a matter of hours. She wasn't sure how she was going to watch Ethan leave. She wasn't sure how she was going to take a "back seat," as Ethan put it, to Chloe. Even though she loved her grandchildren with all her heart and soul, she wasn't sure how she was going to have three young, active children under the age of seven living with her and Don full time.

One thing she knew for sure was that her love and faith in God would see her through. She'd had her whole world turned upside down before and survived. In fact, she'd come out a stronger and better person because of the hardships she'd gone through. Her thoughts carried her back to the darkest time of her life when she hadn't been sure she'd see Ethan grow up.

1976

Betty Jo and Don had just celebrated their first anniversary when she learned she was pregnant. Don was thrilled beyond belief. He was ten years older than Betty Jo and already in his mid-thirties. He hadn't been sure a wife was going to a part of his life, let alone a child. Betty Jo, however, was not quite as excited. It wasn't that she was unhappy about having a baby, but she'd hoped they'd have more time with just the two of them. Having been the oldest of six with three brothers and two sisters, she understood how having a baby would change their lives forever.

When Ethan Donald Breedlow was born and the nurse put him into her arms, he didn't look at all like Betty Jo expected. All her brothers and sisters had been born bald, or at least it looked like they were bald with just a wisp of white blond fuzz on the tops of their heads and reddish pink skin. Her son had a full head of hair as black as coal that stuck out in all directions and a deep olive complexion. When she looked into those big brown eyes of his, she fell hopelessly in love. He became her world.

Betty Jo loved everything about being a mother. She supposed it was because she'd help raise her brothers and sisters, it all came naturally to her. Ethan was an almost perfect baby who cried little and smiled often. When she took him out of the house, which wasn't often, strangers would even comment on what a good baby he was. Don let her know it bothered him he didn't get to spend much time with his boy. He'd been an only child so had no experience with children. Betty Jo wasn't sure she could trust him with their son. But one day, when Ethan was only three months old, she needed to go grocery shopping. She usually took the baby with her, but this time Don convinced her to leave baby Ethan in his charge. She was alarmed when the two of them weren't there when she got home. She panicked, knowing something terrible had happened to Ethan and Don had rushed him to the hospital. This was long before the days of cell phones, so she had no way to contact him. She called the hospital and was relieved to learn no father had brought in a baby. She called everyone she knew to see if they had seen her missing husband and son. She was near hysterics and about to call the police when Don came whistling in the back door with Ethan sound asleep on his shoulder. When Don told her he'd put their son in his little infant seat and taken him out fishing in his boat on the river, she swore he would never be in charge of Ethan ever again. It turned out she was very wrong.

It was a beautiful July morning, and Betty Jo was sitting in her favorite chair, the one her grandmother had once rocked her in, giving six-month-old Ethan his morning bottle when she noticed a "pins and needles" sensation beginning in her feet. She thought it might be because she had her legs crossed and had pinched a nerve. She uncrossed her legs, but the sensation remained. She moved her legs around hoping the movement would make the disturbing sensation go away, but that didn't work either. She decided it might help if she got up and walked. So, when Ethan fell asleep, she went to stand up but found she couldn't. It was as if her legs didn't have any strength in them. Moving Ethan from her arms to her shoulder, she tried once more. She was able to stand, but when she took a step, her legs buckled beneath her. As she fell, she held on tightly to Ethan, whose little head came close to hitting the corner of the coffee table. She was terrified. She'd never experienced anything like that before. She sat in the middle of her living room floor rocking her baby back and forth while they both cried.

Betty Jo wasn't sure how long she sat there, but when Ethan fell asleep once again, she laid him gently on the floor and crawled to the phone. With shaking hands, she dialed Don's work number. When she heard his voice, she broke down and began to sob uncontrollably.

Don's voice was filled with alarm when he asked, "Betty Jo, what's wrong? Is it the baby?"

She managed to choke out between sobs, "C-C-Come h-h-home."

Before he had a chance to respond, she hung up the phone. Crawling back over to Ethan, she'd curled up next to him. That's where Don found the two of them when he came rushing into the living room. It had only taken him five minutes to drive the seven miles home. Leaning down next to his wife and son, he pulled Betty Jo into his arms. She wrapped her arms around his neck and wept into his shoulder. He gently held her as he whispered into her hair, "Shh, don't cry. It's going to be okay."

Betty Jo pushed away from him, her eyes filled with anger. "It's not going to be okay, Don. I almost hurt our son."

Confused by her outburst, Don stared at her.

"I fell down with Ethan in my arms and almost smacked his head on the corner of the coffee table!" Fear began to fill her whole body. "I can't feel my legs, Don! I can't walk!"

Looking down at her legs, Don asked, "What do you mean? They're numb?"

Betty Jo sat up, using her hands to move her lifeless legs in front of her. "It started out as pins and needles in my feet, but then that feeling started moving up my legs. After a while, they just went numb." She was surprised by how matter-of-fact she was able to talk about it.

It seemed to take Don a minute to process, but when he understood what she was telling him, he reacted quickly. "We need to get you to a hospital. I'll call Mrs. Abrams to see if she can watch Ethan."

After their neighbor arrived at the house, Don picked Betty Jo up and carried her to the car. The two of them talked on the way to the hospital. Both were convinced a doctor in the ER would give her a shot that would bring the feeling back to her legs, and they'd be back home in an hour or two to resume their normal lives. However, within minutes of being carried into the ER, she knew their lives would never be normal again.

Chapter Five

"Mom, did you hear me?" Ethan's voice broke through her reliving the past, bringing her to the present.

"Oh, my goodness. I was totally lost in thought." Betty Jo turned toward Ethan. "Say it again."

"It's getting late. I'll need to leave soon."

Ethan had her full attention. "Tonight? I thought you didn't have to be there until tomorrow."

"Tomorrow at zero seven hundred," Ethan reminded her. "We think it'd be best to go on to St. Mary's and spend the night since it's right there at the Kings Bay Naval Base. We don't want to take a chance with morning traffic with people heading to work and all. If it's bad, I could be late if we waited to leave until morning. It'll be less stress to get up there tonight."

Tears began to fill Betty Jo's eyes. "Oh, Ethan, I was thinking we'd be able to spend the whole evening together." She stopped her tears and smiled as she wiped them away. "You're absolutely right though. It'll be better to leave now rather than taking a chance with traffic and all. Do you want your father to take you?"

Ethan grinned. "No, Mom, Chloe will take me. We need this night together."

"Of course, you do." Betty Jo was ashamed she hadn't thought of Chloe. She needed to remember how hard this was going to be for Chloe. "Are you all packed?"

"Packed and ready. I just need to say goodbye to the children." Ethan took a step closer to his mother. "I've already said my goodbyes to Dad and Lily. I wanted to say goodbye to you in private." He leaned down to wrap his arms around her five-foot two-inch frame.

Betty Jo stood on the tip of her toes to get her arms around his neck. She kissed his cheeks. "You take care of yourself. I promise I'll do my best to get along with Chloe. Don't you worry about anything here. You keep your mind on what you have to do to get back home."

Ethan stepped back and looked down at her. "Will do, Mom."

From behind, she heard the squeal of "Daddy!" as all three children ran to him. He got down on one knee and gathered Kelli, Matthew, and Chase in his arms.

"Did you have fun with Pops?"

Betty Jo watched the scene before her as her three excited grandchildren gave the details of their adventure to their daddy. It broke her heart to think of all the adventures they would have that Ethan was going to miss. She was all too aware you never got the time back you missed. It was gone forever.

Don came over to put his arm around her shoulder. "Those kids are really going to miss him."

Betty Jo nodded. When she looked up at her husband, she saw that his eyes were glistening with tears. She took his hand and gave it a squeeze. "We'll need to keep them busy so the time will seem to fly by until he's back."

Her attention was drawn back to Ethan and the children when she heard him say, "It's time for Daddy to go. Now, you remember the three things Mama and Daddy always tell you, right?"

Three little heads nodded up and down as they recited together. "We can do all things through Christ who strengthens us. We are strong together. We are brave."

Ethan smiled. "You make me so proud." Giving each one a kiss, he added, "I love you. Don't ever forget or doubt that."

Six arms wrapped around his neck and they covered their daddy with kisses.

Betty Jo was so engrossed in what was going on with Ethan and the children that she hadn't noticed Chloe coming in the kitchen. It surprised her when she heard her voice. "Come on, my precious little ones, it's time to get ready for bed. Tonight, you have a double special treat."

The children turned around and looked at their mother expectantly as she continued, "You get to sleep in your new rooms, and Gigi, Pops, Aunt Lily, and Kendall are going to put you to bed tonight."

Chase looked back at her with wide eyes. "All of them?"

Betty Jo clapped her hands together. "All of us! Now, give your Mama and Daddy a kiss and head on upstairs. The first one to get their PJs on gets to choose the book we'll read tonight. Aunt Lily and Kendall will help you."

They kissed their mama and daddy before hurrying out of the room with their aunt and cousin.

Betty Jo watched the children leave then turned back to speak to Ethan and Chloe. "Y'all be careful driving to St. Mary's tonight." Looking directly at Ethan, she added, "You take care of yourself, Son. Always know I love you." She quickly left the room.

After the children put on their pajamas and brushed their teeth, they cuddled together in Kelli's big bed. As it turned out, each of the children chose a book they wanted read. Gigi read *The Tawny Scrawny Lion*, Pops read *The Cat in the Hat*, and Kendall read *The Poky Little Puppy*. The kids were amazed the books had once been read to their father way back when he was a little boy. Chase was asleep before Kendall finished reading her book, but it took longer for Kelli and Matthew to settle down.

When they were all asleep or close to it, Betty Jo, Don, Lily, and Kendall went down the stairs and gathered in the kitchen. Betty Jo made hot chocolate for Kendall, coffee for Lily and Don, and a cup of Earl Gray tea for herself. They sat around the table recapping the unexpected events of the day.

Don shook his head. "Well, this sure wasn't the day I'd expected. I thought I'd spend the whole day on the lake with Mark and Alex trading fish stories."

Lily laughed. "Not the way I thought my day would go either, but I had fun getting to know my niece and nephews better."

Kendall gave a dreamy sigh. "They're just the cutest kids ever. Chase is just plain silly, Matthew is so serious, and Kelli is totally precious. I'm so glad they're staying here for a while. I just love them all so much!"

Betty Jo leaned over to kiss the top of Kendall's head as she set the hot chocolate down in front of her. "It is going to be fun to have those sweeties here with us. I'm counting on you to help me with them."

"Just let me know when, and I'll come running."

"Don't worry, I will." She sat down and sipped her tea. "I just hate they're here with us under these circumstances."

"Don't we all!" Don agreed. "We have to do our best to make this as good an experience as it can be for those children and Chloe."

Lily nodded. "You're right, Daddy, but what about Chloe? How is it going to work out between her and Mom?"

Betty Jo took a deep breath before answering her daughter. "Ethan talked to me about that. I'm going to try my best to remember she's in charge of the children, not me."

Lily cocked her head to one side, giving her mother a doubtful look. "Really? You think you can do that?"

Betty Jo put her hand to her chest. "I promised Ethan I would try my best."

"Yeah, well, good luck with that."

"You don't believe I can?"

"If past history is any indication. . ." Lily raised her eyebrows and shrugged. "Just saying."

Don came to Betty Jo's defense. "I believe your mother can keep her promise. I have faith in her. I've learned from past experience, if she puts her mind to doing something, she does it even when everyone around her is telling her it's impossible."

"Thanks, honey." Betty Jo placed her hand on his, giving it a squeeze.

"Okay, I'll give you that, Daddy. But if it's okay with you two, I'll be adding my prayers to help Mom's determination along." She turned to her daughter. "Kendall, it's getting late. I'm beat. Even though you don't have to get up early to go to school, I have to go to work tomorrow. It's time we go home."

Betty Jo and Don walked Lily and Kendall outside. After hugs and kisses, the two got in their car. Don put his arm around Betty Jo as they stood in the driveway waving.

"Well, our world sure changed in one day," Don said thoughtfully.

"In more ways than one."

"In ways I never saw coming."

Betty Jo rested her head on Don's chest. "Oh, Don, what if the air force is sending Ethan into a hostile place where he could get hurt or worse?"

Don remained silent for a few minutes before answering. "We pray for him. We ask God to protect him, to keep him safe, and to bring him back home to his family."

"That's what I've been doing from the minute he told us he was leaving." Betty Jo took a step back to look into her husband's eyes. "The praying is the easy part. The hard part for me is not knowing if God will answer my prayers the way I want them answered."

Don pulled her back to him, holding her close. "You can trust God to keep him safe, Betty Jo. After all, Ethan is His child too."

Betty Jo squeezed him. "How is it that you always seem to know the exact words I need to hear?"

"It's just one of my many talents." He kissed the top of her head as he released her. "It's been a long day. I'm ready to hit the sack."

The two of them walked in the house hand in hand.

While Don locked up the house for the night, Betty Jo headed upstairs to check on the children. She noticed a light shining through the open door of Kelli's room. When she walked into the room, it didn't surprise her to find Matthew and Chase cuddled close to Kelli while she read another book to her brothers. All three looked up when Betty Jo entered the room.

Chase put one finger to his mouth. "Shh, Gigi. Kelli's just getting to the best part."

Kelli put the book aside as she began to explain. "They begged me to read one more book and promised they'd go back to their beds as soon as I finished."

Betty Jo tiptoed to the bed. "Keep reading. I don't want to miss the best part."

Chase scooted over to let her in next to him. Kelli smiled, picked up the book, and began reading again. As she listened to her granddaughter read, Betty Jo couldn't help but feel blessed to be sharing this moment with her precious grandchildren even though she hated the circumstances that had made it possible.

"The end." Kelli closed the book and looked at her two brothers. "Okay, now it's time to get in your own beds. You promised."

Betty Jo gave Kelli a kiss, then stood up. "Come on, you two. I'll tuck you both in." When neither one moved, she began to walk as quickly as she could toward the door. "Bet I can beat you both to your room."

The challenge she'd put down had Matthew on his feet in a flash and racing to his room with Chase close behind calling out, "Oh, no, you can't!"

She laughed as they passed by her. It'd been a very long time since she'd beaten anyone to anywhere. The brothers were in their beds when she finally made it to their room. "Wow! I can't believe how fast you two are." Both giggled with the thrill of having just beaten their Gigi in a race.

Matthew wrapped his arms around her neck as she tucked him in and gave him a kiss. "I love you, Gigi."

"I love you too, Matthew."

She tucked Chase in, but when she leaned over to give him a kiss, he took her face in his hands and looked directly into her eyes. "Gigi, I hate to tell you this, but you're really slow."

Betty Jo could tell by the seriousness in his voice that she shouldn't laugh. "Thanks for letting me know."

"You're welcome."

"You know what, Chase?"

"What, Gigi?"

He was still holding onto her face. She took his hands in hers and kissed him on both cheeks. "I love you."

"I love you too."

She turned off the light after making sure the night light was on, and closed their door.

Don was already in bed when she joined him in their bedroom. He glanced up from his book. "What took you so long? I was beginning to think the children had kidnapped you."

Betty Jo kicked off her shoes and sat on the side of the bed. "I found all three of them in Kelli's room. The boys had convinced her to read them one more book before they would go to bed."

"Well, you can't blame the boys. After all, they've been through a lot today. I'm sure they were both feeling a little insecure and wanted some reassurance from their big sister."

"I'm sure you're right. I tell you, that little Chase is something else." She shook her head as she thought back on Chase's statement to her. "To get the boys moving after Kelli finished reading, I raced them to their beds."

Don chuckled. "You raced?"

"Well, you know how well I race, and Chase noticed. He wanted me know that I'm slow."

"Did you tell him why?"

"No, that's a story for another time."

By the time Betty Jo had changed out of her clothes and into her pajamas, Don was fast asleep with his open book resting on his chest and his glasses still on his face. She closed his book and carefully took off his glasses. She put both on the side table and turned off his light. She crawled into bed and felt sweet relief as the tension of the day drained from her body. She waited for sleep to take her, but thoughts of races she'd never win filled her head, blocking the rest she longed for. She tossed and turned until she gave in and allowed herself to recall the memories of how her life was changed forever.

Chapter Six

1976

Three doctors examined Betty Jo in the ER, and all three doctors walked away shaking their heads. Don did his best to reassure her everything was going to be all right, but she could tell he was as scared as she was. She didn't mention to anyone how after hours of waiting the numbness that had begun in her feet seemed to be spreading throughout her body. She was afraid if she said it out loud it would make it more real. Instead, she kept a brave smile on her face to cover up her fear, all the while silently praying for God to take away the numbness as quickly as it had come.

After hours of waiting in the ER, Betty Jo and Don had run out of things to talk about. They silently sat on the examining table side by side, lost in their own thoughts. Both jumped, startled when a short, stocky man with long, unruly, graying hair flying around his face suddenly marched into her cubicle. He reached out and took both of Betty Jo's hands in his and looked intently at her. "Mrs. Breedlow, I'm Doctor Ronaldi, a neurologist. I have a few questions for you. Have you had a cold, sore throat, or flu-like symptoms at any time during the past two weeks?"

After clearing her throat, she answered, "Yes, sir. I had a sore throat about a week ago.”

"Fever?”

“Yes, sir, but not a high fever.”

“Were you on antibiotics and bed rest?”

Betty Jo shook her head. “I didn't see a doctor. I wasn't that sick, and it went away after a few days.”

The doctor held on to her hands and continued to look directly into her eyes. “I understand you've been experiencing some numbness in your lower extremities.”

“Yes, sir, I have.”

“When did you first notice this numbness?”

“This morning.”

Releasing her hands, Doctor Ronaldi leaned in closer, tilting his head to the side. “Have you noticed any numbness in any other parts of your body?”

His question took her by surprise. She couldn't find her voice to answer.

“It's very important you tell me the truth, Mrs. Breedlow. You need to be completely honest with me.”

She looked over at Don as tears began to fill her eyes. He put one arm around her shoulder. She swallowed hard. “Yes, sir. My hands and arms have that same pins and needles feeling my feet and legs had before they went totally numb, and it's getting harder for me to sit up.”

Doctor Ronaldi gave her a sympathetic smile. “Then it's time for you to lie down, Mrs. Breedlow.”

Betty Jo and Don stared blankly at one another for a minute, then she did exactly what the doctor ordered. Doctor Ronaldi went on to explain. “Your test results are inconclusive at this point. I would like to do one more test, a spinal tap. I believe that will give us the information we need to confirm my diagnosis.”

Things happened very quickly after that. Don barely had a chance to kiss Betty Jo on the cheek before he was shoved out of the room by a large orderly. A nurse instructed Betty Jo to curl up in a ball with her back to the doctor. She was warned if she moved even a fraction of an inch while the doctor was drawing out the spinal fluid the result would be disastrous.

She held her breath in hopes of choking back the sobs that threatened to burst out at any minute.

Doctor Ronaldi gently placed his hand on her shoulder. "You're going to feel pressure as I insert the needle, but try to remain calm and do not move."

Betty Jo caught a glimpse of the needle out of the corner of her eye as the nurse passed it to the doctor. She'd never seen a longer needle in all her life. As blackness began to surround her, she knew she was going to faint. She tried to call out to let the nurse know what was happening to her but found she didn't have the strength to speak.

The first thing Betty Jo noticed when she woke up was an intense light shining in her eyes. Why was there such a bright light in her bedroom? She tried to raise her arms to block out the light, but found she couldn't move. She looked to each arm to see if they'd been tied down while she was unconscious, but saw neither was restrained. The harder she strained to lift them, the heavier they felt. She closed her eyes and moved her head to the side.

"Welcome back, Mrs. Breedlow."

At the sound of the strange voice, her heart was gripped with fear. If she wasn't in her bedroom, where was she? Was someone torturing her by keeping her arms frozen by her side? When she tried to sit up, she found she couldn't. What was happening to her? She opened her mouth to scream, but stopped when she heard Don's familiar gentle voice. "It's okay, Betty Jo. You're in the hospital."

Slowly, she opened her eyes, recalling the numbness, the ER, the spinal tap, the needle, then the blackness that followed. She turned and focused on Don's face. In all the time she'd been with him, she'd never known him to cry, but when she looked at him, his eyes were filled with tears.

In a soft voice, she asked, "Do they know what's wrong with me?"

"I'll let Doctor Ronaldi explain it to you." Don stepped back as Doctor Ronaldi came forward.

"You have Landry-Guillain-Barré Syndrome."

Betty Jo gave him a blank look. "I don't know what that means."

"It's named after the three French doctors who identified the syndrome. It's also known as post-infectious polyneuritis. The cause is basically unknown, but the underlying process involves an autoimmune disorder. Sometimes, after an infection of some kind, like your sore throat with fever, the body's immune system mistakenly attacks the peripheral nerves and damages their myelin insulation or coating, so that when the brain gives a signal to the nerves for the muscles to move, it can't make the connection to the nerve because of the damaged myelin. Therefore, the nerves can no longer move the muscles, which first causes numbness and eventually paralysis."

"Paralysis?"

Doctor Ronaldi nodded as he continued his explanation. "The paralysis usually starts in the feet and hands, then continues to spread throughout the body until the patient becomes totally paralyzed."

Terrifying thoughts swirled around in Betty Jo's mind. *Is he telling me that I am going to be paralyzed? I'm going to lose the ability to walk? Feed myself? Hold Ethan? Talk? Breathe? How can this be happening to me from something as common as a sore throat?* Frantically, her eyes searched for Don. She wondered if his eyes had been filled with tears because the doctor had already told him that she would never again be the woman he'd married. When she caught sight of him leaning against the wall with his head bowed, she had her answer.

"I know this is frightening and a great deal to take in at one time, but before you begin to imagine living your life as a quadriplegic, the paralysis, in all likelihood, may not be permanent."

The only two words Betty Jo heard the doctor say were "quadriplegic" and "permanent." Her mind could not process either.

Don was suddenly at her bedside taking her hand in his. "Betty Jo, did you hear what the doctor just said? There's hope you'll recover from this."

Betty Jo stared at him blankly. "What?"

Doctor Ronaldi smiled down at her. "He's right, Mrs. Breedlow. While the paralysis begins in your feet and continues upward throughout your body, the paralysis, most likely, will leave your body the opposite way, from head to toe. It's just going to take time."

Don looked away from Betty Jo. "How much time, Doctor?"

Doctor Ronaldi put a hand on his shoulder. "I wish I knew."

Betty Jo woke to the sound of Don taking a shower. She didn't know when she'd fallen asleep, but knew she needed more. She started to roll over, but then remembered that she had three small children in her care who would be waking up soon and wanting breakfast. There was no time for more sleep. It was time to get up, get showered, get dressed, and get ready for the day. As she was making the bed, Don walked in the bedroom whistling "Oh, What a Beautiful Morning." She loved hearing his whistling. It always made her smile.

"I hope you're right about that."

He stopped his whistling. "About what?"

"That it's going to be a beautiful morning followed by a beautiful day."

He wrapped her up in a hug, his body still damp from his shower. "You can count on it."

Laughing, she pushed him away. "Don, I don't have time for that. I need to get my shower before those little ones wake up or I may never get another chance."

"It's your missed opportunity," he called out to her as she closed the bathroom door.

By the time she'd showered and dressed, all three children had found their way downstairs. They were sitting on the couch in the living room watching cartoons with their Pops when she came out of her bedroom.

Chase came tattling to her. "Gigi, Pops let me have a cookie."

"Did he now?"

With wide eyes, he answered, "Uh-huh, and I'm not allowed to have cookies for breakfast."

Betty Jo scooped him up. "Well, I'll be sure to talk to him about that. How about some blueberry pancakes for breakfast instead?"

Chase cheered. Betty Jo sat him back on the couch between his brother and sister. She pointed to Don. "You, come with me."

"It was just a small cookie."

Betty Jo laughed. "Let's just hope he doesn't tell his mother about it. Do you want to do the mixing or the cooking?"

"You mix and I'll cook."

As soon as breakfast was ready, they called the kids to come join them at the kitchen table.

"Can we eat in the living room so we can watch TV?" Matthew called back.

Betty Jo put her hands on her hips. "No, we eat together in the kitchen. So, get a move on."

Kelli offered an explanation as she sat down at the table. "Usually, Mama lets us eat in front of the TV. She says she needs that quiet time."

"Oh, I understand, but in this house, we've always eaten breakfast together so we can talk about what's ahead for our day."

Kelli picked up her fork. "Okay, so, what's ahead?"

Don rubbed his hands together. "How about we catch some fish today? We can pick up Kendall on our way to the pond at Kerry Park. Maybe Gigi will even bring us a picnic lunch."

The children squealed in excitement.

Don covered his ears. "The squeals that come from your three little mouths are enough to make a wooden man deaf."

Betty Jo looked at Don. "I think that's a 'yes' to your plans, Pops, but no canoe." She turned her attention to the children. "First you have to finish your pancakes, and then you can go upstairs to get dressed."

The children bombarded their Pops with questions throughout the rest of the meal.

"What kind of fish will we catch?"

"What's the biggest one you ever caught, Pops?"

"Will the fish be so big one could pull me into the pond?"

Betty Jo sat back, enjoying every minute of watching and listening to her three inquisitive grandchildren.

After finishing their breakfast, Betty Jo helped the children get dressed while Don gathered his fishing tackle. Kelli, Matthew, and Chase were waiting on the front porch when Don came out of his shop with his gear. All three rushed to him.

"Can we ride in the back of the truck?" Chase asked.

Kelli gave her brother a serious look. "Don't you even know how dangerous that would be? What if you fell out on your head?"

"She's right, Chase. Everyone rides inside the truck." Don lifted Chase up and buckled him in the car seat Chloe had left.

When all three children were in the truck, Don went back to kiss Betty Jo. "I'll pick up Kendall then head on over to the hardware store to get a couple of smaller fishing poles and some worms and minnows."

"Don, please remember to keep your eye on the kids. You know how quickly they can get away from you and get somewhere they aren't supposed to be. Call me if you need help."

"I promise I'll watch them like a hawk. You do know you worry too much."

"Maybe so, but—"

"I know. I know." Don kissed her before walking back to his truck.

As Don got in, Betty Jo called after him, "I'll be there a little before noon with lunch."

Don smiled and waved as he backed down the driveway. "Don't be late."

Betty Jo stood on the porch watching Don's truck disappear around the corner.

Please, Lord, watch over them. Let them have a good time with their Pops, but please keep them safe.

She wasn't sure why she was worried. It wasn't as if Don didn't have experience taking care of children. He'd watched over Ethan and Lily when they were little, and Kendall had gone fishing with him since she was a toddler.

Betty Jo sat down on the porch swing remembering how well he'd stepped up to take over the care of Ethan those months she was in the hospital with Guillain-Barré. She'd missed out on almost a year of Ethan's life. Even though it was long ago, the memory of that time when she couldn't be there for her son still brought tears to her eyes. She'd missed out on his first words, his fist steps, his firsts of so many things. She recalled what one of her physical therapists had said to her one day when she'd been discouraged by her slow progress.

"Think of what you're going through right now when you're totally paralyzed as the worst thing that will ever happen to you and your family. Guillain-Barré has given you the point in your life when you can say, 'That was the worst.' From this point on, everything will look better because you've already experienced the worst."

She'd thought of those words often through the long months of hospitalization and the years that followed– first in a wheelchair, then in leg braces and crutches, and finally learning to walk again all by herself. Each step was a little better than the one before it. With Ethan's leaving for who-knows-where to do who-knows-what, she hoped and prayed being completely paralyzed would continue to be the worst thing to happen in her or her family's lives.

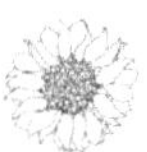

Betty Jo was just finishing up with putting the upstairs bedrooms together when she heard someone pull in the drive. She hurried down the steps praying that nothing had happened on the fishing trip that would have made Don cut it short. Just as she reached the kitchen door, Chloe was coming in the door with her overnight bag slung over her shoulder.

"Chloe. I didn't expect you back so soon."

Chloe dropped her bag to the floor and rushed to Betty Jo. She got out only two words before she broke down in sobs. "Oh, Betty Jo."

Betty Jo wrapped Chloe in her arms and patted her back. "Shh. It's going to be okay."

The two remained like that for several minutes before Chloe stepped back. Betty Jo grabbed a napkin from the kitchen counter and handed it to her. Chloe wiped her eyes and blew her nose. "It was just so hard to watch him leave. I can't believe he's gone."

"Did you find out any more about where they're sending him or for how long he'll be gone?"

Chloe shook her head as she sat down. "They wouldn't tell us anything about that. The only thing they did tell us was to not expect any communication from him."

Betty Jo was stunned. She'd presumed Ethan wouldn't be calling every night to check in, but hadn't expected this. Slowly, she sat down beside Chloe. "Nothing at all?"

"Nothing."

She sat quietly considering the implications of not hearing from Ethan at any time during his deployment. "I'm sure this is for his own safety." She put her hand on Chloe's shoulder. "We're just going to have to put Ethan in God's hands and trust He'll keep him safe and sound." She stood up. "Don has taken the kids fishing at Kerry Park. They're looking forward to a picnic lunch. How about you help me get their lunch ready and take it to the park?"

Chloe stood. "I'd really love to help you, Betty Jo, but I'm beyond exhausted. If you don't mind, I'll just stay here. I need to take a hot shower and a long nap. I don't want the kids to see me like this."

Betty Jo picked up the bag Chloe had dropped at the door and handed it to her. "You go right ahead. Don't you worry about a thing. I know you must be worn out with all that's been going on these past two days." To her total astonishment, Chloe leaned close to kiss her cheek before leaving the room.

She had just finished making the peanut butter and jelly sandwiches for the kids and a turkey salad sandwich for Don when her cell phone rang. She looked down at the caller ID to see that it was Dixie calling. Until that moment, she hadn't realized that she hadn't told any of the Fearsome Foursome about all that had taken place since their Skinny Dippers meeting.

"Hey, what's up?"

Dixie's voice sounded excited. "Do you by any chance remember the little ceremony that group of ladies from the church did for Grace's wedding?"

Betty Jo had to stop to think for a moment. This was not a question she'd anticipated from Dixie. "I'm not sure what you mean."

"I can't remember what it was called, but they gave her some roses and then a Bible at the end."

"Oh, do you mean when they had that shower with the White Bible Ceremony?"

"Yes! That's it! The White Bible Ceremony. I couldn't remember the name, but I was sure you would."

"I may even have the program from it. Why did you need to know the name?"

"Well, I just got to thinking about what Layne said the other day about

Jenny and Aaron dragging their feet with setting a date and all for the wedding. I was thinking maybe if we did something like that for Jenny, it might move them in the marriage direction."

"How so?"

"Well, there hasn't been anything to do with the wedding since we had their engagement party over here. I think it's time we had another event for them."

"I think you've come up with a good idea."

"Every once in a while, I have one." Dixie laughed. "If you're on board, I'm going to give Layne and Nona a call to see what they think. I'll get back with you after talking with them. We'll need to get together to get this thing planned out."

"Count me in, but before you go, I have some news I need to tell you. You can pass it on to Layne and Nona when you talk to them."

Dixie's voice took on a serious tone. "Good news or bad news?"

"Well, I don't know for sure which it is, but the situation with Ethan and his family has changed."

"Go on."

"Ethan isn't going to the Naval Submarine Base at Kings Bay. His orders changed quite suddenly yesterday. In fact, he was here when I got home from Skinny Dippers. He's on TDY, which means temporary duty. He left this morning. We don't know where he's going or for how long or what he'll be doing, but while he's gone Chloe and the kids are staying with us."

Dixie was silent for so long Betty Jo began to wonder if the signal had been lost. "Dixie?"

"I'm here. It's just a lot to take in at one time. That answers another question I meant to ask you about why the fishing trip yesterday was cut short. I don't know exactly what to say, Betty Jo. I'll put Ethan in my prayers. . . And I'll also be praying for you. How has it been going with Chloe so far?"

"It's been okay, but we're only one day into it."

"Well, bless your heart."

Betty Jo laughed. "Amen!"

JOY

Chapter Seven

Dixie remained seated at her kitchen island after she ended her call to Betty Jo. She could tell from the tone in Betty Jo's voice that she was more than just a little concerned about Ethan's assignment. She hadn't asked, but now wondered if he could be in danger. She hoped that wasn't the case, but knew it was a real possibility. Then to top it all off, to have Chloe, who'd never been a fan of Betty Jo's, living right there with her. The only saving grace in that whole situation for Betty Jo was those three precious grandchildren of hers. She hoped they would be the distraction she needed to keep from worrying about Ethan both day and night.

Dixie got up and headed to the back of the house to check on Jason's room one more time. She wanted to make sure everything was in place for his weekend home visit. Her mind had been filled with plans for his homecoming. Both Alex and Hailey had warned her to not make his coming home into one of her big events. They'd stressed to her over and over how Jason's time at home needed to remain low-key. The problem with that was Dixie's mind didn't operate in low-key. She was at her best when planning elaborate celebrations. That was why she was beyond excited about having a White Bible Ceremony for Jenny. Smiling, she picked up her cell phone and punched the speed dial number for Nona's cell.

Nona answered right away. "Hey, Dixie. What's up?"

Dixie took a deep breath. "I need to talk to you about a couple of things. The first is about Jenny. Since Layne talked to us yesterday about Jenny and Aaron dragging their feet on setting a wedding date, I've been brainstorming ideas to get them motivated to set a date. One idea I came up with, which Betty Jo really likes, is reviving the Southern tradition of the White Bible Ceremony like the one Mrs. Nancy Jones had for Grace. I was hoping maybe the three of us could do one for Jenny to help motivate her. What do you think?"

Nona chuckled. "You'll have to give me a minute to process that."

"I know it's a lot, but I think we need to get started with planning and all if we decide to do one for Jenny."

"It was something truly special and very meaningful to both Grace and me when Mrs. Jones did it. I agree with Betty Jo. It is a good idea. If Layne thinks it's a good idea as well, I say, let's do it."

"I'll call Layne right away. Let's go ahead and set a time to meet so we can get our ducks in a row. How would Friday morning at ten here at my house work for you?"

"Let me check my calendar." Nona was silent for a minute. "That works for me."

"Okay, if it checks out with Layne and Jenny, I'll let Betty Jo know. If you don't hear from me, I'll see you at ten on Friday."

"Sounds good. Now, is there something else you wanted to talk to me about? You said you had a couple of things."

"Good grief, I almost forgot. Betty Jo asked me to tell you Ethan won't be going to the Naval Submarine Base like he'd planned. He's being sent on temporary duty. They won't even tell his family where he's going or what he'll be doing or for how long he'll be gone."

"Oh, Dixie, poor Betty Jo. I hate to hear that."

"That's not all."

"There's more?"

"Chloe and the kids are going to be living with Betty Jo while he's gone."

"Nona took a deep breath. "Well, that's a mixed blessing for her. She'll get to know her grandchildren better with them right there in the same house with her, but she'll also have Chloe and her disagreeable attitude living with her as well!"

Dixie chuckled. "It's a mixed blessing, all right. We'll need to say extra prayers for her to get her through this."

"You're right about that."

Dixie's next call was to Layne. She gave her the same news about Ethan she'd given Nona.

Layne reacted as Nona had, seeing the mixed blessings in the situation. "I feel sorry for Betty Jo. She'll be worrying about Ethan and at the same time be dealing with Chloe. Also, having three small children living with her day in and day out for only God knows how long, might be a challenge even for Betty Jo's patience."

"I don't think I could do it," Dixie said shaking her head. "I wouldn't have the energy to keep up with those little ones day after day."

"That's why God gives children to the young."

Dixie chuckled. "Changing the subject, do you remember the White Bible Ceremony Mrs. Jones had for Grace before she got married? She told us all it was an old Southern tradition."

"Boy, that really is changing the subject. Let me think. Oh, yes, I do. If I remember correctly, I cried when they presented her with that beautiful white Bible."

"Well, Nona, Betty Jo, and I would like to do that ceremony for Jenny. I've been wracking my brain trying to come up with something that would motivate her and Aaron to set a date for their wedding, and this came to my mind. What do you think?"

"I love this idea! Oh, Dixie, thank you for coming up with such a great idea. This could be exactly what lights that fire under Jenny and Aaron to get the ball moving."

As soon as she ended her call with Layne, Dixie's mind raced back to making plans for Jason's weekend visit. Maybe she should invite Jenny and Aaron to supper while Jason was home for the weekend. She recalled how Aaron and Jason had been friends when they were young. Maybe she could even invite Lily. Surely, Jason would like to see Lily. She could have a small dinner party for Jason's homecoming with some of his old friends. The more she thought about it, the better the idea seemed to her. She wondered whether she should run that idea by Alex and Hailey. Even they would have to agree it was a great idea.

After Betty Jo finished packing up the lunches for Don and her four grandchildren, she put the cooler in the car and headed to Kerry Park. She parked close to a picnic table and began unloading the car. Before she'd finished setting out the lunches, she heard excited voices coming her way.

Matthew was the first one to reach the picnic table. He shoved an ugly whiskered catfish toward her. "Gigi, I caught the biggest fish! It's even bigger than the one Pops caught."

"Oh, my goodness, that is a big one."

Chase broke loose from Kendall's hand and came running to Betty Jo holding onto a small bluegill. "I caught one too!"

"I can see that."

Kelli joined her brothers. "We all caught one, Chase."

Betty Jo laughed at the competition among the three siblings. "It looks like all of you have learned the secret for catching fish."

Matthew gave her a questioning look. "There's no secret, Gigi. You just bait your hook and throw it in the water."

She shook her head. "That's never worked for me. I can do that all day long and never catch a fish. They just don't seem to like being caught by me."

Don came up behind her. "Your Gigi doesn't have much talent for catching fish, but she's got a special talent for making picnic lunches."

"That I do, so let's dig in."

They all sat down at the picnic table and began eating their lunch of sandwiches, homemade pickles, chips, pouches of yogurt, apple slices, and fresh baked peanut butter cookies. Betty Jo listened with delight to their fish stories. She wondered if this was the first time the children had been fishing. Ethan had practically grown up in a boat fishing alongside his father. She'd have thought he would have taken his own children fishing as often as he could, but maybe the demands of his job had made that difficult or maybe it was the demands of his wife that had made it impossible. She shook her head hoping to shake that negative thought away. It wasn't helpful to her relationship with Chloe to think like that.

"Can we?"

Matthew's question drew her out of her respite. "Can you what?"

Kelli answered for him. "Stay to fish some more?"

"That's up to your Pops."

Don thought for a minute before answering. "Sure, let's stay!"

All four children jumped up from the table and jumped up and down with joy.

Suddenly, Kelli stopped and looked at her grandmother. "Can you stay with us, Gigi?"

As she looked from her husband to her grandchildren, she realized there was no other place she'd rather be. "Okay. I'll stay as long as you don't make me fish."

They remained at the park the rest of the afternoon where the children split their time between fishing and playing on the park's playground equipment. By the end of the day, Betty Jo was worn out. She'd forgotten how much energy it took to keep up with three young children. Four-year-old Chase had given out midafternoon and fallen asleep on his Pops' lap. With Don out of the picture, she was grateful to have Kendall's help.

Kendall, Kelli, and Matthew helped Betty Jo pack up the cooler and get it to the car. The three decided to ride home with Betty Jo while Don carried the still sleeping Chase to his truck and buckled him in his car seat. They arrived home exhausted and grubby from a day of fishing and play. The children were thrilled to find their mother waiting for them on the front porch. Betty Jo had barely stopped the car before Matthew and Kelli were out and running to their mother. She watched as Chloe pulled her children into her arms and listened as they told her about their adventures of the day. She went over to Don's truck to help him get an excited, wide awake Chase free from his car seat. Chase ran to join his brother and sister.

While Don took care of the fishing equipment, Kendall helped Betty Jo carry the cooler to the house. "I had such a good time today, Gigi."

"I'm so glad, Kendall." Betty Jo began unpacking the cooler. "I did too.”

“Do you think they’ll stay here in Kerry?”

Betty Jo stopped and looked at Kendall. “I don’t think they’ll stay here, honey, but we’ve got them with us for a while until your Uncle Ethan comes back.”

Kendall asked softly, “What if Uncle Ethan doesn’t come back?”

Betty Jo hadn’t expected this question. “What made you ask that?”

Kendall’s face turned sad. “I heard Mama talking on the phone, and she said she was worried he might not come back.”

Betty Jo reached out to pull Kendall close. “Oh, Kendall, Uncle Ethan’s going to come back. Your Mama just worries too much.”

Kendall looked up into her grandmother’s face. “Are you sure?”

Betty Jo gave her a reassuring smile. “I’m sure.”

“Then I’m sure too!”

As Betty Jo watched Kendall run out of the house to join her cousins, she hoped she’d given her the right answer.

Layne couldn’t stop thinking about Dixie’s idea of having an old-fashioned Southern White Bible Ceremony for Aaron and Jenny. It seemed like it just might work to get them back on track with their wedding plans. She’d been upset when they first told her they wanted to get married in Bowers, Indiana, but with so much time passing, now she didn’t care where they got married. She just wanted them to seal the deal. She couldn’t wait to run the ceremony idea by Mark. No sooner had she thought of her husband than she heard his truck pull into the driveway. She rushed to greet him at the door.

Mark walked in the back door. his head down as he looked through the mail.

“Hi, honey!”

His head jerked up. “Good grief! Are you trying to give me a heart attack?”

“No, I’m excited to have you home.”

Mark put the mail on the kitchen counter and turned to Layne. “Oh, no.

What's wrong? What's going on?"

Layne gave him an innocent look as she put her hand to her chest. "Are you telling me you don't believe my excitement could be because I'm glad you're home?"

Mark leaned over to kiss her cheek. "Okay, I'll buy that. . . for now." He turned away, picked up the mail, and returned to sorting through it.

Layne waited a minute. "Well, there is something."

"I knew it." Mark turned back, giving her his full attention. "Come on. Out with it."

"You know how it's been bugging me that Aaron and Jenny have been dragging their feet with their wedding plans."

"Yes, even though I've told you over and over that it's none of our business and to stay out of it."

"I have stayed out of it and haven't even said one word about it to Aaron or Jenny."

"Maybe not directly to them, but you've been talking about it with everyone else."

Layne considered his statement for a minute. "Okay, you may be right about that, but Dixie has come up with a plan that I think has a good chance of getting the ball rolling and wedding bells ringing."

"Really? 'Wedding bells ringing'?"

Layne ignored the sarcasm in Mark's voice. "They're going to have a White Bible Ceremony for them."

Mark stared at her blankly. "I have no idea what that is or why you think that will get them down the aisle any faster."

Layne sat down on a stool at the island and patted the one next to her for Mark to join her. "It's an old, Southern, pre-wedding custom that Dixie suggested they revive for Jenny. They're hoping it will help them regain the focus on their love and the spiritual meaning of a wedding. The ladies at the church had a White Bible Ceremony for Grace when she got married. I remember thinking how lovely it was." Layne took Mark's hand in hers. "I think it'll be something beautiful and special for Jenny. It just might get her in the mood to hurry up and marry our son."

Mark squeezed her hand. "I think it's a great idea." Then he added with a glint in his eye, "As long as I don't have to do anything."

Layne playfully punched his arm. "As if they'd ask you."

Rubbing his arm, Mark stood up. "Well, you don't have to beat me up. I just want to make sure it's not one of those ceremonies where you need the sheriff to officiate."

"No, I'm pretty sure they can handle it without getting the sheriff involved."

"I have no doubt the Fearsome Foursome can handle anything they put their minds to."

Chapter Eight

Betty Jo went with Chloe the next day to register Matthew and Kelli at Weldon Academy. She'd assumed the children would be enrolled at Kerry Elementary where both Ethan and Lily had gone, but Chloe insisted they would be more comfortable attending a private school. Even though it was hard to do, she had simply smiled and kept her opinions to herself. While the public school was enjoying their fall break, Weldon's fall break had been the week before. Therefore, the children were starting school that day. Luckily, they'd brought their book bags with their school supplies from their previous school with them.

As Betty Jo drove Matthew and Kelli to the academy, she couldn't help but feel disappointed. She'd hoped she'd have the rest of the week with them before they fell into the routines of school. She'd felt some comfort in knowing that she'd have little Chase home with her, but soon learned that Chloe had already signed him up for the Montessori preschool adjacent to Weldon. She'd arrived at the school with five in the car, but left with only two–Chloe and herself. She couldn't remember a time when it had just been the two of them alone together.

Pulling away from Weldon, she wondered how she was going to handle spending the rest of the day with Chloe. "Oh, my," she said. "It looks like we're going to get some rain. I'm glad I've got a couple of umbrellas in the back."

"Uh huh."

Betty Jo turned on her windshield wipers as the rain began to fall. They rode in silence until it became too much for Betty Jo. "I hope the children have a good day and make some friends."

"Me too."

"I know it's going to be a big change for them going from their school in Virginia to such a small school here in Kerry."

"They'll be fine."

"Did you go to a private school as a child?"

"Yes."

"How was that?"

"Good."

The short, conversation-stopping answers were getting on Betty Jo's nerves, until an idea came to her. "Do you mind if we stop off at Lily's office for a minute? I need to ask her a question."

"Okay."

Betty Jo was thankful they were only a few blocks from Lily's office. As she parked the car, she turned to Chloe. "I can't remember if you've ever been here before."

"I know I've been by it before, but not sure if I've ever been inside or not."

Betty Jo unbuckled her seat belt, reached in the back for the umbrellas, handed one to Chloe, and opened her car door. "Well, here's your chance to see Lily at work."

Lily looked up in surprise as her mother and sister-in-law rushed into the office together. She hurried around her desk. "Let me help you with those." She took their umbrellas, folded them, and set them in the stand. "What are y'all doing out on a day like this?"

"We just enrolled the kids in school and thought we'd stop by for a visit on our way home," Betty Jo explained. "Chloe doesn't think she's ever seen the inside of your office."

Hearing Betty Jo's voice, Nona stepped out of her office. She held out her hand toward Chloe. "Welcome to Kerry and to Foxx and Foxx Law

Firm, Chloe."

Chloe smiled as she shook Nona's hand. "Thank you, Nona." She looked around the office. "It's good to be in a law office again. It looks to be a fine one at that."

"That's right," Nona said. "I almost forgot you're a lawyer. Well, let me show you around."

Betty Jo smiled to herself. Nona had done exactly what she hoped she'd do with Chloe—take her off her hands. With relief, she sat down in the chair next to Lily's desk as Nona led Chloe to the impressive Foxx and Foxx Law Library.

Lily sat down at her desk and leaned in close to her mother. "Rough day, Mom?"

"Does it show?"

"A little, but I think I'm the only one who'd notice."

"It's just that the two of us don't have much to say to one another. The only things we have in common are the kids and Ethan. What in the world am I going to do with her when the kids are at school?"

"If I know you, you'll think of something."

Both Lily and Nona were startled when the office door suddenly opened and Nathan, Layne's son, came rushing in. "Whew! It's really getting bad out there. The rain's coming down hard."

Betty Jo hurried over to him. "Oh, Nathan, you're drenched." She turned to Lily. "He needs a towel or something to dry off."

"You don't need to bother with that, Lily, I'm fine." Nathan took off his rain jacket and hung it up on the coatrack by the door. "It's a pleasant surprise to find you here, Miss Betty Jo. I'd give you a hug, but I'm afraid I might drown you."

"I think you might be right about that." Betty Jo laughed as she went on to explain, "I brought my daughter-in-law Chloe by to see where Lily works. Ethan's been sent off on TDY, so Chloe and the kids are staying with us. She's a lawyer, so I thought she might like to check out one of the finest law offices in Kerry. Nona's giving her the tour."

As if on cue, Nona and Chloe came around the corner and almost bumped into Nathan. Nona made the introductions. "And this, Chloe, is the firm's youngest partner, Nathan Weaver."

Betty Jo watched closely as Nathan reacted to Chloe's attractiveness the way most men did. He stood taller, combed his hair back with his fingers, and set an admiring smile on his face. He reached out his hand toward Chloe. "I believe we met before, when you came to Kerry with Ethan for a visit a few years ago."

Chloe shook his hand, smiling warmly. "I'm sorry, but I don't remember. Ethan introduces me to so many people when we visit."

"I can understand why you wouldn't remember me, but I don't think I could ever forget you."

Chloe's cheeks turned a bright pink. "You're too kind."

Nona cleared her throat. "Chloe's a lawyer, Nathan. She graduated from Columbia."

Realizing he was still holding Chloe's hand, Nathan released his grip. "That's impressive."

"I don't know about that, but I haven't practiced law since my daughter was born." Chloe sighed. "After looking around, I'm realizing just how much I miss it."

Nona looked from Nathan to Chloe. "If you have some free time, maybe you'd like to spend some of that time here with us getting reacquainted with the law. Nathan has a big case coming up. I'm sure he could use some help with his research."

Nathan's face lit up. "I'd welcome your help."

Chloe put her hand to her heart. "Oh, my, I wasn't expecting such an offer."

Betty Jo took a step toward Chloe. "It's something to consider. With the kids in school, I'm sure you could find some time to help Nathan."

Looking around the office, Chloe put her finger to her lips. "You're right about having time on my hands." Chloe turned to Nona. "Thank you, Ms. Foxx. It would be a welcomed distraction to assist Nathan in his research. When would you like for me to start?"

Nona waved her hand toward Nathan. "That's up to Nathan."

Turning to Chloe, Nathan shrugged. "How about tomorrow morning after you drop off your children at school?"

"Sounds good to me," Chloe answered, smiling up at Nathan.

Betty Jo could have hugged Nona and Nathan. With their generous offer, her worries about what she would do with Chloe all day had been taken away.

She could feel the excitement emanating from Chloe as they drove away from Foxx and Foxx Law Offices. "Looks like it turned out to be a good thing we stopped by to see Lily today."

Chloe turned toward Betty Jo. "It was. I never expected I'd be given an opportunity to get back into law in little ol' Kerry, Georgia. I wish there was some way I could tell Ethan about this. He'd be so thrilled for me. He was concerned that I'd be bored out of my mind stuck here in this Podunk town, but it looks like the exact opposite is going to happen, thanks to your friend and her sweet partner. I still can't believe my luck."

Chloe's comments annoyed Betty Jo. She wanted to say something back to her like, *I'm so glad Ethan will be able to stop worrying about you being "bored out of your mind" here in "Podunk" Kerry*–but stopped herself, recalling her promise to Ethan. Instead, she forced a smile as she agreed with her. "Me either. You're one lucky lady."

And so am I!

Nona stood by Lily's desk as she watched Betty Jo and Chloe leave the office. She turned to Lily. "I know you must be wondering why I made such an offer to Chloe when I don't know much about her lawyering expertise. If I remember correctly, her specialty was mergers and acquisitions. Even though Nathan's case is a civil one concerning a personal injury liability, I'm hoping by having Chloe come in here a couple of days a week I can kill two birds with one stone, as the saying goes."

Lily tilted her head. "How so?"

"First of all, it gets Chloe out of the house and out of your mother's hair all day long. And, second, she can help Nathan with the tons of research he has to do to win this case."

Lily smiled. "You're a smart lady, but there's something I need to warn you about when it comes to Chloe. She can be moody and hard to deal with at times."

"So, I've heard." Nona chuckled as she headed to her office.

She had just reached her desk when Lily buzzed her. "Homewood is on the line for you, Ms. Foxx."

Nona picked up the receiver. Was Daddy starting to wonder the halls? Or throwing food? Being rude to the nurses? What could be so important they'd call her at work?

A moment later she was charging out of her office. "Lily! That was one of the nurses from Homewood on the phone. Daddy's on his way to the hospital. They think he may have had a heart attack. I need to get there now." With car keys in hand, Nona stood in front of Lily, frozen with fear as terrifying thoughts began to fill her mind.

It took a few seconds before Lily reacted. She grabbed the keys from Nona's hand. "Nona, you shouldn't drive. I'll take you."

Lily took her purse from her bottom desk drawer. She put a comforting hand on Nona's shoulder. "It's pouring out there. I'll get the car. You wait here. I'll pick you up in front." She grabbed an umbrella from the stand as she rushed out the door.

"What's going on out. . ." Nathan stopped in midsentence when he caught sight of Nona. "What's wrong?"

Nona turned to Nathan as tears began to well up in her eyes. "It's Daddy. They've taken him to the hospital."

Nathan reached out to take her hand. "Oh, Nona, I'm so sorry."

"Lily's pulling her car around to take me to the hospital."

"Do you want me to come with you?"

"No, stay here, answer the phone, take care of clients. I think I have someone coming in around one."

"Don't worry about a thing here. I'll take care of it."

"Thanks." Nona looked up at him. "Nathan, I'm scared."

"Me too." He squeezed her hand. "I'll be praying for Mr. James. . . and for you."

They turned toward the front door of the office when they heard Lily honk the horn. Nona released his hand and started toward the door.

"Wait!" Nathan hurried over to the coatrack, took his jacket down, and handed it to Nona. "You'll need this."

"Thanks." Nona wrapped the jacket around herself as she rushed out the door.

Through the pouring rain, Nathan watched Nona get into Lily's car. As he closed the office door, he prayed that God would be with Mr. James and Nona. Then he went straight to his office. He knew that, besides needing prayers, Nona needed her friends with her. Taking out his cell phone, he called his mother.

Layne answered the phone after the first ring. "Hi, Nathan, I'm glad you called. I want to talk to you about keeping Aaron busy while Jenny's . . ."

Nathan didn't wait for his mother to finish her sentence. "Mom, something's happened with Mr. James. They've taken him to the hospital. Nona just left to be with him."

There was silence on the other end. He hadn't known if coming right out with the news was the best way to handle it, but did know he couldn't make small talk and then break the news to her. He waited.

"Oh, no, Nathan! Thanks for letting me know."

Still holding his cell phone to his ear, it took Nathan a few seconds to realize his mother had ended their conversation. The office phone began to ring. He placed his cell phone on his desk and answered the incoming call. "Thank you for calling Foxx and Foxx Law Offices. Nathan Weaver speaking. How may I help you?"

Nona was silent as Lily drove her to the hospital. At first her mind was filled with terrifying thoughts about life without her father. Then a memory came to her of a day long ago when she was ten years old. She remembered waiting on the front steps of their house for her father to come home so she could show him the first-place spelling ribbon she'd won at school. She hoped he'd be proud of her. When it got dark and the temperature began to drop, her mother urged her to come inside, but she insisted on staying where she was to show him her ribbon the second he arrived home. So she stayed right where she'd been since she'd come home from school, waiting for her father. When she saw his car coming down the street, she was so excited she ran out in to the street waving her ribbon in the air. He'd slammed on his brakes just in time, missing her by mere inches. The man who'd gotten out of the car and headed toward her was nothing like the father she'd always known. This man was red-faced angry.

She recalled the fear she felt when she saw the anger in his eyes. He gripped her by her shoulders and shook her. "Nona, you know better than to run out in the street. What if I'd run over you? I could have killed you!"

She remembered how the hot tears streaming down his cheeks had felt on her face as she stared up at him. Then he'd suddenly picked her up, wrapped her in his arms, and softly whispered in her ear. "I'm sorry I scared you. Don't you know you are more precious to me than life itself? I don't know how I'd go on living without you."

Now, here Nona was wondering the same thing about her father as he had wondered about her all those years ago. *I don't know how I'll go on living without you.*

Lily's voice broke through her thoughts. "Miss Nona, we're here. Do you want me to go in with you?"

Nona hesitated for a moment as she considered Lily's offer, then made her decision. "No, you go on back to the office to help Nathan. I'll be fine."

"Are you sure? I don't mind staying. I don't think you should be alone."

Nona patted Lily's shoulder in hopes of reassuring her. "Thanks, Lily, but I'm sure. " She opened her door and was out of the car before Lily could say anything else. She hurried in the Emergency Room entrance and headed straight to the nurses' station.

A young woman with *Nurse Nace* on her name badge looked up from her desk. "May I help you?"

"Yes, I believe you can. I'm Nona Foxx. My father, James Foxx, was brought here by ambulance. Can you tell me where I can find him?"

Nona tapped her foot on the floor as she watched Nurse Nace shuffle through the papers on her desk. When she took one paper from the stack and began reading through the form, it took all of Nona's self-control not to snatch it out of her hand.

Slowly, Nurse Nace put the form down and looked up. With tenderness in her voice, she said, "You should wait over there, Miss Foxx. Doctor Berry will be with you in a moment."

The look of sympathy that passed over the nurse's face was unmistakable. In that moment, Nona knew with certain clarity that her father was gone from this world. She felt the blood drain from her face. Her mouth went dry. Her heart began to hammer in her chest. She leaned over, struggling to take deep breaths in hopes of calming her racing heart.

Nurse Nace came around the desk. "Are you all right, Miss Foxx?"

Nona felt as if the walls were closing in on her as her breaths became shallower. She gasped for air. "I'm. . . not . . . sure."

"You need to sit down. Let me help you to the waiting room."

Nona gratefully took hold of the nurse's arm and willed herself to put one foot in front of the other. She was looking down at the floor watching her feet as they began to move toward the waiting room when she felt a strong desire to look up. She lifted her eyes to see blessings sent straight from God, as Layne, Dixie, and Betty Jo came through the waiting room door. Without saying a word, the three friends surrounded her with their strength, their comfort, and their love. As Nona fell into their open arms, she felt the full force of her broken heart. The four friends held on to one another, sharing their sorrow and grief until a deep voice, reminiscent of her father's voice, broke them apart.

"Miss Foxx?" the voice asked.

Nona's eyes glistened with tears as she faced the doctor. "I'm Nona Foxx."

She knew the terrible news he was going to tell her. She had the sudden urge to turn around and run, to get as far away from the hospital as she could. With her whole being she wanted to stop him from saying the words that would change her life forever. Then, with a clearness of mind, she remembered the man who had raised her. Mr. James Foxx would never run away. She had always been proud to be his daughter. She would honor her father's memory today by being the strong daughter he had raised her to be.

The doctor took a step toward her. In an even tone, he delivered the news. "Miss, Foxx, I'm Doctor Berry. Your father suffered a massive heart attack. We did all we could to save him. However, he did not survive. I'm sorry for your loss." The doctor shook his head. "I knew your father. Mr. James and I had many a heated political conversation. I'm going to miss his wit and wisdom." With a catch in his voice, he added, "He was a great man."

Nona offered her hand to the doctor. "I appreciate your kind words, Doctor Berry. I agree with you. He truly was a great man."

Doctor Berry shook Nona's hand. "He'll be missed by many."

"Thank you, Doctor Berry."

As Nona watched the doctor leave the room, she straightened her shoulders, wiped away her tears, and took a deep, cleansing breath. When she turned back to her weeping friends who were waiting to console her, she was no longer the grieving daughter, but the no-nonsense lawyer.

"Layne, please call Nathan to let him know about Daddy. Also, tell him that I'll be out of the office for a few days."

Layne gave her a look of concern. "Of course, Nona. Whatever you need for me to do."

"That'll be enough for now."

Nona turned to Betty Jo. "I think the news of Daddy's passing would be easier for Lily if it came from you. Nathan will be too blunt. Also, could you tell Chloe we might need her more days than we originally thought?"

Betty Jo nodded her head. Then in a soft voice, she asked, "Do you want me to take care of things here at the hospital for you?"

Nona considered her offer for a minute. "Thanks, but I'm sure there'll be some papers for me to sign. However, you can call Franklin Funeral Home for me to have them come pick up the. . . body. The funeral arrangements have already been made."

"Of course, I'll take care of it."

Wiping her nose with a tissue, Dixie asked, "What can I do to help, Nona?"

"You can call Brother Richard to let him know. Daddy wants. . .

wanted him to officiate at his funeral. Oh, and would you let our church office know?"

Once again, tears filled Dixie's eyes. "I just wish I could make all of this go away. I'm so very sorry, Nona."

Nona placed her arm around Dixie, patting her on the back. "I know you are." She looked at each of her friends. "I can't thank y'all enough for coming here to be with me, to support me. You three mean the world to me."

Before her friends could respond, Nona turned away, calling back to them, "Let me find out what papers I need to sign to get everything squared away."

She'd only taken a few steps when a thought struck her. She turned back around. "Oh, Layne, I just thought of one more thing you can do for me."

"Anything."

"Would you please inform Grace that her granddad has passed? I believe she would want to know."

Layne reached out to Nona. "Are you sure, Nona? Don't you think news like this should come from you?"

Tears threatened to fill Nona's eyes, but she pushed them back. "Oh, Layne, I don't think she'd take a phone call from me."

"Don't you want to try?"

Nona shook her head. "No, you do it. I need to call Riley, then I'll call Monty." Clearing her throat, she added, "Thank you again for coming. I can't begin to tell you how much it meant to me to see you three walk through that door at just the right time. I love you all so much."

"We love you," Layne, Betty Jo, and Dixie said together as they once again surrounded Nona.

"Would you please pray for Daddy and for me, Layne?"

Layne bowed her head. The other three did the same.

"In Your hands, O Lord, we entrust Mr. James Foxx. In his life, You embraced him with Your tender love. We now ask You to bless him with eternal life. At this time of great sadness for Nona, we ask You to comfort her. Give her the strength and wisdom she needs to get through her fresh grief. In Jesus' name we pray, amen."

81

Chapter Nine

Betty Jo returned home at half past three to an empty house. Don had left early that morning to pick up some plants in Savannah. He'd warned her he wouldn't be home until late that evening. Chloe was probably on her way to Weldon to pick up the children from their first day of school. With so many mouths to feed, she knew she should start supper. After the emotional roller coaster of the day, she decided instead to fix a cup of tea and take advantage of the warm weather by sitting on the back porch. With her cup of Earl Grey, she sat down in the blue Adirondack chair that Ethan had built his junior year of high school. She remembered how he'd taken a woodworking class that year instead of the geography class the counselor had advised him to take. She smiled at the memory of him explaining to her how he was tired of "learning" and needed to be "doing." He was so like his father when it came to "doing." He'd especially liked woodworking, and he'd proven he had a talent for it. Maybe she'd ask him to build her a matching Adirondack chair when he came back from wherever he'd been sent.

A nagging worry about Ethan's not returning home crept into her mind. She pushed it away, forcing her thoughts back to Nona's losing her father. The fact Mr. James had lived a good, long life was comforting, but it was heartbreaking to watch Nona suffer the loss of her father. During her career as a nurse, she'd been a witness to many who had lost a loved one. It had been one of the hardest parts of being nurse. Her mind flashed back to the first time she witnessed a family's loss. She hadn't been a nurse, but a patient.

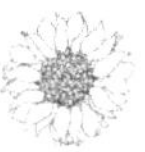

1976

By the time Betty Jo was admitted to the hospital with Guillain-Barré, the only part of her body she was able to move was her head from side to side. When Doctor. Ronaldi sent her to ICU, she was certain she'd been placed there because she was dying. Even though the nurses attending her assured her that was not the case, she couldn't be convinced. With all that had happened to her body in less than twenty-four hours, she was terrified she wouldn't live through the night. When her heart rate and blood pressure escalated to dangerously high levels, her fear of dying became Doctor Ronaldi's fear as well. He had her transferred out of ICU and into a private room. Because the neurology floor was full at the time, she was placed in a room on the cancer floor. Betty Jo hadn't cared where they put her as long as it wasn't back in ICU.

It was well after midnight before the nurses settled her in her bed. Knowing she wouldn't be able to press the call button to summon a nurse if she needed anything, the nurses promised they would check on her throughout the night. When the door closed behind them as they left her room, she'd never felt more alone and frightened in her entire life. She longed for Don's loving arms to hold and comfort her, but he'd left hours ago to pick up Ethan from Mrs. Abrams.

Betty Jo began to cry softly at first, but as the life-changing events of that day filled her mind, she began to sob. Through her sobs, she screamed out to the empty room. "Oh, God! Why have you done this to me? What evil thing did I do to deserve this horrid fate? Why have you abandoned me?"

Betty Jo had been through tough times in her life. She'd lost both of her parents before graduating from high school. She and her brothers and sisters had been separated and dispersed among relatives, and they'd never reconnected with one another. Through those hard time, Betty Jo had vowed to never be one of those people who felt sorry for themselves, but this night she couldn't stop herself. On this night, as she lay there, a quadriplegic without her husband and son, she decided she had every right to feel sorry for herself. The tears rolled down her face and soaked her pillow. Her nose began to run. She cried harder as she realized she couldn't even do something as simple as pick up a tissue to wipe her nose or dry her tears.

Suddenly, she heard a knock followed by a soft voice. "Hello?"

Betty Jo turned her head toward the knock. It wasn't coming from the door to her room, but from her bathroom door. Wide-eyed, she watched as a small, thin middle-aged woman in a much-too-large purple nightgown with matching scarf wrapped around her head came through the bathroom door into her room.

The woman walked over to her bed. "I heard your cries. Are you okay? Can I help you?"

The shock of seeing someone enter through her bathroom door stopped Betty Jo's tears. "You were in my bathroom?"

The woman chuckled softly as she came closer. She answered in a distinctive British accent. "Yes and no. Technically, it's 'our' bathroom. The bathroom connects our two rooms. I'm Mrs. Rebecca Waters. Who might you be?"

Still finding it hard to believe this woman with the British accent had come into her room at one o'clock in the morning, it took her a minute before she could find her voice to answer. "I'm Betty Jo Breedlow."

Mrs. Waters held out her hand to Betty Jo. "It's my pleasure to meet you Betty Jo."

Betty Jo stared at her outstretched hand then turned away, tears filling her eyes once again. "I can't. . . I'm. . . paralyzed."

"Well, then it's a good thing I came over here." Mrs. Waters took a tissue from the box on the bedside table. "Now, look over here at me."

Slowly, Betty Jo turned her head toward her. Tenderly, Mrs. Waters wiped her nose and dried her tears.

She smiled down at Betty Jo. "There, now, that's much better, isn't it?"

Betty Jo smiled a genuine smile for the first time since Don carried her into the hospital. "It is. Thank you."

The friendship that began that night grew through the following weeks as Mrs. Waters did for Betty Jo what she'd done that first night they met—she took care of her. As her paralysis continued to spread to her head, face, and eyes over the next few days, Mrs. Waters was there to help her cope with the changes she was going through and offer her words of encouragement. She sat beside Betty Jo's bed at night telling her stories of her life growing up in London, of how she'd met her husband when he'd been stationed in England, how difficult it'd been for her to move to America, and how she'd loved raising her three daughters. These stories took Betty Jo's mind off what was happening to her body as it transported her into a world she'd never known.

Betty Jo never thought to call Mrs. Waters "Rebecca" or "Miss Rebecca." She was always Mrs. Waters to her. She learned how Mrs. Waters had been in the hospital for two weeks before Betty Jo had been moved into the room next to her. She'd been battling stage four leukemia for over a year. Her hope was to go into remission so she could attend her youngest daughter's wedding five months away. Her husband was still in the Air Force, but stationed in Florida. He came every weekend he could to spend it with her. It was obvious to anyone who saw the two of them together that their love was strong. Betty Jo could feel the disappointment that Mrs. Waters tried to hide when her daughters didn't come to visit as often as she hoped they would.

Betty Jo's favorite days were those when Don brought Ethan to the hospital. Even though it was hard not to be able to hold Ethan or give him his bottle, she found such joy to simply be in the same room with him. It was Mrs. Waters who played with Ethan so Don and Betty Jo could have some time alone. It didn't take long for both Don and Ethan to think of Mrs. Waters as part of their family.

Whenever Betty Jo began to lose hope and felt the darkness of despair, it was Mrs. Waters who lifted her spirits and prayed for and with her. It was Mrs. Waters who cheered her on when the paralysis began to recede and the pain-filled days of physical therapy began. Betty Jo was given the chance to return encouragement to Mrs. Waters when her leukemia advanced and stronger chemicals had to be pumped into her body to kill the deadly blood cancer. Even though she couldn't offer physical help, she could give her spiritual and emotional help. When Mrs. Waters was too weak to get out of bed, Betty Jo asked one of the nurses to wheel her over to the older woman's room in her wheelchair. Sitting beside her bed she'd read the Bible or an inspirational story or tell her jokes to make her laugh.

As Betty Jo got stronger, Mrs. Waters became weaker. Mrs. Waters tried to warn her how her prospects for a full recovery were not likely, but Betty Jo wouldn't allow such negative talk. The truth was she didn't know how she could go on without Mrs. Waters beside her. She'd been the source of her courage when she hadn't believed she had the strength to continue.

Late one night, just as Betty Jo was falling asleep, she thought she heard Mrs. Waters call out her name. She blocked out all other sounds as she listened intently for her voice. She heard Mrs. Waters call out weakly, "Betty Jo."

Using the bar above her bed, Betty Jo pulled herself up and, with the transfer board, lowered herself into her wheelchair. As quickly as she could, she wheeled herself into Mrs. Waters' room and up next to her bed. "Mrs. Waters, are you okay?"

Mrs. Waters clasped Betty Jo's hand in hers. Her voice was so soft and weak that Betty Jo had to lean in close to hear her. "You have to keep going even if I'm not here with you, Betty Jo. You must keep working and getting stronger so you can walk again. You need to do it for Don and Ethan. They're counting on you."

Betty Jo squeezed Mrs. Waters' hand tightly as tears began to sting her eyes. "Don't talk like that. You have to beat this leukemia so you can dance at your daughter's wedding. If you promise to keep fighting, I promise I'll work hard so I can be there to dance with you."

Mrs. Waters smiled as she patted Betty Jo's hand. "Oh, Betty Jo, I do love you so very much. I'd love to dance with you, but I don't think it's in the cards for me. However, I need you to promise me that you'll be there and dance for me."

Betty Jo put her face next to Mrs. Waters to kiss her cheek. "I promise."

"Don't you ever forget God loves you. He didn't give you Guillain-

Barré, just like He didn't give me leukemia. Try not to look at what's happened to you as a tragedy, but as a blessing which has made you stronger."

"How will I ever go on without you?"

"You don't have to. I'll be right up there in heaven watching over you and Don and little Ethan every day for the rest of your lives."

Mrs. Waters passed away later that night with her family by her side.

Betty Jo hoped that Mrs. Waters was still watching over Ethan. She heard the kitchen door slam, announcing the arrival of Chloe and the children. She wiped away her tears.

"Gigi!" Chase, Matthew, and Kelli called as they ran out on the back porch.

Betty Jo put down her tea cup just in time to catch Chase when he jumped in her lap. "I had the best day ever. I made three friends– Jane, Leah, and Lyla."

She hugged her grandson. "I'm so glad, Chase."

Matthew sat down on the arm of her chair. "Ooo, those are all girls!"

Chase looked at his big brother. "What's wrong with that?"

"Nothing is wrong with that," Kelli said as she sat down on the other arm of her chair. "Girls are the best."

"Friends are the best," Betty Jo said, hoping to stop an argument.

Turning to Matthew she asked, "So, how was your day, Matthew? Did you make any friends?"

Matthew folded his arms. "It's a stupid school with stupid kids."

Kelli put her hands on her hips. "Well, I liked it."

"That's because you're stupid."

Kelli stuck her tongue out her brother.

Betty Jo slapped her hands together. "Okay, that's enough. Who wants a snack?"

Nona was right about having to sign papers. She was almost finished with the paperwork when she noticed a young nurse walking towards her.

"Mrs. Foxx?"

Nona looked up. "Yes?"

"Would you like to see your father before he's taken away? We've got him cleaned up for you."

Nona stared blankly at her. The thought had never entered her mind to even ask to see her father. It hadn't occurred to her seeing him would be an option. As she considered the nurse's question, she wasn't sure how she felt about it. There was a part of her that wanted to see him one more time, but there was another part of her that wanted to remember him as she'd seen him that morning sitting in his recliner reading the paper. After all, it really wasn't her father in that room, only the shell of the man he'd once been. The father she'd known was no longer in this world. She remembered going with him when he made the arrangements with the funeral home to be cremated. He hadn't wanted a viewing where people would take turns walking by his casket, making comments about how he looked. Instead, he'd wanted a celebration of his life.

Nona made her decision. "Thank you for the offer, but I'm going to decline. I choose to remember him as I saw him last."

The nurse walked away as Nona put her signature on the final document. She picked up her purse, took the papers to the nurses' station, and walked out of the hospital into the fresh air. When she looked out at the parking lot searching for her car, she suddenly remembered Lily had brought her to the hospital. She didn't have her car here. She'd sent everyone away and left herself stranded.

As she stood at the top of the steps just outside the emergency room door, thinking about her situation, she started to giggle. Soon the giggle became a chuckle, which bloomed into full-blown, bent-double laughter. She couldn't stop herself. She sat down on the concrete steps and crossed her legs hoping that would keep her from wetting her pants. Tears were streaming down her face. Realizing how she must look to anyone passing by made her laugh harder. She wrapped her arms around her aching stomach wondering if anyone had ever died from laughing too hard when her cell phone rang out the ringtone she'd programed for Monty's calls. She sat up, taking in several deep breaths, hoping to get herself under control before answering.

"Hello, Monty."

"I just heard the news about your father. I'm so sorry."

Hearing the genuine concern in Monty's voice brought her back to reality.

"Nona, are you all right?"

She wiped the tears from her cheeks and took in another deep breath before answering. "To tell you the truth, I'm not sure how I am."

"I'll be right over."

"Actually, would you mind stopping by Kerry Memorial on your way?"

"Of course. Do I need to pick up something for you there?"

"Yes. . . me."

Once the children had eaten their snack, they disappeared into different parts of the house, which left Betty Jo and Chloe sitting alone at the kitchen table.

"I'm so sorry about Mrs. Foxx's father."

Betty Jo gave Chloe a questioning look.

"Lily called me to tell me. She was pretty upset about it. I guess they were close."

Betty Jo nodded. "Mr. James is the one who hired Lily. He knew what a rough time she was having after her divorce and offered her a job." She sighed. "He was a good man who'll be missed by many."

"I'm sorry I didn't get the chance to know him."

"Me too. You would have liked him."

"I'll go into the office tomorrow to help Nathan any way I can."

"I know he and Nona would appreciate that."

Betty Jo got up from the table. "I'm going to make my special homemade lasagna for our supper tonight. I'll make a little extra to take to Nona."

"I know the kids love their Gigi's lasagna. I'm going to check on them. It's too quiet and the silence has me worried."

Chloe left the kitchen as Betty Jo began to prepare the lasagna. She was putting the layers of noodles and sauce together when she heard Don's truck come down their driveway. She'd called him to tell him the news of Mr. James passing right after she'd broken the news to Lily. She looked up when he walked through the kitchen door.

She was assembling the final layers of the lasagna. "You're just in time to help me. Can you get the bag of shredded mozzarella cheese out of the drawer in the refrigerator for me, please?"

"Sure thing." Don took the cheese out of the drawer and handed the bag to her. "What would you do without me?" He kissed her cheek.

"I truly don't know, and I don't intend to find out."

He chuckled. "I'm all for that."

Betty Jo sprinkled a generous portion of cheese over the top of the large pan of lasagna and then over the small dish she'd prepared for Nona's supper. She put the large pan of lasagna in the oven and set the timer. She turned back to Don. "I'm taking supper over to Nona."

"That's nice of you." Don shook his head. "I still can't believe Mr. James is gone."

"Me either. I think it's going to take a while before it truly sinks in. After I got home from the hospital, memories of Mrs. Waters came flooding back to me. I was thinking of the last thing she ever said to me."

Don came over to stand beside her. "What was that?"

"That she'd be in heaven watching over you, me, and Ethan."

Don took Betty Jo in his arms. "If I know Mrs. Waters, that's exactly what she's doing."

She held him tightly. "Oh, Don, I hope she's up there with God, and they're both watching over Ethan."

"No doubt about it." Don squeezed her. "None at all."

"Would you do a favor for me?"

"Anything."

"Keep an eye on the lasagna in the oven while I run this over to Nona's."

"I'm pretty sure I can handle that much."

"Thanks. I shouldn't be long." Betty Jo gave Don a quick kiss and headed out the door to her car.

It took Betty Jo less than fifteen minutes to get to Nona's house. She wasn't surprised when she saw both Layne and Dixie's cars parked in the driveway, but was surprised when she found both sitting on the steps outside the back door. They waved to her as she got out of the car holding her lasagna.

"Is Nona not home?"

Layne shrugged. "Her car's not here, so I guess she's still at the hospital."

"Surely not," Betty Jo said as she joined them. "It wouldn't take this long to get everything squared away. Have you called her?"

Dixie nodded as she held up two fingers. "Two times and left messages. It could be her cell phone died. That happens to me sometimes late in the day."

Betty Jo said, "I don't know about y'all, but I can't wait much longer. I have lasagna in the oven."

Layne stood up and looked around. "I was going to say we leave the food, but I don't see anywhere we could put it that it would be safe. We might have to bring this food to Nona another time."

The three gathered up the dishes they'd brought and were heading to their cars when they heard a car coming down the driveway. They were surprised to see that it was Monty's car and confused to see Nona sitting in the passenger's seat. They watched as Monty parked his car under the carport. Within a minute, Nona emerged from the car.

"I'm surprised to find y'all here," Nona said as she got out of Monty's car.

Betty Jo held up her pan. "We've brought you supper. You're going to need your strength to get through the next few days."

Nona looked at the pan of lasagna. "You didn't have to do that."

Dixie smiled at Nona. "We know we didn't 'have to do' anything, but that's what friends do for friends."

Nona simply smiled at her friends.

Monty stepped up beside Nona as he reached out for Betty Jo's lasagna. "I think what she wants to say is thank you."

At Monty's words, Nona snapped out of her reverie. "That's exactly what I want to say. Thank you all so very much."

"You're so very welcome," Layne said as she set her dish on top of the pan Monty was holding.

"I baked some bread," Dixie said, adding her contribution.

"Won't y'all come in for a little while?" Nona asked.

"Oh, I wish we could, but we need to get home. You take care of yourself. Call if you need anything," Betty Jo said as she gave Nona a quick hug.

Chapter Ten

Betty Jo's special homemade lasagna was a hit with all three children. Each asked for seconds, which she was more than glad to put on their plates. What was even better than watching them clean their plates was listening to their excited chatter as they each shared their day with their Pops and her. It'd been a long time since she and Don had this much energy around their kitchen table. Chloe hadn't joined them for supper. She'd sent a message with Kelli saying she wasn't feeling well and was going to bed early. Betty Jo wondered if she was truly sick or simply didn't want to spend time with the whole family. Either way, she was glad to have this time with her grandchildren and not have everything she said or did be scrutinized or criticized by their mother.

After everyone had finished eating, Betty Jo began to clear the table. "Who wants to help me clean up the kitchen?"

All remained silent until Don asked, "Who wants to help me out in the greenhouse?"

All three children answered at once. "I do!"

Don looked to Betty Jo. "Is that all right, Gigi?"

Kellie, Matthew, and Chase all looked to Betty Jo. "It's fine with me, but after y'all finish out there it'll be time for baths and bed."

They were out the door in a flash. As she watched them follow Don,

Betty Jo shook her head. "Wish I had half their energy."

By eight o'clock all three children were bathed, in their pajamas, and ready for a bedtime story—Betty Jo's favorite part of the bedtime routine—when Chloe came out of her room. She looked from the children to Betty Jo. "You have the children ready for bed?"

"I do." Betty Jo was proud she'd been able to get all three ready for bed on time. When they'd come back from the greenhouse wet and dirty from helping Don fill pots with soil, she hadn't been sure she'd be able to manage such a feat.

Turning away from Betty Jo, Chloe clapped her hands together. "Y'all go jump in my bed and I'll tell you a bedtime story."

The children squealed and took off running to their mother's room. Without saying a word to Betty Jo, Chloe followed them into her room. Betty Jo watched with disbelief as Chloe closed the door, leaving her standing alone in the hall. She was left with the distinct impression she'd done her duty and had just been dismissed by Chloe. Her first thought was to walk right up to that closed door, knock, and demand to be allowed to give her grandchildren a hug and goodnight kiss. Determined, she started toward the closed door, but her second thought stopped her. Even though this was her house and she had just fed and bathed the children, Chloe was their mother. Betty Jo knew she needed to keep that thought foremost in her mind. She turned around and walked slowly down the steps to join Don in the living room.

She plopped down on the couch next to Don and sighed. "Well, the kids are all bathed and ready for bed."

Don paused the sports program he was watching. He looked at his wife with concern. "Do you want me to go up there to tuck them in?"

"No, they're with their mother right now."

"She's awake?"

"Seems she was able to get herself up just in time to read a bedtime story to her children." Betty Jo knew she sounded bitter, but couldn't seem to shake the disappointment she was feeling.

Don put his arm around her and pulled her to him. "It's not a competition, you know."

Anger flashed through Betty Jo, and she leaned away from him. "Don't you think I know that?"

"I just thought it needed to be said." Pulling her back onto his shoulder, he added, "You do know those children love you."

He was right. She was overreacting. Resting her head on his shoulder, she said, "I do know that, but with all that's happened today with Nona's father dying and worrying about Ethan and thinking about the past, I guess I was feeling a bit insecure."

Don wrapped both arms around her. "I understand. You've gone through a lot in one day."

"Thank God today is over. Here's hoping for better days ahead. How about a cup of decaf before we call it a night?"

"Sounds good to me."

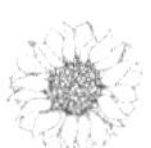

Betty Jo woke up to a rainy, cold Friday morning that matched her mood. If it wasn't a school day, she'd rolled over and go back to sleep, but there wasn't time for that. From the sounds floating down from the floor above, she knew the children were getting ready for their second day at Weldon Academy. She was heading toward the stairs to see what she could do to help them get ready for school, but changed her mind as an idea come to her. The best thing for her to do was to prepare a hearty breakfast for Kelli, Matthew, and Chase to help them get a good start to their day. As she walked in the kitchen, she decided this would be the morning for French toast with cinnamon and powder sugar topped off with warm syrup. Lily and Ethan had always loved what they called "French toast mornings." She hoped Ethan's children would like it as much as he had.

She was flipping over the final four pieces of French Toast when Chloe entered the kitchen with Kelli, Matthew, and Chase following close behind.

"You're just in time for a special breakfast," Betty Jo said as she put the toast on a plate. "I've made what was always your daddy's favorite breakfast."

Chloe stopped and put her hand to her chest. "Oh, no, Betty Jo, my bad. I should have told you we always have breakfast out on Fridays. It's one of our family traditions we started long ago before the children even started school. Ethan has always said this is one of his favorite traditions we created. You wouldn't want me to confuse the children by breaking their daddy's favorite tradition just because he's not here to go with us, would you? Maybe we can talk about modifying our tradition later without the children present. Let's go, children."

Matthew folded in his arms and loudly protested, "But I want Gigi's toast!"

Chloe took hold of his arm and began leading him out the door. "You can have Gigi's toast another day." Chloe called out on her way out the door, "Oh, by the way, I'm going to go to the Foxx Law Firm to see if there's anything I can do to help. I'll probably be there the rest of the day."

Before following her mother out the door, Kelli ran back to Betty Jo to give her a quick hug. "I love you, Gigi."

Betty Jo stared in disbelief as Chloe took her grandchildren away. She looked back at the kitchen table with its five plates of cinnamon- and powdered sugar-sprinkled French toast and mumbled, "You're so wrong about this not being a competition, Don."

She stacked all five plates up and carried them to the sink and began angrily scraping the untouched French toast into the garbage disposal. She pushed back her threatening tears as she watched all ten pieces slowly grind down the drain. She refused to give Chloe the power to make her cry. Don was always reminding her to put things in perspective and not overreact. She needed to take his words of advice to heart today. She took a deep breath. This was only a breakfast, and going out for breakfast had been a tradition the children had shared with Ethan. She had a choice as to how to react to the situation. She could let it become a big deal or she could let it go. She took another deep breath and prayed for the blessing of an understanding, forgiving heart. After her prayer she knew the right choice was to let it go. She made a mental note to check with Chloe to find out which day would be the best day to fix French toast for the kids. She began to hum as she put the dishes in the dishwasher. Suddenly, the day didn't seem as dreary as it had only moments before.

Betty Jo glanced at the kitchen clock on the wall to check the time. She needed to get moving. She had less than an hour to shower, dress, pick up Nona, and get to Dixie's house to plan the White Bible Ceremony for Jenny. She was still amazed that Nona insisted they keep this planning meeting. Betty Jo didn't know where she found the strength. She hoped Dixie had found the time to get the program of the one they did for Grace from Mrs. Nancy Jones. It'd help to have a model to go by when they began planning for this one. She dried her hands and headed toward her bedroom to shower and dress for the day.

Betty Jo picked up Nona and they arrived at Dixie's house with five minutes to spare. Normally, they would have gone in the house though the door in the garage, but after parking the car, the two noticed the garage door was closed. They walked around to the front of the house, rang the doorbell beside the front door, and waited for Dixie to answer. When Dixie opened the door, both Betty Jo and Nona were taken aback to find Dixie in her bathrobe, hair uncombed, and eyes red-rimmed. They stood, staring, unable to move. It was obvious to both that something unsettling had happened to their friend.

Dixie broke down in sobs when she saw her friends. Betty Jo immediately took Dixie in her arms, holding her close.

Nona took a step closer. "Oh, Dixie, what's happened? What's wrong?"

Dixie answered between sobs. "Jason. . .can't. . .come. . .home."

Betty Jo's heart broke to see her upset like this. "I'm so sorry, Dixie. I know how much you were looking forward to having him home for the weekend."

Dixie stepped away from Betty Jo. Taking a tissue from her bathrobe pocket, she wiped her eyes and blew her nose. "I made plans. It was going to be the perfect weekend."

Putting her arm through Dixie's, Betty Jo led her into the house. "Let's go in the kitchen. I'll fix us all a cup of tea and you can tell us what happened."

Betty Jo sat Dixie at the kitchen island and went in search of tea and cups. Nona sat down next to Dixie and took her hand. "Do you think you can talk about it?"

Dixie wiped her nose and took a deep breath. "We got a call last night from the NextStep Center. We thought they were calling to let us know what time we could pick Jason up, but that wasn't what they were calling about at all."

Nona sat quietly and waited for her to continue.

Dixie looked up at Nona with tear-filled eyes. "They called to tell us Jason doesn't want to come home this weekend." She pulled her hand away from Nona's, buried her face in her hands, and began to cry once again. "It just doesn't make sense to me. Why wouldn't he want to come home?"

Nona put a comforting arm around Dixie's shoulder. "I wish I knew,"

As Betty Jo took mugs and tea bags out of the cabinet, she was once again amazed at how quickly life can change. It'd been only a few days ago when both Nona and Dixie had been happy, and now their worlds had been turned upside down and their hearts broken. The whistle of the teakettle startled Betty Jo. She poured the boiling water into the three waiting mugs and carried two of them to the island. She set one mug down in front of Dixie and the other she handed to Nona.

Betty Jo dunked her tea bag up and down in her own cup several times considering what she could say to help ease Dixie's pain. "I don't know why this has happened, Dixie, but I do know Jason loves you. He's shown just how much he loves you by working hard to overcome his addiction. I don't think he's telling you he doesn't want to come home. I think he's telling you he's not ready to come home."

Dixie slowly lifted her head, giving her full attention to Betty Jo.

Betty Jo continued, "I think you need to trust he knows what's best for him and for you. I'm sure he doesn't want to hurt you any more than he already has. I believe he's doing this out of the love he has for his family. "

Dixie looked directly into Betty Jo's eyes. "Do you truly believe that's the reason?"

Betty Jo put her hand over Dixie's and gave it a squeeze. "Without a doubt." She could almost see the wheels turning in Dixie's mind as she considered her statement.

With tears still glistening in her eyes, a smile began to spread across Dixie's face. "I am totally ashamed of myself. I immediately jumped to the conclusion that Jason was rejecting his family. The thought never crossed my mind he might be staying away out of his love for us." She reached out to take both of Betty Jo's hands in hers. "Thank you, Betty Jo. Thank you so very much. You're a blessing sent by God."

Feeling embarrassed by Dixie's emotional outpouring, Betty Jo gave a nervous laugh. "Aren't all friends blessings from God?"

Dixie squeezed her hands. "Yes, they are. They truly are."

Nona cleared her throat. "I hate to break up this lovefest, but as your friend, Dixie, I have to be honest with you."

Dixie dropped Betty Jo's hands as she turned her attention to Nona. "About what?"

Nona blurted out, "You look awful!" Dixie stared at Nona. "You're still in your robe. Your hair is a mess. Your eyes and skin are blotchy from all the crying you've done. You've got to do something now!"

Betty Jo nodded in agreement. "She's right."

Wide-eyed, Dixie walked over to mirror beside the door. When she caught sight of her reflection, she gasped. She looked to Betty Jo, who looked to Nona, who started to giggle. Soon, all three were bent over double, laughing so hard they could barely catch their breath. Tears of laughter streamed down their faces. Each time they tried to stop, they'd look at one another and start up again.

"We have to stop or I'm going to wet my pants," Betty Jo said wrapping her arms around her stomach.

"I think I already did!" Dixie confessed as she hurried down the hall to her bedroom.

"Oh, no!" Betty Jo and Nona said together. Then looking at one another, they burst out laughing again.

Betty Jo and Nona were discussing the White Bible Ceremony and taking notes when Dixie emerged from her bedroom dressed, made up, and with her hair styled. "Tada!" she said as she entered the kitchen with arms spread out.

Nona clapped. "There's the Dixie we all know and love."

"The one and only and, thanks to y'all, I'm feeling much better than I did an hour ago!"

"It's about time you got out here. We need fresh eyes to look this over." Betty Jo slid her notebook toward Dixie.

Dixie looked from the notebook to Betty Jo. "What's this?"

"We've planned out Jenny's White Bible Ceremony."

"We followed the basic outline you got from Mrs. Nancy," Nona said, "but we've changed some things to make it our own since we're not giving her only roses like they did for Grace. We've already called Michael at The Columns to make sure they have the date open. He's already emailed us food choices and prices. We need your expert eye to look it over."

With notebook in hand, Dixie pulled up a chair to join her friends at her dining room table. She read through their notes then closed the notebook and slid it across the table to Betty Jo.

"Well?" Betty Jo and Nona asked together.

Dixie smiled. "I like it. It's simple and straightforward. What I remember about the one Mrs. Nancy did for Grace was that it was formal, which was fitting for her, but I think the changes you've made are just right for Jenny."

Betty Jo smiled back. "Great! That's what we were aiming for."

"Then that's a wrap." Nona stood up from the table. "I don't mean to rush y'all, but I have a great deal to take care of at home. Monty went to get Riley at the airport. I want to be there when they get to Dad's house. . . I mean my house."

Betty Jo took in the sad look on Nona's face. She'd almost forgotten the grief Nona was carrying. She stood. "I know you do. Let's get you home."

Dixie walked the two of them to the door. She took Nona's hands in hers. "Thanks for coming. Please, let me know if there's anything I can do to help you in any way."

Nona leaned down to kiss her cheek. "Thanks. I will."

When they got into her car, Betty Jo said, "I hope she feels better about

Jason's decision."

"I think you helped her see another side to his staying at NextStep this weekend."

Betty Jo smiled. "That's how friends help one another."

Nona turned away and looked out the car window. Betty Jo could hear the emotion in her voice when she spoke. "I don't know how people get through life without the love and support of good friends."

"Me either."

They were silent for the rest of their ride to Nona's house.

Chapter Eleven

After dropping Nona off at her house, Betty Jo stopped by Harris Grocery. She knew how much the children loved Harris's homemade corn dogs. She could fix them corn dogs for supper and get pork chops for the adults in the family. There was no way Don would be happy eating a corn dog. She'd call Lily when she got home to ask if she and Kendall would join them for supper. Since it was Friday night, maybe Kendall could stay to spend the night with her cousins.

As she drove home, she thought about Nona and Dixie. Even though her life had been turned upside down in the past week, she wasn't going through anything as tough as what they were going through. This was one of those times she needed to stop and thank God for the blessings in her life. Immediately, a big smile spread across her face as the sweet little faces of her grandchildren popped into her thoughts.

Thank you, God, for giving me this unexpected opportunity to spend time with my grandchildren so I can shower them with my love and together we can create treasured memories.

She was still smiling as she turned into her driveway. When she noticed two men in uniform step out of the black car parked in front of her house, her smile quickly faded. Her mouth went dry as she stared straight ahead, unable to move. The two uniformed men stood next to their car. They appeared to be Air Force officers, but she wasn't sure of their rank. Ethan had explained to her many times how to tell rank, but her mind was blank now as she studied them closer. A sudden urge came over her to back the car out and drive as far away from the news the two officers had to give her as she could get. Then she thought of Ethan, her strong, determined son. He'd always faced difficult situations head-on. He'd be disappointed in her if she ran away. She took a deep breath, opened her car door, stepped out, and on shaking legs walked toward the officers.

As she approached the two officers, each removed his hat and placed it under his arm. The taller of the two spoke. "Good afternoon, ma'am. I'm Lieutenant Colonel Wilkerson and this is Captain Reeves. Are you Mrs. Breedlow?"

She tried to keep her voice steady, but it cracked, filling with emotion as she answered, "Yes, I'm Mrs. Donald Breedlow. Are you here about my son, Lieutenant Colonel Breedlow?"

"Yes, ma'am, we are. You might be more comfortable if we went inside."

Betty Jo shook her head. She didn't want to have the memory of the moment they gave her bad news, perhaps devastating news, about her son associated with any room in her house. "No, please say what you've come to tell me right here." She braced herself for the words that could possibly change her world forever.

Lieutenant Colonel Wilkerson stepped closer. "We regret to inform you that your son, Lieutenant Colonel Ethan Breedlow, is missing in action."

Betty Jo stared at the lieutenant colonel, sure she hadn't heard him correctly. Gripping his arm tightly, she looked up into his face, and asked, "He's missing? Not. . .dead?"

"Ma'am the only official information we have at this time is Lieutenant Colonel Breedlow is missing in action, MIA."

As Betty Jo's legs buckled, Captain Reeves came up quickly beside her. Together, the two officers helped her to the wicker chair on the front porch. She buried her head in her hands and cried tears of relief for Ethan being alive and tears of despair for his missing in action. She didn't know how long she cried, but when she finally looked up, the two officers were still standing at her side.

Taking the handkerchief Lieutenant Colonel Wilkerson handed her, she wiped away her tears and blew her nose. "I'm sorry. I thought you were going to tell me my son had been killed in action. I know 'missing in action' is not the best news, but hope comes with that news where with the other. . ." Her voice trailed off.

"Yes, ma'am."

"Can you tell me where he went missing, the country or region?"

This time it was Captain Reeves who spoke. "I'm sorry, ma'am, but that information is classified."

"How long has he been missing?"

"I'm sorry, ma'am, but that information is classified."

Betty Jo stood to face the officers. "What was he doing when he went missing?"

"I'm sorry, ma'am, but that information is classified."

In a demanding voice, she asked, "What can you tell me?"

Lieutenant Colonel Wilkerson answered this time. "We are sorry, ma'am, but we do not have information that can be shared with the family at this time. However, our job is not finished here. We need to inform Lieutenant Colonel Breedlow's wife the status of her husband. Do you know where we can find her?"

Betty Jo put her hand to her mouth and fresh tears began to fall down her cheeks as she thought about Chloe, Kelli, Matthew, Chase, Don, Kendall, and Lily receiving the news about Ethan. "Oh, my, of course you do. This is going to be devastating to her." She looked down at her watch to check the time. It was fifteen minutes before two. Chloe would be picking up the children from school at three. She shouldn't be with the children when she was given this news. "She's helping out a friend at the law offices of Foxx and Foxx. I can show you where that is."

"That's not necessary."

Betty Jo wasn't sure of the protocol the two officers had to follow, but she knew without a doubt she needed to be with Chloe when they gave her the news of Ethan missing in action. "I understand it isn't necessary, but I need to be there with her when you tell her."

Lieutenant Colonel Wilkerson studied her for a moment before stepping back and returning his hat to his head. "Yes, ma'am."

The two officers turned away from her and walked to their car.

Betty Jo looked to the heavens, calling out to God, "Dear Lord, be with Ethan wherever he may be. Protect him and direct his path home to his family. Give me strength and courage to hold my family together during this crisis. I ask this in the precious name of my Savior and Lord, Amen."

With renewed strength, Betty Jo stood up from her chair and followed the officers.

The drive to the law offices of Foxx and Foxx took only a few minutes. On the way, Betty Jo tried to think of some way the news the officers were about to deliver to Chloe could be softened. In the end she realized this kind of news was going to be hard to take no matter how it was delivered.

When they stopped in front of the law office, Captain Reeves got out and opened the door for Betty Jo. She looked up at him. "Would y'all let me go in first and then the two of you can follow after a few minutes?"

Captain Reeves looked to Lieutenant Colonel Wilkerson who answered her question. "Yes, we can do that."

Betty Jo stopped before opening the door. She knew the first person she would see would be Lily. She didn't want to alarm her, so she plastered a smile on her face, took a deep breath, and pulled open the door. She dropped her smile when she found Lily wasn't at her desk. The office was eerily silent. The first thought that came to her mind was that somehow Chloe and Lily had found out about Ethan and had been so upset by the news they'd rushed out leaving the office unattended. She was turning back to the door when her ears caught the faint sound of laughter deeper in the office. She followed the sound around the corner, past two open doors until she came to a closed door. The laughter was coming from the office behind the closed door.

She tapped on the door. "Lily? Chloe? Nathan?"

There was no answer, only more laughter. She knocked louder. "Hello, it's Betty Jo."

The laughter stopped abruptly. Betty Jo had her hand up ready to knock once more, when the door suddenly opened.

Nathan straightened his tie and began rambling, "Oh, Betty Jo, I bet you're looking for Lily. We sent her to the courthouse to get copies of some documents we need. I didn't think about the fact there was no one in the front office."

"Actually, I'm looking for Chloe. Do you know where I can find her?"

"I'm right here." Chloe came from behind the door to stand next to Nathan. When she looked at Betty Jo, she came out of the office and grabbed hold of Betty Jo's arm. "Oh, Betty Jo, what's wrong? Is it the kids?"

Realizing her façade had failed to keep the concern and worry from her face, tears began to fill Betty Jo's eyes. She shook her head, but before she could answer, she heard the clicking footsteps of the two officers coming down the hall toward them. She put her arm around Chloe's shoulder.

"Mrs. Breedlow?"

At the sound of Lieutenant Colonel Wilkerson's voice, Betty Jo held her tighter. They stood together in the hall facing the two officers.

Betty Jo could feel Chloe's body begin to shake. "Yes."

Lieutenant Colonel Wilkerson stepped closer. "We regret to inform you your husband, Lieutenant Colonel Ethan Breedlow, is missing in action."

Wide-eyed, Chloe looked from Lieutenant Colonel Wilkerson to Captain Reeves. Betty Jo noticed the color draining from Chloe's face as her body crumbled. Betty Jo reached out to stop her fall, but it was Nathan who rushed forward, easing her gently to the floor. Betty Jo knelt beside her.

"Oh, no, dear God! Not Ethan!"

They all turned to see Lily standing behind Captain Reeves. No one had noticed she'd been there when Lieutenant Colonel Wilkerson gave Chloe the news about Ethan. She stood staring at the scene before her. Betty Jo quickly stood and hurried to her daughter. She wrapped her arms around her. "He's going to be okay, Lily. They're going to find Ethan and bring him home. We have to believe that."

Lily buried her face in her mother's shoulder and began to cry. Betty Jo patted her back rocking her back and forth. Over and over she said, "Shh. It's going to be okay." Not sure if the words she repeated were said to comfort Lily or to convince herself.

"Should I call for an ambulance?"

At Captain Reeves' words, Betty Jo was brought back to the situation with her daughter-in-law still lying unconscious on the floor. She took Lily by the shoulders and looked directly into her eyes. "We cannot fall apart, Lily. Chloe and the children need us to be strong. Ethan is counting on our strength. We can't let him down." Lily wiped the tears from her cheeks and nodded.

Betty Jo once again knelt next to Chloe, then looked to Nathan, who was now holding Chloe's head in his lap. "We need a cold compress for her forehead."

Nathan thought for a moment. "There's a first aid kit in the break room."

In a flash, Captain Reeves was on his way, looking for the break room. Nathan called out to him, "Third door on the right. I think it's on the second shelf of the first cabinet."

Lily quickly fell in behind Captain Reeves. "I know where it is. I'll get it."

Lily returned with the first aid kit and placed it on the floor as she knelt next to Chloe. It didn't take her long to locate the instant ice pack, activate it, and place it on Chloe's head. All eyes were on Chloe's still body when her eyes began to flutter open. With a moan, she put her hand up to her forehead and looked up at Nathan with confusion. "Ethan?"

Gently taking Chloe's hand in hers, Betty Jo said, "Chloe, you fainted, but you're going to be fine."

Captain Reeves leaned down to hand Betty Jo a cup of water. She gave him a puzzled look, but then realized he must have gotten it when he went in search of the first aid kit. Together, she and Nathan helped Chloe sit up. She handed Chloe the cup of water. "Here, you need to drink this."

Sitting up, Chloe took the cup from Betty Jo. As she sipped the water, she looked around. When she noticed Lieutenant Colonel Wilkerson standing to the side, the cup slipped from her hand. With a shaking finger, she pointed at him. "You told me Ethan's missing."

Lieutenant Colonel Wilkerson stepped forward. "Yes, ma'am."

Betty Jo squeezed her hand. "Ethan is missing, Chloe, but they're going to find him and bring him home to you and the children."

Chloe turned her head, unblinking. She stared at Betty Jo for a long minute and then took hold of her hand. "The children. We can't tell the children." Pulling Betty Jo closer and taking both of her hands in hers, she pleaded, "Oh, Betty Jo, the children must never know their daddy is missing. Promise me you won't let them ever know."

Betty Jo's heart went out to Chloe. She could see that panic and pain were filling her mind. "I won't tell the children, Chloe, I promise."

Releasing her grip on Betty Jo, Chloe buried her face in her hands and broke down in sobs that shook her whole body.

As Betty Jo got up from the floor, she wondered how she could ever hold true to her promise of keeping this a secret from her three inquisitive, observant, sensitive grandchildren.

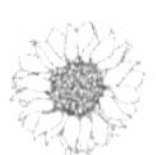

It took several minutes before Chloe was calm enough to get up off the floor and be helped into a chair in Nathan's office. Betty Jo stepped out of the room, leaving Chloe with Nathan and the two officers. Lily had gone up front to close the office for the day. It was obvious that no one was in any shape to deal with clients.

Betty Jo picked up her purse from the floor in the hallway where she'd dropped it when Chloe fainted and was heading to the front to talk to Lily about the situation Chloe had put her in with the children when her cell phone began to ring. Taking it from her purse, two important facts came to her attention– it was Don calling, and it was five minutes before three. Without a doubt, she knew Don would know something bad had happened as soon as she said "Hello." There was no way she could make her voice sound normal. She also knew someone needed to be at the school to pick up the children. She quickly realized her best bet would be to send him a text.

With the phone still ringing, with hands shaking, she began typing in her text.

Sorry, can't talk. Need you to pick up kids at school by three.

She pressed the SEND button, and with her heart pounding prayed he'd read it. In only a few seconds, his answer came back.

Ok. Is everything all right?
Betty Jo quickly responded.
Will explain later.

With a great sense of relief, Betty Jo leaned against the wall, looked up to heaven, and prayed a prayer aloud she never thought she would. "Thank you, God, for texts."

Seeing her mother leaning against the wall, Lily hurried toward her. "Mom, are you okay?"

Betty Jo pushed off from the wall. "Truthfully, I'm not sure how I am. If my phone hadn't rung a few minutes ago, Kelli, Matthew, and Chase would have been standing outside of the school wondering if we'd forgotten about them. But now your father is headed their way to get them."

"Oh, Mom, Daddy doesn't know yet. How are we going to tell him about Ethan and not let the kids know?"

Betty Jo let out a sigh. "I don't know. We'll just have to take it one step at a time. The first step is to get those kids home. I think our second step must be getting Chloe calmed down enough to take her home. Then the third step is making sure things remain as normal as possible at home. And that's where you and Kendall come in."

Lily put her hand to her mouth. "Oh, Mom, what do I do about Kendall? Do I tell her and then expect her to keep it a secret from her cousins, or do I keep it a secret from her and hope she understands why I didn't tell her?"

Betty Jo thought for a moment. "I think for now, you keep it a secret from her."

Lily nodded. "Now, tell me what Kendall and I can do."

Betty Jo plopped down in one of the chairs across from Lily's desk. "I just picked up corn dogs and pork chops from Harris's when I came home to find those two officers waiting for me. I'm sure they've spoiled in the trunk of my car." She shook her head, then went on with her explanation. "I was planning on having you and Kendall over tonight for supper and then ask Kendall to spend the night."

Lily smiled down at her mother. "We can still do that, Mom. In fact, that all sounds like a good diversion for everyone. Let's throw in a movie and popcorn for the kids tonight, and we've got a plan. I'll pick up more corn dogs and pork chops, get Kendall packed up to spend the night, and be at your house by five. You take Chloe home and straight upstairs. Tell the kids she's caught something and might be contagious, so they leave her alone. Send them out to play while you tell Dad what's going on with Ethan."

Even though Betty Jo's heart was broken, she couldn't help but smile with relief. "Thank you, sweetheart, for coming up with a plan. With all that's happened, I wasn't sure what to do next."

Lily anxiously glanced down the hall. "The first thing we need to do is get Chloe out of here and home, hopefully before the children get there."

Betty Jo looked up at the clock on the wall behind Lily's desk. "Oh, I don't think that can happen. I'm sure your dad is almost home with the children."

Lily thought for a moment. "Don't they usually have a snack as soon as they get home?"

Betty Jo nodded. "They're usually starving."

"If they have their snack in the kitchen, then you can take Chloe in through the front door and up the stairs without anyone seeing her. If any of them even get a glimpse of her in the state she's in, they'll know something is terribly wrong."

Betty Jo looked down. "I'm afraid the same thing is true if they see my face. I'm not sure I can hide the worry and fear I'm feeling."

"If we're to honor Chloe's wishes to keep this a secret from the children, you have no choice, Mom."

Betty Jo stood-up, straightened her clothes, and brushed through her hair with her fingers. "You're right. I can do this. I'll use the tricks I've used when dealing with terminally ill patients. I'll put a smile on my face and fake a positive attitude."

"We can do this, right?"

"Right, but first we need to get Chloe." Betty Jo held out her hand to Lily.

Lily put her hand in her mother's, and together they walked down the hall to Nathan's office. Both were relieved to find Chloe sitting at Nathan's desk calmly talking with Captain Reeves. Nathan was sitting on the corner of his desk, listening to their conversation. Lieutenant Colonel Wilkerson was standing off in the corner away from the group, talking on his phone. As soon as Chloe saw Betty Jo, she motioned for her to join them.

"Captain Reeves was just telling me he'll be staying here in Kerry to support us through this difficult time. He was also telling me not only is the Air Force searching for Ethan, but also the army and the marines. I think that's a good thing, don't you?"

Betty Jo looked to Captain Reeves. "That's hopeful news. What else can you tell us?"

Captain Reeves shook his head. "Nothing else at this time, ma'am."

"You're staying here in Kerry?"

"Yes, ma'am. I will be staying. However, Lieutenant Colonel Wilkerson will be going back to Langley Air Force Base."

Timidly, Betty Jo asked, "So, Captain Reeves, will you be staying with us?"

Captain Reeves smiled. "No, ma'am. I'll be getting a room nearby."

"I was wondering which child I was going to have to make move out of their bedroom." Betty Jo laughed with embarrassment. "How do we get in touch with you?"

"I will be staying in touch with you," Captain Reeves assured her. "You are also welcome to call either one of us." Both Captain Reeves and Lieutenant Colonel Wilkerson handed her and Chloe cards with their contact information.

"Thank you. I appreciate how you've handled this situation." Betty Jo turned to Chloe. "Don is picking up the children from school. Lily is going to pick up Kendall, then they'll be joining us for supper." Taking a step closer, she added, "I don't have my car here, so I thought we could go home together. I was thinking we could get you upstairs to your room before the children see you. We can tell them you're not feeling well so they won't bother you."

Chloe's head jerked up as her eyes pinned on Betty Jo. "How could you ever think that my children 'bother' me?"

Betty Jo, stunned by Chloe's reaction, hurried on to explain. "I didn't mean that they are a bother to you. I meant that they wouldn't. . ." She paused, searching her brain for a better word to use. "I meant that they wouldn't disturb you. You could have some time alone to process everything that's happened."

Lily, who had been standing behind her mother, came around to stand next to Chloe. She placed her hand on her shoulder. "We're worried about you, Chloe, that's all. We know this isn't easy for you, and your concern is evident. If you want us to keep this news from the children, you might want to take some time alone to get yourself together. I don't think it'd be good for them to see you right now. You know how sensitive they are. After one look at you in the state you're in, they'd know something was wrong. Mom's just trying to help."

Chloe reached up and patted Lily's cheek. "Maybe I do need some time alone to get myself together before I see my children." Looking back at Betty Jo, she added, "Let's go home."

JOY

Chapter Twelve

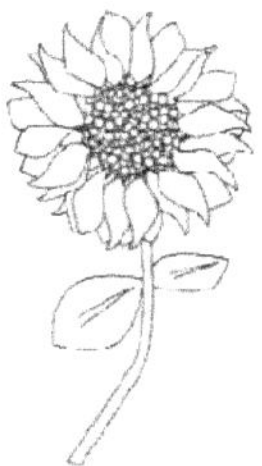

As soon as Betty Jo dropped her off at her house, Nona did the two things she always did when she got home. The first was to take off her watch, which she rarely set down in the same place twice. She would have to search for it the next time she left the house. The second was to head straight to her bedroom to take off her shoes and put on her well-worn leather slippers Bill had given her many years ago for Christmas when he'd grown tired of looking at her old ones. As she headed down the hall to her bedroom, she smiled, wondering what he'd think of those same slippers today.

Her smile faded as she walked past her father's closed office door. She'd closed that door the day she'd taken him to live at Homewood. She couldn't handle seeing his empty chair behind his walnut desk. She'd even closed the blinds on the office window so she couldn't see the emptiness of his office from the garden. She stopped and placed her hand flat on the door as tears began to roll down her cheeks. It was hard to know her father would never step foot inside his office ever again. Even after taking him to Homewood, she'd imagined he'd one day come back to his office. She'd known that was highly unlikely, but she'd held out hope. Now, that hope was gone. She had to face the reality and the finality that he'd never sit in his office chair again.

"Hello?" Monty called out.

Hurriedly wiping away her tears with the back of her hand, she headed back down the hall to the kitchen. "I didn't even hear you come in."

Monty stood in the kitchen holding a suitcase in each hand. "We really made good time. Believe it or not, the traffic around Atlanta wasn't a problem. Now, where do you want me to put these." He held up Riley's suitcases.

Nona pointed to the room off the kitchen. "In the room he usually stays in. It's all ready for him." Looking around, she asked, "Where is he? You didn't leave him sitting in the car, did you?"

Monty called over his shoulder as he carried the suitcases to Riley's room. "I thought he was right behind me. He must still be outside."

"What's he doing out there?" Nona wondered aloud. She opened the back door and looked around. Glad to see he wasn't sitting in the car, she called as she walked outside. "Riley? Where are you?"

"Over here."

Nona followed his voice around the corner of the house. She found Riley, his head in his hands, sitting on the bench in their mother's rose garden. She'd known that Riley would have a hard time with their father's death. She sat down beside him, and put her arm around his shoulder. "Oh, Riley."

His face streaked with tears, Riley turned to her. "Oh, Nona."

As brother and sister, they sat on the same bench where their mother and father had once sat together. Holding on to one another, they wept.

"I can't believe he's. . . gone," Riley said in a halting voice. "I'm truly sorry I left you to deal with all of this alone, Nona."

She squeezed his shoulder. "I was never alone, Riley. God's been with me the whole time along with Monty, Layne, Betty Jo, and Dixie. Plus. . ." She stood, and with a teasing smile held out her hand to her brother. "We all know you're a wimp!"

Ignoring her hand, Riley stood too. "Wimp! That's not a very nice thing for a little sister to say to her big brother."

Nona started walking back to the house while continuing her teasing. "I call 'em like I see 'em, Brother!"

Riley called after her. "Well, you never did have good eyesight." Hurrying to her side, he wrapped her in his arms. "Truthfully, I want to thank you for handling everything."

Nona kissed her brother's cheek. "You're very welcome." She leaned back so she could look directly in his eyes. "Honestly, it was my pleasure and honor. You hungry?"

"I'm starving."

"Let's go in and see what we can scrounge up for lunch."

Holding hands, the two slowly walked to the back door.

Monty met them at the door. "Where have you two been? I'm heating up the leftovers from the meal Dixie, Layne, and Betty Jo brought over the other night. I was beginning to think I might have to eat it all by myself."

Nona and Riley laughed as they stepped into their father's house together. They had just walked into the kitchen when Nona's cell phone began to vibrate. She looked at the screen to see that it was Nathan calling. She was about to hit the DECLINE button for the call to go to voice mail, when she had the overwhelming feeling she needed to answer his call. She pressed ACCEPT and put the phone to her ear.

"Hello, Nathan."

"Nona, I don't want to alarm you, but we have a situation that has made it difficult for me to keep the office open for business the rest of the day."

Nona was instantly filled with apprehension. "What's happened, Nathan?"

Alert, both Monty and Riley moved closer to Nona to listen to her conversation.

"As you know, Chloe was here at the office working with me today. We came out of my office and. . ." Nathan paused.

"Yes, and?"

"These two Air Force officers along with Betty Jo came to tell her Ethan is missing in action. Nona, Chloe fainted dead away right there in the hallway when she heard the news about Ethan. I've never seen anyone just fall over like that. It truly scared me."

Nona gasped, "Ethan's missing?"

With a look of disbelief, Monty stared at Nona and repeated what he'd just heard. "Ethan's missing?"

Nona held up one finger as she pressed the speaker button on her phone so Monty and Riley could hear Nathan's explanation.

"They said he's missing in action. They couldn't or wouldn't tell us where he was when he went missing or how or why or anything else, just that he's missing."

"How is Chloe now?"

"Better. Betty Jo took her home. After Lily found out, she left too. So, it's just me down here, and to tell you the truth, I don't think I'm the best for our clients right now. If it's okay with you, I'd like to close the office early for the weekend."

"Of course you can, Nathan. I wouldn't expect you to stay down there after all that's happened."

Monty leaned in closer to Nona's phone. "Nathan, this is Monty. Did the Air Force officers say anything about keeping in touch or give a number where they can be reached?"

"I think so. I saw them give their cards to Betty Jo and Chloe. Those cards must have their phone numbers. They also said they would keep the family informed."

"What about Don and the kids? Do they know?" Nona asked.

"I don't know about Don, but Chloe doesn't want the children to know anything about Ethan being missing."

"That's interesting," Nona said more to herself than to Nathan. "Thanks for letting me know, Nathan."

"Did Riley get there okay?"

"I'm here, Nathan," Riley said into the phone.

"That's good. I'll talk to y'all later." Nathan ended the call.

Nona put the phone on the counter. Shaking her head, she looked to Monty. "This hasn't been a good week for the Fearsome Foursome."

Layne spent most of the morning with Madison, her three-year-old granddaughter, at her pediatrician's office. It wasn't at all the morning she'd planned. When her daughter Blair called her before seven in the morning to tell her Madison was running a fever and complaining about her throat hurting, what could she do but offer to take her to the doctor so Blair wouldn't have to miss a day of work. As a retired teacher, Layne was aware of the hassle it was to take a day off as a teacher. You had to write up lesson plans for a substitute to follow and pray they could and would follow those plans so the students wouldn't miss an entire day of instruction. She remembered many days when she'd dragged herself out of bed and to school not feeling her best just so she wouldn't have to write up substitute plans.

Luckily, Madison's pediatrician, Hailey, who happened to be Dixie's daughter, had been able to work her in first thing. When trying to get a sick child seen by the doctor as soon as possible, it helped to be friends with the doctor's mother. She learned two important things from Hailey that morning. The first was that Madison had a virus, which Hailey assured her would run its course in short order with bed rest and ibuprofen every four hours. The second was that Jason wouldn't be spending the weekend at home as Dixie had planned, which according to Hailey, had left her mother devastated.

Layne had no doubt Hailey was right after witnessing Dixie's excitement about Jason's weekend visit only a few days ago. It broke her heart to think about the disappointment Dixie must be feeling. She'd hoped as soon as she got Madison settled in bed she'd be able to give Dixie a call to let her know she was in her thoughts. Her plan hadn't worked out as she hoped. She'd spent the rest of her day rocking Madison, who'd cried every time she tried to put her in bed. By the time Blair picked Madison up, Layne was exhausted. She didn't even encourage Blair to stay and chat as she normally would. Instead, as soon as they'd gotten out the door, she was walking down the hall to her bedroom to get in a quick nap before Mark came home. She was stopped by the familiar ringtone she'd set for her oldest son.

"Nathan, can I call you back? I've had Madison all day and was just on my way—"

"Mom."

Layne fell silent. She could tell by the tone of Nathan's voice that something was very wrong. Her heart began to race. "What's wrong?"

"It's Ethan. He's missing."

"Missing?"

"Mom, Ethan is missing in action."

"Oh, Nathan."

Nathan went on to explain. "Chloe was helping us out here today when two officers from the Air Force came and told her Ethan is missing in action."

Layne sat down on her bed as the reality of what Nathan was telling her became clear to her. "Did they tell Chloe where he was when he went missing?"

"They couldn't say. They said it was classified."

"Do Betty Jo, Don, and Lily know Ethan is missing?"

"Miss Betty Jo was with the two Air Force officers. I'm pretty sure they went to her house first and then came here together. Lily was here at the office and heard the news. I don't know if Mr. Don knows or not."

"Do you know if they've told the children?"

"Chloe doesn't want the children to know anything about this. She made that very clear to all of us."

Layne stood up and began to pace. She knew Betty Jo well enough to know how hard a secret like that would be for her to keep. "Does she really think she can keep this a secret from them? They'll need to know at some point. He's their father."

"Mom, it's her decision to make for her children. We need to respect that."

Layne shook her head. "Maybe, but I think it's a mistake. I've found secrets have a way of coming out when you least expect them to."

"That may be true, but that's none of our business."

Hearing how he clipped his words, she could tell her response had irritated him. She took a deep breath. "You're right. I'll respect Chloe's wishes, but that doesn't mean I agree with her."

"You don't have to agree, Mom, just remember not to say anything about Ethan being missing in front of the children."

"I promise I won't. Thanks for calling to let me know." She sat back down on the bed as she ended the call.

It was alarming how many life-changing events had happened to her friends in only a few days—Mr. James passed away, Jason wouldn't be coming home for the weekend, and Ethan was missing. They were going to need her to be strong and clear minded. She bowed her head.

Dear Lord, be with Ethan wherever he may be. Provide him the strength and courage he needs to get through the situation he's in. Be with those who are searching for him that they may find him and bring him home to be with his family and friends. Fill Betty Jo and her family with hope and peace as they wait for Ethan to come home. Help me to be the friend Betty Jo, Nona, and Dixie need. In Jesus name I pray, Amen.

Dixie couldn't believe how much better she felt about the situation with Jason after her visit with Betty Jo and Nona. When she'd gotten the call informing her Jason didn't want to come home for the weekend, she'd taken it personally. She'd immediately thought he didn't want to be with her or the rest of the family. She'd never once considered it an act of love. When she thought of him staying away because of his love for her and for his family, that changed her whole outlook on the situation. It was as if a weight had been lifted from her shoulders.

As soon as Betty Jo and Nona left, Dixie pulled out her Kitchen Aid mixer, yeast, flour, sugar, and salt. She was going to bake four loaves of her delicious—according to everyone who'd ever tasted it—crispy French bread. It'd go great with the homemade lasagna she planned on preparing next. When Alex left that morning, she'd been inconsolable. She couldn't wait to see the look on his face when he got home that evening to find she'd fixed him one of his favorite home-cooked meals and was in a better mood.

She'd just put her bread in the oven to bake when the house phone rang. It was her habit to ignore calls on the landline since they were usually someone soliciting for something she didn't want or need. Most of the time it was some company asking her to purchase a warranty for her Kia she'd traded in over three years ago. She wasn't sure why, but for some unknown reason this time she decided to answer.

"Hello."

"Miss Dixie?"

The voice on the phone was a young woman's with a slight Southern accent. The voice sounded vaguely familiar, but she couldn't put a name with it.

"Yes, this is Dixie Bradley. Who's calling, please?"

"This is Grace Harris-Bannerman. Nona's daughter."

The phone dropped from Dixie's hand as she fell into the closest chair. Her breath caught in her throat. It took her a few seconds to recover from the shock of Nona's estranged daughter calling her before she was able to pick the phone up from the end table where it'd landed.

"Grace, you caught me by surprise. I wasn't expecting. . . you know. . . It's just I can't believe it's you calling me." Dixie knew she was rambling. She was searching her brain trying to come up with any reason Grace would call her. They'd never been close.

Grace chuckled. At least it sounded like a chuckle to Dixie. "I'm sure you're wondering why I'm calling you out of the blue like this."

Knowing the heartache Grace had caused Nona these past few years, she kept her voice neutral, void of warmth or emotion. "Yes, Grace, I am wondering that very thing."

"I had a message on my cell phone from Mom's friend Miss Layne telling me my granddad passed away. I just couldn't make myself call Miss Layne. She's too close to my mother. I'm calling you because you're the only one of Mom's other friends I could find who was listed in the phone book. I'm wondering when the funeral will be. The message didn't mention anything about the funeral."

Had no one called Grace to let her know about the arrangements for Mr. James? How sad she'd cut her family out of her life and had to learn about his death through a voice mail message. She remembered Nona saying that since Grace was his only grandchild, they had been very close once upon a time.

Dixie's heart went out to her. She softened her tone. "I'm so sorry you had to find out about his death that way, Grace." She had a strong urge to remind her it was her own fault her mother had felt uncomfortable with calling her, which was the reason she didn't know any of the arrangements. Instead, she took a deep breath. "You know how he was. Your grandfather didn't want a traditional funeral. Instead, he requested a celebration of his life to be held at his house at least ten days after his death. He didn't want tears or anyone making speeches or tributes to him. He asked that only family and friends come by the house for barbecue, cake, and whiskey, and share their most outrageous stories about him with one another."

When Grace finally spoke, Dixie could hear the emotion in her voice. "That's my granddad for you. He was one of a kind."

"You know your mother has had a very hard time with losing her father." Dixie wasn't sure if she should say anything about how much Grace had hurt her mother, but decided she couldn't make the strain between the two any worse. "And the fact is, you've broken her heart by the way you've cut her out of your life."

Totally ignoring Dixie's last statement, Grace asked, "Do you know when they'll have Granddad's memorial?"

"They haven't decided. Your mom is waiting for your Uncle Riley to get here so they can decide together. I'll be glad to call you to let you know when they set the date."

"Thank you, I'd appreciate that." She gave Dixie her phone number, and Dixie wrote it down.

Dixie was sure Grace was ready to end the call, but she had one more thing to ask before she did. "Does that mean you'll be attending his memorial?"

Grace hesitated before answering. "I'm not sure. Goodbye, Miss Dixie."

"Goodbye, Grace."

Dixie put the phone back in its cradle. She took it as a hopeful sign that Grace hadn't said that she wouldn't be attending, only that she wasn't sure. Now the question was, should Dixie tell Nona about the call, which could get her hopes up of a reconciliation, or wait to see if Grace actually showed up at the memorial?

The timer sounded on the oven. Her bread was finished. She hurried to the oven. She took the bread out, put the lasagna in, and set the timer for seventy minutes. When she noticed her cell phone on the counter to the left of the oven, she took it as a sign.

Nona answered before she'd even heard the phone ring. "Oh, Dixie, I'm glad you called. Have you heard the news about Ethan?"

All thoughts of Grace vanished from her mind. "No, what's happened?"

"He's missing in action."

"Missing? Oh, poor Betty Jo."

"I know. Listen, Riley's just gotten here, and we've got a lot to talk about. Let's talk later."

"That's fine."

They ended the call. It wasn't until later that night Dixie realized she hadn't said anything to Nona about Grace's call. Maybe that was for the best after all.

Chapter Thirteen

*I*t was a silent drive home with both Betty Jo and Chloe deep in thought. When Betty Jo turned into the driveway, she was relieved to find they had made it home before Don and the children. She got out of the car and was halfway to the door before she noticed Chloe was still sitting in the car. She'd hoped she could get Chloe settled upstairs as quickly as possible, but it seemed Chloe wasn't in as much of a hurry as she was. She counted to ten to calm herself before going back to the car.

She opened Chloe's door and leaned in. "Come on, Chloe. We really need to get you in the house before Don pulls in here with the children."

Chloe slowly turned toward her. "The whole way over here the same thought has been turning over and over in my head." Her tear-filled eyes met Betty Jo's. "What will I do if they never find him? What if he's. . ." Her voice trailed off.

Betty Jo sighed. *How could any of them get through this if they allowed such negativity to take over their thoughts?*

She had the sudden urge to grab Chloe and shake her. Instead, she reached out and, taking Chloe gently by the shoulders, said sternly, "You cannot allow yourself to think like that, Chloe. We must believe they're going to find Ethan. He will come home."

Chloe stared back at her blankly.

Betty Jo continued, "Now, if you want to keep what's happened to their daddy from your children, I suggest you get out of this car right now. I guarantee you if those children see you in the state you're in, they would know beyond a shadow of a doubt that something very bad has happened."

Betty Jo stood up, turned away from Chloe, and began walking back to the house. After a few minutes, she heard the car door shut. When she looked around, she was thankful to see Chloe was behind her. She waited for her at the back door.

Taking Chloe's hand in hers, she smiled. "How does a hot bath sound?"

Chloe gave her hand a squeeze. "Perfect."

After getting Chloe safely out of sight upstairs, Betty Jo busied herself in the kitchen hoping she could distract herself from thoughts of what Ethan might be going through. She was emptying the dishwasher when she happened to glance up at the kitchen clock. It was almost four thirty. She couldn't imagine where Don and the children could be. This was the first time he'd overseen all three by himself. She pulled her cell phone from her pocket and called him.

A young, sweet, bright, cheery voice answered, "Hi, Gigi!"

"Kelli, how'd you know it was me?"

"Your picture came up on the screen. Pops put me in charge of his phone."

"Where is Pops?"

"He's paying for his plants he bought. He got some pink roses for me to plant and take care of all by myself." Betty Jo could hear the excitement in her voice.

That told Betty Jo all she needed to know about where Don had taken the children and why he'd been gone so long. He'd gone to Myers Feed and Seed Store, his favorite place to shop, which was out by Weldon Academy. He'd be hard-pressed to drive by Myers without stopping to see what new plants they had gotten in since his trip there last week.

"That's great, Kelli. Where are your brothers?"

"They're helping Pops carry all the plants out to the truck."

"Okay, then. You tell him I called, okay?"

"Yes, ma'am, I'll tell him."

"Love you."

Kelli ended the call with, "Love you too, Gigi."

Betty Jo knew how happy buying plants made her husband. He'd be in a great mood when he came home. That made her heart even heavier knowing how sad the news she had to give him about Ethan would make him. She considered for a moment how it might be better to tell him about Ethan when they went to bed later that night, but quickly dismissed it as a bad idea. It wasn't right to keep such news about their son from him. She didn't have that right.

She was taken out of her reverie when she heard Lily's voice calling out at the back door. "A little help here, please."

Betty Jo hurried out to find both Lily and Kendall loaded down with bags of groceries. She took the bag Lily handed to her as she held the door open for them.

Lily plopped her bags on the kitchen counter. "I might have gotten a little carried away with the grocery shopping. Everything looked so good."

"I told her we had enough, but she wouldn't listen to me," Kendall added as she unloaded her burden of overfilled grocery bags.

Betty Jo glanced at the bags covering her counter. "It's okay. I'd rather have too much than not enough."

Kendall stood beside her grandmother. "I think we have more than enough."

"How's everything with Chloe?" Lily asked.

Betty Jo didn't want to alert Kendall about what was going on with Chloe. She forced a smile as she answered, "She's taking a relaxing bath."

Lily looked at Kendall. "You can help Gigi put the groceries away while I go upstairs to check on Chloe."

"What's wrong with Aunt Chloe?" Kendall asked with concern.

Lily looked to her mother to answer Kendall's question, "Nothing bad. She's just feeling a little under the weather."

All three turned toward the sound of the back door opening and watched as Matthew and Chase came running in.

"Wait till you see what we got!" the boys called out as they grabbed Kendall's hands and began pulling her toward the door.

With pleading eyes, Kendall looked to her mother and grandmother. "Can I go see?"

Betty Jo nodded her head. "Of course, go see!"

Lily laughed. "Now, that's excitement. It's exactly what we need to get us through this night." As she walked out of the kitchen, she added, "I'll come back to help you put all of this away after I check on Chloe."

Betty Jo was finishing putting the last of the groceries away in the refrigerator when Don came walking in the kitchen.

"Well, look who's here, finally."

Don went straight to the sink and began explaining as he washed his hands. "I thought the kids would enjoy a trip to Myers to help me pick out some plants after a long day at school. I was right too. They had a ball." As he dried his hands, he walked over to where Betty Jo was standing and wrapped his arms around her. "Were you missing me?"

Usually, their hugs were short, but this time she pulled him closer. "You'll never know how much."

He leaned back to look in her eyes. "Is something wrong?"

She buried her face in his chest. She tried to hold back her tears, but in the comfort of his arms, she couldn't stop them. He held her tighter and waited.

It took several minutes before Betty Jo was able to speak. As she pulled away from his embrace, she took his hand in hers and led him to the kitchen table. "Let's sit down and I'll explain everything." They sat at the table beside one another.

Still holding his hand, she began, "This isn't going at all the way I planned. In my plan, I was strong and in control of my emotions, but when you put your arms around me. . ."

"Betty Jo, what is it? Tell me what's happened."

"It's our son. Don, Ethan is missing in action."

Don gave her his full attention as she recounted the events from the moment she'd pulled in the driveway to find the two Air Force officers waiting until she'd helped Chloe upstairs less than an hour ago. She told him how Chloe didn't want the children to know their father was missing.

When she finished, Don sat silently beside her staring down at the floor. Still holding his hand, she put her other hand on his shoulder. "Are you okay?"

After several minutes of silence, Don shook his head. "I don't know what to say."

He looked up at Betty Jo and squeezed her hand. "It's hard to believe this is really happening. You hear about something like this happening to other people, but never think it can happen to you. It's like when you were paralyzed from Guillain-Barré. It was hard to believe that such a thing was happening to us."

Betty Jo could see tears filling his eyes. He took a deep breath before continuing. "But you know, after that tough time we went through together with Guillain-Barré and then my being falsely charged with a DUI, I've been thinking of myself as a strong person. But, Betty Jo, right now, I'm not sure I'm all that strong."

Betty Jo hitched her chair closer to Don's and took both of his hands in hers. "Don, you are strong. With God's help, we got through those tough times together, and with God's help, we'll get through this rough time together. We must keep the faith that they will find Ethan, we must believe that God is right there looking after him, and that Ethan will be back with his family once again."

With tears streaming down his face, Don looked down at the floor. "Betty Jo, it's always been you who's been the strong one. You're the one who got us through all of the hard times."

Betty Jo shook her head. "No, Don, you're wrong. It's always been God who got us through those hard times. I believe God will get all of us through this one. Please tell me you believe that too."

Don looked up into Betty Jo's eyes. "I do believe, Betty Jo. I believe God will lead all of us through this."

They stood up quickly at the sound of excited children running in the back door. Betty Jo smiled over at Don, who forced a smile on his face as he wiped his tears away. "Here we go. Let's see how well we can convince four youngins that every thing's fine and dandy at the Breedlow household."

Friday night went better than Betty Jo had hoped. Don kept the children busy in the greenhouse with the new plants while Lily and Betty Jo cooked the corn dogs and grilled the pork chops. The children talked excitedly all the way through supper, giving great details about their adventurous day. After supper they spent the rest of the evening curled up together on the couch watching the movies Lily had rented for them.

Lily and Betty Jo cleaned up the kitchen after supper while Don finished up in the greenhouse with the planting he and the children had started.

Lily tiptoed into the living room. She wanted to check on the children before leaving for home. Little Chase was sound asleep on Kendall's lap and it looked like Matthew would soon join his brother.

"Well?" Betty Jo asked as she put the last of the dishes in the dishwasher.

"I can tell you for certain that Dad did an excellent job of wearing those children out."

"They're asleep already?"

"If not already sleeping, they will be before long."

Betty Jo rolled her eyes in relief. "Thank heavens!"

Don came in the house soon after Lily left. He and Betty Jo carried Chase and Matthew upstairs to bed. Kendall and Kelli decided to continue watching their movie in Kelli's room, which was fine with Betty Jo. She'd checked in on Chloe and was careful not to make any noise as she opened the door. She found the room dark as pitch. She could make out Chloe's shape curled up in her bed. It was good she was sleeping. She needed the rest after the shock she'd had. She closed the door and went down the stairs to the kitchen.

The weekend passed without anything new about Ethan from Captain Reeves. He'd checked in every day just to let them know the search for Ethan continued. Chloe had remained sequestered in her room all weekend. Betty Jo had taken her meals, but each time she retrieved the tray she noticed very little had been eaten. Surprisingly, the children had left their mother alone. That was due to how busy their Aunt Lily kept them with the numerous activities she'd designed for them throughout the weekend.

Betty Jo was grateful that Lily had kept the children busy. It allowed her the time alone she needed to keep from falling apart in front of them. Don had kept busy all weekend with his projects either in his greenhouse or his shop. They'd spoken to each other very little during the day, but held onto one another tightly throughout the night.

The children were dressed, ready for school, and eating their breakfast on Monday morning when their mother walked into the kitchen dressed in an attractive navy-blue suit complete with jewelry and high heels.

All three children jumped up from the table and ran to her. Chloe sat down on the closest kitchen chair and pulled Chase and Matthew onto her lap. Kelli stood to her mother's side with her arm wrapped around her shoulder. "I missed you all so much," Chloe said as she kissed each child's cheek.

Wiping off his mother's kiss with the back of his hand, Matthew looked at her, worry in his eyes. "Are you still sick?"

Chloe chuckled and planted another kiss on his cheek. "I'm all better. In fact, I'm going to take you to school on my way to the office."

Kelli stepped away, withdrawing her arm from her mother's shoulder. "Office?"

Chloe stood up so fast that Chase and Matthew almost fell to the floor. Red-faced, she turned to Kelli. "Yes, 'office'! It's where I'm working for now!"

Betty Jo wondered why Kelli's question seemed to instantly anger Chloe. It wasn't an unreasonable question, since she hadn't gone to an office to work in Kelli's lifetime. She could see the hurt and confusion on the children's faces as they stood watching their mother leave the room.

Betty Jo clapped her hands together hoping to break the tension. "Come on, y'all need to sit down and finish your breakfast. Don't you worry about your mother. She's still a little tired."

Her eyes overflowing with tears, Kelli looked up at Betty Jo. "Gigi, she yelled at me and hurt my feelings."

Seeing her granddaughter upset broke Betty Jo's heart. She leaned down and smoothed Kelli's hair away from her face. "I know she did, sweetie. That can happen after someone has been sick for a few days and still isn't feeling well. I'm sure she didn't mean to yell and is sorry."

Chase came over to give his sister a hug. "It's going to be okay, Kelli. I won't yell at you."

Kelli returned her brother's hug. "I know you won't, Chase."

"Ha, ha! I'm going to finish my breakfast first and be the winner," Matthew called out from the table. "You two are losers."

"I'm not a loser," Chase said as he hurried to the table. "Am I, Gigi?"

"No, Chase, you're not a loser. You're all winners."

Things remained about the same for Betty Jo and her family for the next two weeks. The children continued to go to school each day. Betty Jo and Don continued to do everything they could to keep the children busy and Chloe's secret safe. Chloe continued to work at Foxx and Foxx Law Offices each day. Captain Reeves continued to give the same report about Ethan—missing in action—although he was no longer staying in Kerry. He'd returned to Langley Air Force Base where he delivered his report via phone instead of in person.

Betty Jo spent most of her day cleaning up after the four extra people in the house, doing laundry for four extra people, and feeding the four extra mouths breakfast and supper each day. Her understanding of why God gave children to the young was becoming clearer with each passing day. Her friend, Marci, the charge nurse for the pediatric wing at the hospital, called her several times begging her to take a shift. Even though Betty Jo missed her job as a nurse, she explained to Marci that her job at home took priority. The only good thing she found that came from her exhaustion was that when she fell into bed each night, she was asleep almost before her head hit the pillow, which meant she didn't lie awake worrying about Ethan or imagining what fates he might be suffering.

Those first few nights after Betty Jo and Don learned Ethan was missing, they had worried much and slept little. They knew they wouldn't be much help to Chloe, the children, or Lily if they continued with their sleepless nights. After Don had questioned his strength and belief when he'd first heard about Ethan, she was surprised when he proposed the solution to their problem after suffering through another long, restless night. Thinking back on their conversation that night, Betty Jo smiled. She was sure it was proof that God was working through him.

"Betty Jo, I think we need to give our worries and fears over to God each night before we go to bed."

Betty Jo remembered sighing. "Don, I'm praying to God day and night. I'm telling Him about my worries and my fears for Ethan. Although it brings me comfort to pray, it hasn't helped me sleep."

Don shook his head at her words. "I didn't say we need to pray more, Betty Jo. We need to do more than pray. We need to trust God to answer our prayers. We need to give over to Him all our worries and fears, and then trust Him with them. We haven't been trusting Him like He tells us to."

Betty Jo recalled how a Bible verse, or "heart verse" as Brother Richard called those Bible verses that were committed to memory, had come to her.

Trust in the Lord with all thine heart and lean not unto thine own understanding.

It was in that moment she realized how much she'd been leaning on her own understanding of what was happening to Ethan and not trusting God to answer the prayers she'd been praying for him. That was the reason for her constant worrying even though she'd been constantly praying. She'd left out trust. That night, in the quiet of their bedroom, she and Don began their routine of praying prayers of thanksgiving and entrusting their son to God's care. Since they'd made their commitment to trust God, they'd both been sleeping better.

Chapter Fourteen

Betty Jo was having one of those days when she was feeling overwhelmed by the long list of chores she still needed to complete before picking up the children from school when she heard a knock at the back door. She froze in place. She wasn't expecting company. The first thought that flew into her mind was that it was Captain Reeves. Her second thought was that he would have called if he had good news to share with the family.

"Betty Jo, are you going to answer the door or just leave us standing out here in the cold!"

She hurried to open the door, recognizing the sweet Southern tones of Dixie's voice calling out to her.

"I'm coming!"

When she opened the door, she was beyond thrilled to find not only Dixie, but also Layne and Nona standing at her back door. Even though her friends had called her at least once a day to check on her, this was the first time she'd seen any of them in person.

"Well, are you going to invite us in or not?" Nona asked.

Betty Jo stood aside as she held the door for her friends to enter. "Please, come in!"

She closed the door and followed them into the kitchen. "I'm so glad to see y'all."

Layne set a brown bag on the kitchen table before walking over to Betty Jo to give her a hug. "We've brought you lunch."

"From the Rustic Bistro," Dixie added as put down her bag next to Layne's.

"Chicken salad?" Betty Jo asked hopefully after accepting a hug from Dixie.

"On croissants and with a side of homemade chips," Nona said, reaching out for her hug.

Betty Jo beamed at her friends. "I can't believe you're here. Y'all couldn't have picked a better time to come."

Layne pulled out a chicken salad sandwich from the bag and placed it on one of the paper plates she'd brought. "Let's all sit down and eat."

Dixie sat down at the table. "You don't have to tell me twice. I'm starving."

After all were seated and their plates were filled, Layne prayed, "Dear Lord, we ask that you be with Ethan and bring him home soon. Bless this food to the nourishment of our bodies and our bodies to your service."

Betty Jo quickly added, "And thank you for my amazing friends. Amen."

"Have you heard anything more about Ethan?" Layne asked.

Betty Jo shook her head. "Nothing has changed since they gave us the news that he was missing. I get frustrated at times with not knowing, but then I think about that old saying 'no news is good news,' and realize I'd rather have no news than bad news." She turned to Nona. "I think working at your firm is helping Chloe keep her mind off of what's going on with Ethan."

Nona nodded and took a bite of her sandwich.

Dixie jumped in. "Oh, I think it's a true blessing that she's able to help Nona."

Once again, Nona simply nodded as she put a chip in her mouth without giving her opinion.

Nona's silence confused Betty Jo. "Don't you think it's a blessing for both Chloe and you, Nona?"

Nona swallowed her chip and gave Betty Jo a smile. "Sure."

Betty Jo put down her sandwich and cocked her head to one side as she took a closer look at Nona. "Okay, tell me what's going on."

Nona put down her sandwich and leaned back in her chair. "Okay, but it's nothing, really. It's just that Chloe's putting in so many hours at the office that I worry about all the time she's spending away from her children. I mean, don't they need her?"

Truth be told, Betty Jo had those same concerns. Most nights she was the one putting the children to bed before Chloe got home. Her excuse for being late was always that she, Nathan, and Lily were working overtime in order to be ready for the court date that was fast approaching. "Yes, they do need their mother, but I think Chloe is afraid if they spend too much time with her, they'll see she's worried, and then they'll ask questions she doesn't want to answer."

"So she's still not telling them about their daddy?" Layne asked.

Betty Jo sighed. "No, she's standing firm on not letting them know what's going on. Don and I are doing our best to keep them busy and distracted, but we're about to run out of ideas and stamina!"

"I'm sure you are," Dixie sympathized. "That's a strain on the two of you."

"It's fine. We're fine. I'm just glad we can help."

Layne began clearing off the table. "Speaking of help, is there anything any of us can do to help you tomorrow with Mr. James's celebration of life ceremony, Nona?"

Nona chuckled. "You could come take Riley far, far away until tomorrow at two. He's about to drive Monty and me nuts, coming in behind us and changing things after they've all been arranged." She shook her head before continuing. "Daddy and I talked about what he wanted. You know Daddy. He wrote most of it out, and I'm going to honor his wishes. Sweat's Barbecue is doing the barbecue, Brunswick stew, baked beans, and slaw. Monty's taken care of getting the Jack Daniel's Old #7 Tennessee Whiskey—Daddy's favorite—and soft drinks for those who don't want to partake. Dixie has offered to make three cakes."

Layne turned to Dixie. "Which three did you finally decide to make?"

"I've made a red velvet cake with ermine frosting, and Mr. James's favorite carrot cake with cream cheese icing, and a Chocolate Ice Storm Cake. Actually, I've made two Chocolate Ice Storm Cakes, one for the celebration and one for the White Bible Ceremony."

"That all sounds delicious, but what in the world is ermine icing?" Layne asked. "I don't think I've ever heard of that."

"It's a boiled frosting. You'll love it."

"I'm sure I will."

Nona looked around at her friends. "There is something y'all can do for me tomorrow."

"Name it," Layne said.

"Come early and stay late."

Layne laughed. "We can do that. Mark and I will be there right before two and stay until you shoo us out."

Dixie nodded in agreement. "Alex and I will do the same."

"Don and I will be there too." Betty Jo hesitated a minute before asking Nona the question that had been on her heart. "Have you heard anything from Grace?"

Nona ran her hands through her hair. "Not a word. It doesn't make sense to me. Through her actions she's made it crystal clear she doesn't want to have anything to do with me, but she was so close to her grandfather. I thought she'd want to at least honor his memory. I guess I don't know my daughter anymore."

Betty Jo could hear the sadness and disappointment in Nona's voice. She placed her hand on Nona's back. "I'm sorry."

Layne crossed her arms. "Well, it doesn't make sense to me either. I called her the day Mr. James passed away, but she didn't answer. I got her voice mail. I didn't want to leave a message like that, so I asked her to call me. When she didn't call that day, I called her several times the next day. Still no answer. She was making it very clear that she wasn't going to answer any of my calls. I finally left the news of her granddad's death in a message."

"There was nothing else you could do, Layne. Who knows what Grace is thinking? Certainly not me," Nona said

Betty Jo noticed how Dixie was staring down at the floor and was unusually quiet. "Are you okay, Dixie?"

Dixie slowly raised her head to look at Nona. "I should have told you days ago . . ."

Nona raised an eyebrow. "Told me what?"

Dixie breathed in deeply then slowly let the air out. "Grace called me."

"Grace called you?" Nona repeated in disbelief. Frowning, she leaned forward. "About what?"

"She wanted to know the arrangements for the funeral. She told me she'd gotten a message that her granddad had passed away, but the message didn't say anything about the funeral. She wanted to know when and where it was. She called the same day we found out Ethan was missing. I called you to tell you, but then you told me about Ethan, and I just forgot to tell you then. I'm sorry."

Nona put her head in her hands.

Betty Jo sighed. "Oh, Dixie, you should have made it a point to tell Nona."

Shaking her head back and forth, Dixie stood up and began to pace. "I know I should have, and I'm so sorry I didn't. She even asked me to call her when the arrangements had been made, which I did as soon as I found out."

Nona lifted her head to ask, "So you talked to her last week?"

Dixie pulled out the chair next to Nona and sat. "No, I didn't talk to her, but I left a message."

"So she knows it's tomorrow at the house?"

Dixie nodded.

"Is she coming?"

Dixie averted her eyes. "I don't know."

The ride back from Betty Jo's house was nothing like the one going to her house. Of course, Nona was upset with Dixie. However, she wasn't sure if she was upset because Dixie had kept it from her that she'd talked to Grace or because Grace had chosen to call Dixie instead of her. She'd hoped that as soon as Grace learned of her granddad's death, she would call her. She had to accept the fact that she hadn't wanted to talk to her.

Logically, Nona was aware how Grace not calling her wasn't Dixie's fault, but she couldn't stop herself from blaming her.

Layne tried her best to fill the awkward silence between Nona and Dixie, but as soon as Dixie was dropped off at her house, Layne turned to Nona. "I cannot believe Grace called Dixie, of all people. She barely knows Dixie. Why didn't she call me?"

Nona could hear the hurt in her voice. "I couldn't begin to explain anything Grace does."

"It's just that I always thought Grace and I had a bond. I remember how she used to come to my house when she was upset with you or her Dad. I'd fix hot chocolate and we'd talk it out."

"I guess she's put you over on my side. If you're on my side, then you're not on hers."

Layne considered this for a moment. "I guess that makes sense."

Nona's voice was filled with anger. "None of this makes sense, Layne. I don't even know why we have sides. I've always believed if you're family, then you're on the same side."

Nona pulled into Layne's driveway and turned off the engine. Layne released her seat belt and turned to Nona. "Do you think she'll come tomorrow?"

"I honestly don't know."

"Do you want her to come?"

Nona considered her question before answering, "I don't know." She went on to explain, "Tomorrow's not going to be an easy day anyway you look at it. I'm not sure if I could handle the emotions I would be feeling if Grace showed up."

Layne reached out and patted Nona's hand. "We'll be there to help you through it if she does."

Nona put her hand over Layne's. "Thanks, I'm counting on y'all."

As Nona drove home, she closed down her thoughts of Dixie and Grace that had been running through her mind. She had enough drama to deal with at home with Riley. He hadn't been his normal big-brother self since he'd arrived. Even though it had been his choice to return to Seattle so he wouldn't have to witness his father's decline as Alzheimer's took away his life, he seemed upset with her for being the one who'd stayed. He was going through something that was all his own and that she couldn't understand. She wasn't sure what she could do to help him through whatever it was, and her patience was wearing thin.

When she pulled into the driveway, she was disappointed she didn't see Monty's car. She'd hoped Monty would be there when she got home. She'd hoped he would handle Riley while she finished preparing the house for tomorrow's event. After parking the car, she was searching in her purse for her cell phone to call Monty when she heard it ring.

She was so sure it was Monty she didn't check the screen to see who was calling. "Please tell me you're on your way."

"Okay, I'm on my way."

She almost dropped her phone when she recognized the voice. "Why are you calling, Bill?"

"Don't tell me you're not happy I'm on my way."

Hearing the playfulness in his voice annoyed her. "What do you want?" she snapped.

Bill snickered. "I can tell you're not in the mood for conversation."

"Bill, I'm really busy. Did you have a reason for calling?" Nona didn't even try to keep the irritation she was feeling out of her voice.

"As a matter of fact, I do."

She waited for several seconds for him to continue. "Are you going to tell me or am I supposed to guess?"

"It's just that now I'm talking to you, I'm not sure how to ask you what I've called to ask you."

"Bill, you're babbling. Just ask." Nona was sure Bill was calling to ask if he could come to her father's memorial. What she wasn't sure about was what her answer was going to be.

"Okay, let me just come out with it. Will it be all right with you if I come tomorrow and . . . bring Grace with me?"

The air left her lungs as the shock of his question settled on her. Her heart began to race. His words swirled around in her mind—*come tomorrow and bring Grace with me.* Her hands were trembling as she set the phone down on the car seat beside her and grabbed hold of the steering wheel with both hands so hard her knuckles turned white. After all Grace had put her through by turning away from her and her granddad when they'd both needed her, was she ready to welcome Grace into her home?

Bill's voice broke through her thoughts. "Nona? Are you all right?"

She glared at the phone. She didn't have an answer to his question. She needed time to think about it. She wanted to talk it over with Monty and her friends.

"Nona, are you still there?"

All of a sudden, she realized the one person she desperately wanted to talk it over with was her father. Tears began to well up in her eyes. She leaned her head on the steering wheel. What would he tell her to do? Her thoughts traveled back to the many times his words had helped her through life's dilemmas. She whispered to herself, "Oh, Daddy, what do I do about Grace?" As soon as she said Grace's name, she knew her answer. He would want her to show Grace, grace, the same grace God had shown her time and again. Taking a deep calming breath, she picked up the phone and placed it to her ear. "I'm still here. Of course, you and Grace are welcome to come tomorrow."

As soon as Nona ended the call, she heard Monty's car pull in behind her. The sound of his car engine had become a familiar one to her. When she glanced up at her rearview mirror, she could see Monty was out of his car and walking toward hers.

He tapped on her window. "What are you doing just sitting out here in your car?"

She opened her car door and stepped into his arms. "Oh, Monty, I'm so glad you're here."

"I'm glad I'm here too. Now, tell me what's going on."

Nona wrapped her arms around him more tightly. "Just hold me for now. I'll explain everything later."

Chapter Fifteen

As Betty Jo drove to Weldon Academy to pick up the children, the scene that had taken place in her kitchen between Dixie and Nona kept playing in her mind. Her heart went out to both of her friends. Dixie was sorry, but it was understandable why Nona would be upset with her for not telling her about her conversation with Grace. She could still feel the tension between the two when they left her house. She hoped when Nona had time to think about what Dixie had done, she would see she hadn't meant to hurt her.

Kelli and Matthew were in the car before she'd come to a full stop. "Whoa, what's the hurry?"

Kelli answered as she pulled on her seat belt. "Don't you remember? Pops said we could help him with a project in his shop as soon as we got home."

Matthew added, "Yeah, but he wouldn't tell us what it is."

Betty Jo smiled. "Knowing Pops, I'm sure it's going to be something special."

When Betty Jo pulled up to Chase's Montessori preschool, she saw him waiting under the portico, but he didn't see her. He was giving his full attention to a little boy who appeared to be about his age and looked vaguely familiar. She waited as his teacher called him away from his conversation and walked him to her car.

As soon as he was buckled in his car seat and the door was closed, Betty Jo asked, "Who was that little boy you were talking to?"

"Gigi, don't you remember? Last week I told you I had a new friend."

Thinking back, she recalled one night after a very long day while she was getting him ready for bed, he had mentioned something about a new friend. She looked at him in her rearview mirror. "Sorry, Chase, I forgot. What's his name?"

"It's okay." He looked out of his window and sighed. "Grayson, but I don't think I want him to be my friend anymore."

Matthew looked over at his little brother. "Why're you dumping him?"

Kelli scowled. "Matthew! He's not dumping him."

"Yes, I am," Chase declared. "He's a liar."

"All little kids lie," Matthew proclaimed as if it was common knowledge.

Kelli smacked Matthew on the arm. "They do not!" She turned to Chase. "What do you think he lied about?"

"He said my daddy isn't ever coming home."

Betty Jo was only half-listening to the bantering of her grandchildren, but when she heard Chase's words, she slammed on her brakes, throwing the children forward and then back against their seats.

"Gigi!" all three yelled as one.

She said the first thing that came into her mind. "Oh, sorry, there was a cat walking across the road that I almost hit." She was thankful there hadn't been a car right behind her or she would have more explaining to do.

Trying to keep her voice even and calm, she asked Chase, "What exactly did Grayson tell you?"

"He said that my daddy was lost and would never come home."

Matthew glared at Chase. "Grayson is a stupid liar! Our daddy is the smartest man in the whole world. Only dumb people get lost, isn't that right, Kelli?"

Kelli crossed her arms. "That's right! Right, Gigi?"

Betty Jo's mouth went dry as her mind raced for an answer. "Your daddy is one of the smartest men in the whole world. If he ever got lost, he'd find his way home." Her answer seemed to satisfy the children for now. She wondered how Grayson had come up with something that was way too close to the truth of what had happened to their daddy.

"Chase, do you know Grayson's last name?"

Chase shook his head. "I just know that Mommy works with his daddy."

His name popped into Betty Jo's head—Grayson Weaver, Nathan's son. That explained why he'd told Chase about his father. Nathan must have said something about Ethan being missing in front of his son. She wanted to drive straight over to Foxx and Foxx to have a word with Nathan, but drove home instead.

As soon as she stopped the car, Matthew and Kelli were out and running to their Pop's shop. As she got Chase out of his car seat, she called after them, "You have to change your clothes before you can help Pops." She watched as they changed their direction away from the shop and toward the house.

As soon as Chase's feet hit the ground, he took off running after his brother and sister. "Wait for me!"

Betty Jo needed to talk to Don about what she'd just learned from Chase. She headed to his shop hoping she would find him there.

She was surprised when Don met her at the door. "What's with all the commotion out here?"

Betty Jo grabbed him by the arm to pull him back in his shop. "Don, we've got a problem."

Wrinkling his brow, Don asked, "What's happened?"

"Nathan's son told Chase that Ethan is missing." She hurriedly went on to explain the conversation that had taken place in the car.

Shaking his head, Don walked over to his workbench and plopped down on his stool. "So, for now, they're satisfied to believe that boy is a liar, right?"

Betty Jo walked over to stand next to him. "For now, I think so."

"Then I think we just leave it at that."

Betty Jo began to pace. "I just hate that it makes me feel like I'm the one who's the liar."

At that moment, three children filled with anticipation burst through the door.

Matthew ran to his grandfather. "What's our project, Pops?"

Don stood up and gave Betty Jo a quick kiss. "It'll be all right."

He turned his attention to the children and clapped his hands together. "Are you ready?"

"We're ready!" Matthew answered.

The children followed as Don walked to the back of the shop. In one swift motion, he yanked off the tarp that had been hiding their "project." "Ta Da!"

Kelli screamed, "It's a go-cart!"

Don hurried to explain, "It's not ready to ride yet. You've got a lot of work to do to fix it up before you can take it out."

Matthew looked up at his grandfather with awe. "Do you mean we're going to do the work?"

Smiling down at Matthew, Don patted him on the back. "You bet you are. It's a project for all three of you."

Betty Jo reached out to steady herself on the stool her husband had vacated. "Oh, Don, not Ethan's old go-cart." She remembered how thrilled Ethan was the day Don had brought it home. Ethan and Don had fixed up a track that weaved around and through the trees, garden, and shed. Ethan would come home from school, throw his books on the table, and head out to the shed to get his go-cart. Then he'd ride around and around on that track for hours. That happened every day for a month until the day of the near tragic accident. She could recall that day as if it was yesterday.

Lily had been playing with her kitten, Snap, on the side porch. She'd never liked the sound of the go-cart as it zoomed around the track, so she always kept her distance. On that day, however, Snap jumped out of her lap, ran straight for the track, and ran right out in front of Ethan as he rounded a corner. He swerved to the left to miss her and the go-cart flipped over. Luckily, Ethan had been able to pull himself out from under it without a scratch. The go-cart wasn't as lucky. The gas leaked out from the tank onto the hot engine, and the go-cart caught fire. Lily screamed, which brought Betty Jo running out of the house. When she saw the fire, she picked up the garden hose and was able to put it out. That was the end of Ethan's adventures with the go-cart. He pushed it back into the shed, and Betty Jo hadn't seen it since that day.

Don hadn't discussed having the children fix up Ethan's go-cart with her and, most likely, not with their mother. What if one them wrecked it, but wasn't as fortunate as their daddy had been? However, seeing the excitement on the faces of her grandchildren as they jumped up and down around their grandfather, she had to admit this go-cart might just be the distraction they needed.

Betty Jo left Don and the children in the shop busy making plans for how to fix up their go-cart and went to the house to start supper. She was pretty sure she couldn't count on Chloe to feel the same way she did about the go-cart being a welcome distraction for her children. She needed to think of how to present it to her in the most positive way. When she saw Chloe's van pull down the driveway, she realized she needed to think fast.

She waved as she waited by the kitchen door. She called to Chloe as she got out of the car and walked back to open the rear door, "Hey, can I help you with anything?"

With her arms full, Chloe closed the car door with her knee. "No, I've got it."

Betty Jo hurried to the kitchen door and held it open. "Let me get the door for you."

"Thanks." Chloe walked in the house and unloaded her burden on the kitchen table. "Whew! That was heavier than I thought it would be."

"I would have helped."

Ignoring Betty Jo's comment, Chloe looked around the kitchen. "Where are the children?"

"They're with their Pops." Hoping to distract her from going in search of the children and seeing what was going on in Don's shop before she had a chance to explain, she offered, "How about a cup of tea or maybe a glass of wine?"

Chloe took off her coat and put it on the back of the chair before sitting down. "Thanks, I'd love a glass of wine."

Betty Jo took out two wine glasses from the corner cabinet. "Rough day?"

"Long week is more like it."

Betty Jo got the white wine out of the refrigerator, filled the glasses, carried them to the table, and took the seat across from Chloe. "We sure haven't seen much of you these past two weeks."

Chloe took a sip of wine and looked directly at Betty Jo. "I've been busy, but I don't expect you to understand."

Betty Jo didn't look away. "I understand more than you might think I do. You've been spending a great deal of time with Nathan."

Chloe crossed her arms. "He needs my help with this case."

"Which means you haven't been spending time with your children, who also need you. I wonder if you even have time to think about your missing husband." The moment she spoke those words, she knew she'd gone too far.

Chloe's face turned red with anger. "Are you accusing me of neglecting my children and not caring about my missing husband?"

In a much gentler voice, Betty Jo answered, "No, I'm not." She leaned across the table toward Chloe. "I'm sorry. I shouldn't have said that. It's just that something happened today that upset me."

When Chloe didn't say anything, Betty Jo continued. "Did you know that Chase has a new friend?"

Chloe shook her head. "No, he didn't tell me anything about having a new friend."

"His new friend is Nathan's son, Grayson. They're in the same class at Montessori."

Chloe leaned back in her chair. "Okay."

"When Chase got in the car this afternoon, he was upset by what Grayson told him today."

"Which was?"

Betty Jo could hear the annoyance Chloe was feeling toward her. She hoped she was doing a better job of hiding the anger that was building inside her toward her daughter-in-law. She cleared her throat and took a sip of wine.

"He told Chase that his daddy was lost and wasn't going to come home.”

In one swift move Chloe sat up, uncrossed her arms, and stared open-mouthed at Betty Jo for several seconds before crying out, “What?”

Betty Jo nodded. “I couldn’t believe it either, but that’s what Grayson told him.”

Chloe buried her face in her hands. “Why would he tell Chase such a thing?”

“I have no idea why he did it, but I’m sure he heard about what’s happened to Ethan from Nathan.”

Chloe quickly stood up from the table, almost knocking over her chair. “I’ve got a few things to say to Nathan and that son of his.”

Betty Jo grabbed hold of Chloe’s wrist as she hurried past. “You need to stop right there.”

Chloe tried to pull away, but Betty Jo held tight. “Before you overreact, you need to sit back down, calm down, and listen to the whole story.”

“Which is!” Chloe snorted.

Betty Jo pointed toward the chair beside her. Chloe looked from Betty Jo’s determined face to the chair several times before resigning herself to sit. “So, tell me.”

She released Chloe’s wrist from her grasp. “Right now, it isn’t an issue. The children worked it out in their minds that Grayson is a liar. They are certain their daddy is way too smart to get lost. At this moment, all three are as happy as they can be in Don’s shop working on a project he’s set up for them. I’m afraid if you confront Nathan, then it might become a problem. The children might think there is some truth to what Grayson said if they know you’re angry about it.”

Chloe stared at the floor. “Nathan shouldn’t have said anything about Ethan in front of Grayson.”

“True, but you know how children can overhear things they were never meant to hear. Nathan and his wife could have been discussing what’s happened to Ethan and thought Grayson was out of the room or in bed. I’m sure they don’t even know Grayson heard them talking.”

Chloe looked up at Betty Jo. “You may be right. I’ll let it go for now.”

“I think that’s the right thing to do. Now, how about you help me get supper ready?”

Chloe leaned over the table to gather her things. "Okay, but let me get this stuff out of your way and get out of these clothes first. I don't think a suit is the proper attire for cook's assistant." She was almost out of the kitchen when she suddenly turned back to Betty Jo. "By the way, what is the project that Don has the kids working on?"

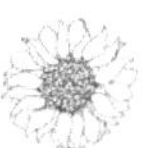

Every day and night since Betty Jo had learned Ethan was missing in action, she'd given it her best effort to not question God and to trust He was watching over Ethan. She held on to her faith that He would bring Ethan home. Sometime during this night she'd allowed doubts and fears to creep into her thoughts. They'd robbed her of both trust and faith and invaded her mind with what ifs. *What if Ethan is injured? What if Ethan has been captured? What if Ethan's being tortured? What if Ethan's never found? What if Ethan's children have to grow up without him?*

She tried to reattach her mind on comforting, trusting thoughts, but it kept returning to the what ifs. She'd finally given up finding peace in sleep, grabbed her grandmother's quilt from the bottom of the bed, fixed a pot of coffee, and curled up on the back porch swing to await the sunrise.

Betty Jo found the back and forth motion of the swing calming. Her mind drifted back to Chloe's reaction to Don and the children's project of fixing up Ethan's wrecked go-cart. When Chloe had stormed out of the kitchen door on her way to Don's shop, Betty Jo had been sure Chloe would put a stop to their work. But once Chloe witnessed the children's enthusiasm firsthand, she became a fan of the project. All through supper, the children talked nonstop to their mother about the work they were doing on the go-cart and the plans they had for it when it was finished. By the rare smile on Chloe's face, it was evident she was pleased to have three happy children.

At the sound of the back door opening, Betty Jo turned to see Don coming towards her with a cup of coffee in hand. "Mind if I join you?"

"Please do." Don sat down beside her, and Betty Jo rearranged the quilt to cover both of them.

Don put his arm around her. "Are you okay? I got worried when I woke up and found you weren't beside me."

Betty Jo leaned her head on his shoulder. "It was just one of those nights."

"I thought that might be it." He pulled her closer. "It's all going to be all right, Betty Jo. We have to keep believing that."

Betty Jo sighed. "I know. I just forgot for a minute."

Don kissed the top of her head. "It's okay to have doubts. The trick is not to dwell on them."

Betty Jo cuddled closer. "I'm not going to."

"Good."

The two swung back and forth as the day dawned bright and beautiful.

Chapter Sixteen

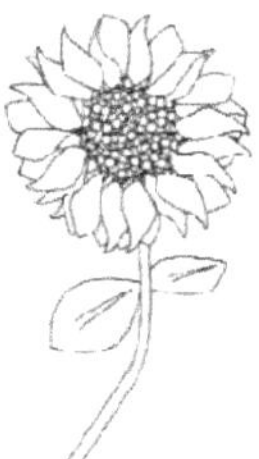

When Nona went to bed the night before her father's memorial, she was sure she wouldn't be able to sleep, but, just in case, she set her alarm clock. She was surprised when the annoying buzzing of the alarm woke her. She'd slept the entire night without getting up, not even for her normal once a night bathroom trip. She was amazed, what with all that had gone on the day before and all that would be going on today, that she'd slept. Maybe it was a sign things were going to work out for the best today.

She took her time showering and dressing before leaving her room. When she opened her bedroom door, she was met with the welcoming aroma of fresh brewing coffee and frying bacon, which she hoped meant that Riley was making her favorite bacon waffles. As she passed her father's office on her way to the kitchen, she placed her open palm on the closed door. "We're celebrating you today, Daddy."

Imagining her father behind the door at his desk leaning back in his chair, she smiled. He'd always enjoyed celebrations. He'd always been especially fond of the ones that celebrated him. She was sure, if at all possible, he'd be there today with them for this most special of celebrations.

As expected, Nona found Riley busy in the kitchen preparing their breakfast. Without saying a word, she walked over to the cabinet above the coffeemaker, took out two cups, and filled them to the brim. Picking up one cup, she took a sip. "You want yours in hand or at the table?"

Riley broke two eggs in the bowl and began to vigorously beat them into the mixture. "Table. Can't you see my hands are busy?"

Nona carried both cups to the table and sat down. "Have I ever told you how much I love to watch you cook?"

Picking up the bowl while continuing to stir, he turned to his sister. "Well, someone around here has to do the cooking, or we'd starve to death."

Before taking another sip of coffee, Nona looked at her brother over the top of her cup. "Not as long as there are places that'll deliver."

"Very funny." Riley turned back to the counter, put the spoon to the side, poured some of the mixture into the waiting waffle iron, and added two pieces of bacon before pulling the top down. Taking the towel he'd draped over his shoulder, he wiped his hands. "Will Monty be joining us for breakfast this morning?"

Nona set down her cup. "Not this morning. He's busy running errands. He'll be here around noon to help us set up."

When the buzzer sounded on the waffle iron. Riley hurried over to take out the four waffles. He placed them on a plate and carried them to the table. "I think these four will be enough for us. I'll save the rest of the batter for another day."

Riley pulled out the chair next to Nona and sat.

Nona placed two waffles on her plate. "Oh, Riley, these smell wonderful."

Riley watched as Nona took a bite. "I wanted to do something special for you today."

With her mouth full, Nona smiled. She swallowed and said, "Well, this is for sure something special."

Riley put the remaining waffles on his plate. "I'm glad."

When Nona finished eating, she carried her plate to the sink and poured herself another cup of coffee before sitting back down at the table.

"Are we ready for today?"

"Good grief, Riley, we've been over everything umpteen times. If we're not ready now, we never will be."

"I'm not talking about that kind of ready. I know we're physically ready. I mean, are we ready for what today will bring emotionally?"

Putting her elbows on the table, Nona folded her hands together. "I hope and pray we are. I'm determined to honor Daddy's wishes by making today a joyful day of celebrating his life."

Riley reached out and put his hand over hers. "I know you are, Nona. So am I, but I know it's going to be a challenge for you to keep it joyful when both Grace and Bill will be here."

Unfolding her hands, Nona said, "When Bill first mentioned he wanted to come and then when he said he wanted to bring Grace, it felt like a bomb had been dropped on me. I wanted to scream at him, but then I remembered something Daddy said to me when I was going through that awful time with Amy and divorcing Bill."

"I remember how horrible that was for you. What did he say?"

"He told me that the most important thing to remember when I'm going through unwanted or unexpected life events is to have God by my side. He told me to remember that He is our hope and strength when we face any of life's challenges."

Riley nodded. "That sounds like something our father would say."

"He said the best way to react to life's challenges is not with anger and resentment, even though the person might have earned a great deal of anger and resentment, but to always choose grace, God's grace. I knew right then with Bill on the phone I needed to show my Grace, God's grace by choosing to forgive her for the hurt she's caused me. After all, if I was able to show Amy—the 'other woman'—God's grace, then I can surely give His grace to my own daughter. Don't you agree?"

"I do, Nona, I truly do. And I'll do the same for Grace." Riley stood up and took his plate to the sink. "However, I can't say I can do it for Bill."

To everyone's surprise, Kendall's father, Matt, volunteered to keep all four children for the afternoon while Betty Jo, Don, Lily, and Chloe attended Mr. James's Memorial. Betty Jo had worried that Chloe might turn down Matt's offer to watch the children because they'd only met one time, but was pleased when she agreed without having to be convinced.

Betty Jo, Don, Lily, and Chloe arrived at Nona's house fifteen minutes before two. Don drove around to the back of the house to park the car as Nona had instructed, anticipating how most of the guests would be parking in the front. Betty Jo was surprised that they'd arrived before Dixie's and Layne's families since she was often known as "the late Betty Jo."

Don had just cut off the car engine when Monty was beside the car. He opened Don's door and shook his hand. "I'm sure glad to see you, Don. You're just in time to help me get some tables and chairs out of the garage. Nona's decided she wants to set some up on the front porch since it's such a nice day."

Monty hurried around the car to help Betty Jo out of the car. She gave him a quick hug. "How's she doing?"

"She's actually doing pretty well. You know Nona. She's determined to fulfill her father's wishes and make this a day of celebration. And I need to fulfill her wish of getting some tables set up. Are you with me, Don?"

"Right behind you, Monty."

Betty Jo stared after the two as Monty led the way with Don following close behind. "Nona may be doing 'pretty well,' but I think Monty might be a tad nervous about today."

Lily and Chloe looked at one another and laughed.

Betty Jo shook her head as she started toward the back door. "Let's see what we can do to help Nona."

The three stood at the door to the kitchen savoring the sweet, smoky aroma of Sweat's barbecue. Lily put her hand on her stomach. "I didn't realize it until now, but I'm starving."

"Me too," Chloe agreed.

Betty Jo put an arm around each and turned them away from the kitchen. "Sorry, but we're going to have to wait until the guests get here."

They found Nona in the living room arranging a vase of white camellias.

Betty Jo walked up beside her. "Oh, Nona, those are beautiful."

Nona took a step back to admire her work. "Aren't they though! Riley cut them this morning from the bushes out back. There's a vase filled with Mama's pink camellias that are just as beautiful in the dining room."

Betty Jo glanced around the room. "It looks like every thing's ready. Tell us what we can do to help."

Chloe moved around Betty Jo to take Nona's hands in hers. "I'm so sorry for your loss."

Nona smiled. "I appreciate that, Chloe, but this day is not about being sorry for losses. This day is for celebration." She turned her attention to Lily. "Lily, Riley could use your help setting up the bar. You'll find him in Daddy's office. We decided his office would be the appropriate place to serve drinks since Daddy usually ended his day there with his whiskey on rocks in hand."

Lily smiled recalling the many times she'd worked with Mr. James in his office. "I'd be glad to help Riley."

Nona turned to Betty Jo. "I thought I'd station you and Layne at the front door as greeters. I'm sure that between the two of you, you'll know everyone who comes through the door. Where's Don? I thought he and Mark could be here with you and Layne."

"He's helping Monty with getting the tables and chairs for the front porch. I'll let him know where his duty station is for the day. I'm sure you have other things that need your attention."

"Thanks, I do need to check on the food." Nona turned to leave.

"Wait, you forgot about me," Chloe called out. "You haven't told me what I can do to help."

Nona hesitated. "I could use some help putting out the plates and napkins in the dining room."

Dixie's and Layne's families were at Nona's five minutes before two. As soon as Dixie arrived, Nona put her in charge of the kitchen. Dixie immediately enlisted Alex's help in making sure there was always plenty of food on the buffet table . Layne and Mark, along with Betty Jo and Don, were at the front of the house by two o'clock welcoming guests. By two thirty, the house was over-flowing with people from all walks of life who were there to honor and celebrate the life of Mr. James Riley Foxx III.

Nona and Riley were overwhelmed by the outpouring of love and respect so many had for their father. They spent the afternoon enthralled by people's humorous and tender stories about him. Their father's idea of food, whiskey, and stories turned out to be the perfect combination for celebrating a life well spent.

Nona was busy telling stories, listening to others tell stories, and laughing at many of those stories all afternoon. It wasn't until Dixie brought her a plate of food and insisted she sit down for a few minutes to eat that she realized Bill and Grace hadn't come to the celebration as Bill had said they would. In a way, she found it to be a relief she hadn't had to deal with the possible drama that could have come from the two of them attending. She had just taken a bite of Dixie's Chocolate Ice Storm Cake when she heard a voice she recognized coming from the front room. She put down her fork. Her heart began to race as she prayed silently. *Dear God in heaven, help me to give grace as you give grace.*

Gathering her courage, Nona walked into the front room where she saw Bill and Grace, with their backs to her, engaged in conversation with Betty Jo, Don, Layne, and Mark.

With her heart pounding in her chest, Nona walked up to the group. "Grace."

Grace slowly turned to face her. "Mother."

It was Grace's tone and formal "Mother" that stopped Nona from going closer to her daughter. She crossed her arms in front of her. "It's good to see you."

Grace looked down at the floor as she took a step back toward her father. "I'm sorry about Granddad. I realized too late I should have been here for him."

Nona had a strong urge to grab Grace by her shoulders and shake her, demanding an explanation as to what reason she could possibly have that had kept her away from her granddad and her mother for the past three years. She closed her eyes, recalling her father's words of forgiveness and grace. Taking a deep, calming breath, she let the desire pass. She opened her eyes to look at her daughter. "Granddad knew you loved him, Grace.

Let's not have any regrets today."

Nona could see relief wash over her daughter's face as she understood her mother wasn't going to reprimand her for her behavior. "Today's a day for celebrating your granddad's life. I know for a fact you were his most treasured blessing. That's what we need to remember."

Their eyes met, and Nona could see the sadness in Grace's eyes. She opened her arms and held them out to her daughter. With only a moment of hesitation, Grace walked into her mother's arms. As Nona held Grace, she whispered in her ear, "I've missed you." She drew her closer. It felt good to hold her daughter once again. For the first time that day, tears filled her eyes.

Bill cleared his throat. "Uh, don't forget there are other people here to pay their respects."

Grace broke away from her mother's embrace. "Sorry, Dad, we didn't mean to exclude you."

Nona wiped away her tears as she turned her attention to her ex-husband. She offered him her hand. "I know my father would have appreciated your coming, Bill."

Bill stared at her hand for a moment before taking it. "I will miss his stories and his words of wisdom."

Nona forced a smile. "Yes, as we all will."

Turning away from Bill, Nona reached out for Grace's hand. "Let's go in the kitchen. Uncle Riley is there, and I know he can't wait to see you. Plus, there's someone special I want you to meet."

Grace looked back at her father as she reached a hand up to fidget with the locket that hung on the gold chain around her neck. Nona smiled as she recognized the locket her mother, who had passed away before Grace was born, had always worn around her neck. It held a picture of Nona's mother and father on their wedding day. Nona's father had given it to Grace on her sixteenth birthday. When he'd put it around her neck, Grace had vowed she'd wear it forever. Like most teenagers would, she'd broken that vow. After a few years, she'd put it away. Nona wondered if wearing the locket today was Grace's way of saying she was sorry for cutting Nona and her father out of her life for the past three years. It gave Nona hope that Grace was back in her life to stay—not for just this one day.

Still holding out her hand to Grace, Nona said, "Please, come with me, Grace."

Grace turned away from her father and took her mother's outstretched hand. "Of course I'll come with you, Mom."

As Betty Jo watched Nona take Grace from the front living room, she wiped the tears from her own eyes. When she glanced over at Layne and saw her doing the same, she laughed with embarrassment. "That really got to me."

"Me too," Layne agreed. "That's not what I was expecting."

Bill shook his head. "Me either. Grace and I worried all the way here about what horrible things her mother might say to her."

Stunned, Betty Jo stared at Bill in disgust. "Nona would never say horrible things to her daughter."

Bill's lips curled up in a grin. "If you think that, then you don't know her like I know her."

Fury poured through Betty Jo's whole body. Taking a step closer to Bill, she took her index finger and poked his chest, accenting each word she spoke. "You're right about that. I know her better."

Bill grabbed Betty Jo's hand and Don stepped between the two. "I wouldn't do that if I were you."

Layne took Betty Jo by the shoulders and led her toward the kitchen. "Let's go check on Dixie."

Mark chuckled. "Well, Bill, you sure know how to win friends and influence people. How about we step outside so you can cool off?"

"I think that's a good idea," Don agreed.

When Layne had Betty Jo in the hall, she stopped and leaned against the wall. "Betty Jo, that scared me. I thought Bill was going to hit you. What in the world got into you?"

Betty Jo bent over, taking deep breaths and trying to calm her racing heart. "I'm not totally sure. He just made me so mad with that comment about Nona. It was as if he hoped things would go badly between Grace and Nona."

"What comment?"

Betty Jo and Layne looked up to find Dixie standing in front of them with her hands on her waist.

Betty Jo put her hand over her heart. "Oh, Dixie, you missed the whole thing."

"Well, I knew something big had happened, because Nona just fixed a plate for Grace. Now, they're sitting at the kitchen table talking with Riley and Monty."

Layne clapped her hands together. "That makes me so happy,"

Betty Jo put her arms around Dixie and Layne. "Let's go into Mr. James office. We can get Lily to fix us a drink while we tell you all about how I put Bill in his place."

Nona couldn't stop smiling as she watched Grace. When Bill first told her he was bringing Grace with him today to her father's memorial, she'd imagined many things happening. In her wildest imagination, she'd never imagined Grace sitting at the same table with Monty, listening to his stories. It was even more than a dream come true, because she'd never dared to dream this. It was almost as if the past three years hadn't happened—almost.

Nona couldn't deny she'd been hurt by Grace's refusal to have any contact with her. She could almost understand why Grace had taken Bill's side when they'd separated since she'd always been closer to her father than she was to Nona. She was well aware it was her own fault. She'd spent a great deal of her time and energy making partner in her father's law firm instead of with her daughter. Grace made it clear on many occasions how much she resented Nona for pursuing her career.

Grace had been a gifted child both academically and musically. Her musical talents were evident from an early age when at five years old she'd sat down at the piano and played a hymn by ear that she'd heard Nona play only minutes before. That next week, Nona had enrolled her daughter in piano lessons. It'd been Nona who'd encouraged her to work harder, practice more, and never settle for average when she could be exceptional. Bill complained, often in front of Grace, about how much pressure she was putting on Grace. As soon as Grace had proven herself to be an extraordinary pianist, she'd turned her back on her musical talents. It'd broken Nona's heart to watch her daughter toss aside her remarkable talent. At first she'd believed it was somehow her fault. Her father had been the one who'd helped her understand she'd done what she was supposed to do as a parent by providing her daughter with opportunity and support. What Grace did with her talent was her choice to make, not Nona's.

The fact that Grace had chosen to became friends with Amy, the person whose affair with her father had ended her parents' marriage and who'd plotted to destroy Nona's life, was still hard for her to wrap her mind around. Through Bill, she'd learned about Grace seeing a life coach in Atlanta. According to him, this life coach convinced Grace how much her life would improve if she stopped all communication with her mother. Nona never understood how a strong-minded person like Grace could be influenced to such an extent that she would turn away from her own mother. Nona had to remind herself that was then, and right now, Grace was sitting at the table with her.

Nona turned her attention back to her daughter. "Can I get you anything else, Grace?"

Grace pushed back from the table. "I couldn't put another bite in my mouth."

"Not even Dixie's Chocolate Ice Storm Cake?"

"That's not fair. You know I can't turn down Miss Dixie's Ice Storm Cake."

Before Nona could get up, Monty stood. "Let me see if I can get you a piece." He left the table in search of a piece of Dixie's famous cake.

Grace leaned in. "He seems like a nice man."

Nona smiled. "He is, and he's very special to me."

"Oh, so he's more than your attorney. Didn't he represent you when you divorced Dad?"

"He was my attorney, but our relationship has evolved into something more."

An uneasy stillness fell over the table. Nona was relieved when Riley broke the silence. "Grace, I've told you all that's been going on with me.

Tell us what's been going on with you?"

Grace considered his question for a moment. "The biggest news is that Adrian and I just purchased a new townhouse in Buckhead. We move in next week."

Nona looked at her with disbelief. "What? You sold that beautiful loft you spent a fortune renovating! I thought you both loved living in downtown Atlanta."

"We did, but it just wasn't right for us anymore."

"In what way?" Nona asked.

Grace stared down at the napkin she'd been twisting around her finger. "It didn't have enough bedrooms."

Nona wrinkled her forehead. "Couldn't you have just carved out a space and called it a bedroom?"

Grace looked up to meet Nona's gaze. "Not really, since we're going to need a nursery."

Nona stared intently at Grace, unsure if she'd heard correctly. "A nursery?"

A smile slowly spread across Grace's face as she nodded. "A nursery for our baby."

"Baby! That's awesome!" Riley shouted.

Nona's breath caught in her throat. She remembered the failed attempts and heartbreak Grace had gone through with fertility doctors. She stared unblinking at her daughter. "I thought the doctors told you and Adrian you couldn't have children."

Grace's eyes glistened with tears. "I know, but they were wrong, Mom. Our baby is a miracle. A true blessing from God."

Nona sprang up from her chair and wrapped her arms around her pregnant daughter. Her heart was filled with so much emotion, she wasn't sure she could speak. "Oh, Grace."

Grace put her arms around her mother. "That's one of the reasons I came today."

Nona released her hold on her daughter to sit down next to her. "You came here today to share the good news that you're pregnant with me?"

Grace took both of Nona's hands in hers. "Yes, Mom. I know I hurt you and Granddad. I could give you a bunch of reasons and excuses for why I felt justified in cutting you both out of my life, but I was wrong. After I learned the truth about Amy, I was ashamed of my behavior, but I was too proud to tell you I was sorry. When Adrian and I found out we were pregnant, you were the first person I wanted to call to share the news, but I didn't know if you'd even want me back in your life after the hurt I'd caused you. I'm truly sorry, Mom. When I remembered the love and acceptance I had from Granddad, I knew I had to get you back in my life. Even if you can't forgive me, I want your unconditional love as a grandparent to be showered on my baby."

Tears of joy were streaming down Nona's face as she kissed Grace on both cheeks. "Your baby already has my love, as do you."

Nona shook her head as she handed Betty Jo another plate to dry. "I still can't believe Grace is going to have a baby!"

Betty Jo chuckled. "None of us can, but it's such a blessing for everyone. This baby is going to be the best reason to heal your relationship with Grace. Her coming here to tell you means the healing has already begun."

Dixie took the dry plate from Betty Jo, added it to the stack, and carried them to Layne." I sure didn't see that announcement coming."

Layne picked up the plates and put them away in Nona's china cabinet. "I'm just so proud of the way you handled Grace and Bill today. I know that took a great deal of restraint on your part to not give them both a piece of your mind, which they both deserved, by the way."

With her hands deep in the dishwater, Nona washed another plate, "It was Daddy's words coming back to me that stopped the words I truly wanted to say from coming out of my mouth."

Betty Jo put the dish towel over her shoulder. "Thank heaven for your memory. Otherwise, it could have been a nasty scene, just like the one Bill hoped for."

Nona jerked her hands out of the dishwater, showering Betty Jo with soapy water. "What do you mean 'just like the one Bill hoped for'?"

Betty Jo took the towel from her shoulder to wipe the suds from her face. "You know how Bill is. He thought you'd say something nasty to Grace so they could leave, and you'd be out of her life again."

"Bill wanted that to happen?"

Betty Jo nodded. "That's basically what he told us after you took Grace out of the living room."

Nona turned back to the sink. "He's a piece of work. How in the world did I ever stay married to him for forty-two years!"

Betty Jo patted Nona on the back. "Forget the past with Bill and look to the future with Monty. You do want a future with him, right?"

Nona grinned at Betty Jo. "I do."

Betty Jo squeezed her shoulder. "Okay then, let's get this kitchen cleaned up so we can join our men who've been lounging by the fire pit for the past hour."

Layne put her hands on her hips. "Remind me again why is it they aren't in here helping us?"

Dixie crossed her arms. "We wanted to keep Nona's mother's china in one piece."

"Oh, yeah, I remember now."

They all laughed.

Once the dishes were done, the leftovers stored away, and the kitchen put back in order, the Fearsome Foursome left the house to join the men around the fire pit in the backyard.

Don stood up when he saw Betty Jo coming toward him. "We're glad to see y'all. We were beginning to wonder if you were ever going to finish up in the kitchen."

Betty Jo gave Don a quick kiss and sat down in the seat he'd vacated. "We can relax now that everything's back in its place."

Don pulled up an empty chair next to Betty Jo. "We've been discussing the events of day." He turned to Nona, who was sitting next to Monty. "I have to hand it to your father, Nona. He knew how to arrange a great memorial."

Mark nodded in agreement. "It was by far the best one I've ever attended."

Laughing, Alex slapped his knee. "I have to tell you, Nona, after hearing so many stories about Mr. James today, I feel like I know him better now than I did when he was alive."

Monty stood and held out his glass in a toast. "Let's drink to Mr. James and his choice of beverage. It was the perfect choice for a day of celebration and reminiscing."

Getting to their feet, Don, Alex, and Mark joined Monty in his toast as they touched their glasses together and drank.

Betty Jo frowned at her husband. "Just how many glasses of Mr. James's favorite beverage have you had?"

Don looked down at her. "A couple."

Betty Jo stood. "That's what I was afraid of. You know it's not good for you to drink with your diabetes." Taking Don by the arm, she led him away from the fire pit and their circle of friends. Stopping by Nona's chair on their way out, she leaned over to kiss her cheek. "It truly was a joyous day of celebration, and I hate for it to end, but I need to take this guy home."

Nona reached out and took Betty Jo's hand in hers. "Thank you for your help today. I don't know what Riley and I would have done without you two."

Don patted Nona's shoulder. "Glad we could help."

Betty Jo held out her hand to Don. "Give them to me."

"What?" Don asked.

Betty Jo snapped her fingers. "You know what."

Don dug in his pockets for the car keys and turned them over to his wife, and the two walked to the car hand in hand.

As Betty Jo started the car, she realized that she hadn't thought about Lily or Chloe since early in the afternoon. "Don, do you know how Lily and Chloe got home?"

"I know Lily caught a ride with Aaron and Jenny because she made it a point to let me know she'd found a way home and not to worry about her. I believe Nathan took Chloe home."

"You believe? You don't know?"

Don shrugged. "She didn't let me know she was leaving. I'm assuming Nathan took her home, because she was with him all afternoon."

"Now that I think about it, whenever I looked for Chloe, she was with Nathan, but I don't remember seeing Heather anywhere."

"That's because Heather didn't come. Nathan said Grayson wasn't feeling well, so she stayed home with him."

"That's interesting."

"What's interesting? That Grayson was sick?"

"No, that Chloe had Nathan take her home after spending the entire day with him."

"Now, Betty Jo, don't go reading something into that. I'm sure it was because Chloe didn't know anyone else and felt comfortable with Nathan."

"That's what's bothering me, Don. She's comfortable with Nathan, who happens to be a charming, handsome man."

"Don't be silly. She and Ethan are happily married with three beautiful children. And Nathan is happily married and has a beautiful son. I'm sure Chloe and Nathan are friends, nothing more."

"I hope you're right."

Betty Jo truly did hope Don was right and she was just being silly to think something might be going on between Chloe and Nathan, but she wasn't convinced she was the one who was being silly.

Chapter Seventeen

Betty Jo was not surprised when Don fell asleep on their short drive home. However, she was surprised to find Lily's parked car in the driveway when they arrived there. She tapped Don on the shoulder, waking him up. "It's almost midnight. I wonder why Lily is still here I would have thought she'd want to get home as soon as she could since she'll have the house to herself. Wasn't Matt taking Kendall home with him tonight?"

Don stretched. "I thought that was the plan."

Betty Jo parked the car next to Lily's. As soon as she shut off the engine, she grabbed Don's arm. "You don't think something's wrong, do you?"

Don patted her hand. "I'm sure everything's fine."

"Oh, Don, maybe there's news about Ethan, and Lily's waiting here to tell us."

Offering a comforting smile, he gave her hand a squeeze. "Well, I don't think we're going to find out sitting here in the car."

They hurried out of the car and into the house. As soon as she opened the kitchen door, Betty Jo called her daughter's name softly so as not to wake the children she assumed would be asleep at this hour. She stood still, listening for Lily's voice. The only sound she could hear was the beating of her heart and Don's heavy breathing. They looked at one another. "Don, something's wrong. I just know it is."

"Let's not—" Don stopped talking when he heard footsteps running down the stairway.

Lily rushed into the room. "Is she with you?"

"Who?" Don asked.

"Chloe, did she come home with you?"

Betty Jo shook her head. "No, she's not with us. I thought Nathan brought her home hours ago."

Lily's eyes darted back and forth between them. "No one's brought her home. She's not here."

Betty Jo could hear the panic in Lily's voice. She took her daughter by her shoulders and gently sat her down at the kitchen table. "Take a deep breath and calm down." She turned to Don. "Get her some water."

She sat in the chair next to her daughter and leaned in. Don handed Lily a glass of water. Betty Jo watched as Lily took a drink. "Now, do you think you can tell us what's going on?"

Lily nodded. "After I helped Riley straighten things up in Mr. James's office, it was getting late. I was worried that Matt might be getting tired of taking care of the kids and all, plus I was beat and ready to go home. I could tell you and Dad weren't ready to leave. That's when I saw Aaron and Jenny getting ready to leave. I asked them if they would give me a ride to your house. They said they'd be glad to. I knew Chloe was probably ready to leave as well, so I went to find her so she could go with us. I looked all around Nona's house, but couldn't find her anywhere."

Lily stopped to take another drink. Betty Jo and Don waited. "I was asking everyone if they'd seen her. Finally, Mr. Montgomery said he saw her leave with Nathan. I figured she'd have Nathan bring her here, but she wasn't here when I got here. At first I wasn't worried. I figured maybe they went out for coffee or something like that and would be back soon. I told Matt to go ahead and take Kendall home with him. I figured Chloe would be home any minute. I could tell the kids were ready for bed. I tried calling Chloe's cell, but there was no answer. I called Nathan's cell, but no answer on his phone either. I finally put the kids to bed. But, Mom,

I've called and called their cell phones and left voice messages as well as text messages, but they haven't called or texted back."

The slump of Lily's shoulders told Betty Jo how tired and frustrated she was with Chloe.

"Mom, it's late. I can't imagine where they could be. What if something awful has happened to them? What if those children were left without either parent?"

Don gave Lily's shoulder a squeeze as he took out his cell phone. "I'm sure they're fine, Lily. They're probably sitting at The Grill or some other restaurant and lost track of the time. Let me give them a call." He stepped away from the table.

Betty Jo held Lily's hand in hers. "Your Dad's right. They've lost track of time, that's all it is."

Lily widened her eyes as she leaned forward. "For six hours! That doesn't make sense."

Frowning, Don returned to the table. "No answer. I think Lily's right. It doesn't make sense. It's time to call Mark."

Betty Jo grabbed his arm as he started to walk away. "Don, don't you think you're overreacting? Do we really need to get the police involved?"

Don scratched his head. "I'm not going to call Mark because he's the sheriff. I'm going to call him because he's Nathan's father. I thought maybe he'd have an idea where Nathan might be at this hour."

Betty Jo put her hand to her mouth. "Sorry, I didn't think about that. You should go ahead and make that call."

At the sound of the back door opening, Betty Jo, Don, and Lily all swung around and stared, openmouthed, as Chloe stepped into the kitchen.

Lily jumped up and wrapped her in a crushing hug. "Thank God you're home, Chloe! I've been worried sick."

Chloe blushed. "I'm sorry, Lily. I didn't mean to worry you. Time got away from us."

Don pulled out a chair for Chloe. "Why don't you sit down and tell us about it."

Chloe took off her jacket and put it over her arm. "Oh, I'd love to, but I need to check on my children."

Betty Jo pursed her lips together as she patted the seat of the chair Don pulled out. "The children are fine. Lily's been watching after them. You need to sit down and explain to us just where you've been and why you didn't bother to call or answer Lily's calls, before you do anything else."

Chloe slung her jacket across her lap as she sat. "Okay, but I'm not sure why you're so upset, Betty Jo. Nathan and I simply stopped by the office to get some work done on that case that's coming up next week. We didn't have our phones with us because we purposefully left them in the car. We didn't want to be disturbed. We got lost in the work and didn't notice the time."

Betty Jo raised an eyebrow. "You're telling us that you and Nathan decided to go to work on a Saturday evening after attending the memorial of the senior partner of Foxx & Foxx."

Chloe smoothed out the jacket on her lap. "Well, when you say it like that, it sounds like we did something wrong. Let me start from the beginning. After we left the memorial, Nathan and I got to talking about the adjustments I've had to make since moving from a big city to a small town. I mentioned how much I missed Starbucks coffee. Nathan asked me if I'd ever been to the Dream Bean Coffee Shop. He claimed they have the best coffee in the state. So, to prove it, he insisted we get a cup. By the way, I'm convinced it is the best in the state. While we were there, we started going over some points of the case that weren't coming together like we'd hoped they would." She turned to Lily. "You know what I mean? Right?" She didn't wait for Lily's answer. "Anyway, that's why we went back to the office to work on the case."

Betty Jo cocked her head. "Interesting."

Chloe stood. "It is, isn't it? Now, if you've finished with your inquisition, I'm going upstairs to kiss my children good night."

All six eyes followed Chloe as she walked out of the kitchen.

Lily sat back in her chair. "Whew! That was some explanation."

Betty Jo crossed her arms as she leaned back. "Yes, it was. Now, the question is, do we believe her?"

Don gazed at his wife and daughter. "I don't think we have a choice but to believe her, Betty Jo. I'll admit it sounds a bit strange, but I say we leave this alone and not discuss it further."

"I'm good with that, Dad." Lily stood. "Now, if y'all don't mind, I'm going home." She gave her mother a kiss and her father a hug before going out the door.

Don put his hand on Betty Jo's crossed arms. "What about you? Can you leave it alone?"

Betty Jo didn't believe Chloe's story any more than she believed in the Easter Bunny, but she knew it wouldn't do any good to say that to Don. She bit down on her lip. "I'll do my best."

"I'm sure you will." Don held out his hand. "Come on. Let's go to bed. It's been a long day."

Betty Jo smiled as she took his hand. "I'm with you."

Sleep escaped Betty Jo. She envied Don, who seemed to have fallen asleep before his head hit the pillow. Images of Chloe and Nathan together in various compromising ways kept popping in her mind the second she closed her eyes. Rationally, she was aware there was not a shred of evidence Chloe had been anything but truthful about the time she'd spent with Nathan that evening and well into the night. Yet, an uneasy feeling that Chloe was violating the absolute love and trust Ethan had shown her throughout their lives together kept creeping into her thoughts. With Ethan missing in action, how could Chloe even think about being with another man? Was Nathan taking advantage of Chloe's vulnerable state of mind? She'd always believed Nathan to be an honorable, ethical man. Yet, after the events of the day, she was reevaluating her opinion of him and his motives.

She needed a distraction, something that could provide her with a break from the images and thoughts that were running through her mind. She glanced around the bedroom searching for a diversion. She considered turning on the TV or the radio, but quickly reconsidered, knowing the sound would disturb Don's rest. She took her Kindle from the nightstand, switched it on, and began reading. When she'd read the first page through three times without remembering a word she'd read, she gave up. She was coming to the understanding there were few options of distraction available to her in the middle of the night.

She was about to give sleep another try when the bathtub through the open bathroom door caught her attention. When they'd remodeled their master bath, Don surprised her with the biggest jetted spa bathtub she'd ever seen. It was something she was certain she wanted and would enjoy, but in reality, she hadn't bathed in it more than a half-dozen times in the two years since the renovation. It was just quicker and easier to use the shower. However, tonight seemed like the perfect time for a long soak in her spa tub, complete with bubbles.

As the tub filled with hot water, Betty Jo stripped off her pajamas. She caught a glimpse of herself in the mirror, something she usually tried to avoid. It was disconcerting to see how much her body had changed through the wear and tear of aging. She didn't often compare her body to others', but she was well aware that her body had never been a source of attraction to the opposite sex like Nona's and Layne's were– at least at one time. As a person of shorter statue, it seemed as if every pound gained showed. She'd been on the heavier side of average most of her life except when she'd been paralyzed. She remembered being weighed in the hospital and learning she'd lost eight pounds of muscle mass in one day. As she gingerly stepped into the hot water, she chuckled at the memory, realizing she'd have a hard time these days to lose that much weight in a month.

As she eased her body down through the bubbles, she could feel her muscles and mind begin to relax. She leaned her head back, closed her eyes, and sighed, certain this was exactly what she needed. When she inhaled the aroma of the jasmine bubble bath she'd chosen, she was transported back to summer nights when Ethan and Lily were young, and they were a family of four. The fence that outlined their property had been covered with confederate jasmine. From early spring to midsummer, when the jasmine bloomed, its intoxicating scent enveloped all who stepped out their back door. After the supper and the dishes were cleared away, they'd hurry outside to sit on the swing that hung on the back porch. Ethan and Lily's favorite game was hide-and-seek. When they grew tired of playing with only the two of them, they'd beg their parents to join in, which they did on most nights.

One night in particular now flooded Betty Jo's memory. It was the night they'd lost Ethan. The game started out in its usual way with Betty Jo being "It" and counting while the others hid. She'd easily found Lily in her usual hiding place behind the wheelbarrow that stood up against the shed. She'd taken Lily's hand as they set out to seek the other two. Lily had been excited when she'd spotted her daddy hiding behind the maple tree. The three of them went in search of Ethan, who on most nights was the last to be found. He had a knack for hiding in the most unusual places. They searched together at first, but soon separated so they could widen their search area. After almost twenty minutes, they'd given up and called out to Ethan to let him know he was the best at hiding and had won the game. She and Don began to worry when Ethan didn't come out from his hiding place to claim his victory.

It'd grown dark outside with no moon to light up the night. Don had gone in the house to get a flashlight while Lily and Betty Jo continued to call out to Ethan as they searched. She remembered the fear that had gripped her heart as she imagined some stranger finding him and stealing him away from his family. That was when Don had called out to her and Lily that he'd found Ethan. Holding hands, they'd run to Don. They saw where Ethan had burrowed in behind the confederate jasmine, which had completely covered him with its low hanging vines, and fallen sound asleep. To this day, she could recall the relief that poured over her when she saw Don holding Ethan safely in his arms.

She sat up with the sudden revelation that God had given her this memory on this night to let her know Ethan was safe. He wanted her to remember how Ethan had always had a knack for hiding. That's what he was doing. Ethan was hiding from whatever danger was out there waiting to harm him. With complete certainty, she knew in her heart that God was sending her a message that He was watching over her son.

Betty Jo hurried to dry off. Still damp from her bath, she pulled on her pajamas and opened the bathroom door. She stopped when she heard Don's soft even breathing of a restful sleep. For one brief moment she considered waiting until morning to share with him God's message, but then decided the news couldn't wait.

In only a few quick steps, she was beside him. Putting her face down next to his, she kissed his cheek. "Don, wake up. Have I got a story for you!"

Chapter Eighteen

Betty Jo only got three hours of sleep, but with God's assurance Ethan was safe, her mind was clearer. With her mind sharper, she was wondering what had possessed her, Nona, and Dixie to set the White Bible Ceremony for Aaron and Jenny the day after Mr. James's memorial, and on a Sunday afternoon. For the life of her, she couldn't remember why they'd chosen this day. She realized the "why" didn't matter; it was today and that was that. The good thing was they were ready for the event. She needed to stay positive by reminding herself it was going to be a special day.

The blueberry pancakes she made for breakfast were getting cold. She'd called up the stairs two times already letting the children know their breakfast was ready and to hurry on down. As she headed back through the living room to the stairway, she hoped they hadn't gotten back in bed. If they didn't come now, they were all going to be late for church.

"Kelli, Matthew, Chase, get on down here now!"

"Coming, Gigi," Kelli called back. "Matthew's trying to tie Chase's shoes."

"Matthew, Pops can help you with that. Come on. Y'all need to get some food in you before church."

She was heading back to the kitchen when an unexpected voice coming from upstairs stopped her in her tracks.

"I'm herding them on down to you, Gigi," Chloe sang out.

Stunned, Betty Jo made her way in through the kitchen door where she found Don sitting at the kitchen table.

"Was that Chloe?" Don asked as he poured syrup over his plate of pancakes.

"I believe it was." She busied herself with making coffee.

Don took a bite of his pancake. "Huh, do you think she's going to church with us?"

Betty Jo carried a cup of coffee to the table and set it down in front of him. "Your guess is as good as mine."

Don turned toward the sound of thundering footsteps as the children ran down the stairs. "Get ready. Here they come."

Kelli, Matthew, and Chase, dressed in their Sunday best, slowed their steps as they entered the kitchen.

Betty Jo kissed each one on the top of their head as they passed by her to join their grandfather at the table. "Good morning."

Matthew put three pancakes on his plate. "Yum, pancakes."

"Don't take more than you'll eat," Chloe cautioned as she joined her children at the table.

Chloe was dressed in a tailored teal-blue suit complete with a pearl necklace and matching earrings. Betty Jo thought she looked stunning in her stylish outfit. The necklace and earrings made her think of the first time they'd met. She remembered thinking to herself how beautiful Chloe was. She had to admit, she was still a beauty.

Betty Jo took the orange juice from the refrigerator and began filling the juice glasses. "Eat up. We only have twenty minutes until church starts."

Don finished his pancakes, pushed his plate aside, and leaned back in his chair. He glanced around the table. "Well, aren't y'all looking rather dapper this fine Sunday morning?"

"What's 'damper,' Pops?" Chase asked through a mouthful of pancakes.

Matthew turned on his little brother. "It's not 'damper,' dummy. It's 'dabber,' 'cause we're dabbing our pancakes in syrup."

Kelli looked over at her brother as if he had two heads. "You're the dummy! He didn't say 'dabber'. He said, 'dapper,' and that means—"

Before Kelli could finish her sentence, Chloe set her juice glass on the table with such force Betty Jo feared it was going to shatter into a thousand pieces. "Enough already! Nobody is a dummy! Now, put your plates in the sink and get your coats on."

Shocked, all three children stared at their mother for a minute before moving. They each mumbled a "Yes, ma'am," as they left the kitchen to get their coats.

Chloe picked up her plate and glass and carried it to the sink. "Sorry about their rude behavior. They do know better."

Betty Jo caught a glimpse of Don, who was trying his best to suppress a grin. She gave him a warning look before turning her attention back to Chloe. "They're just being children."

"Well, that's not how I expect MY children to act." Chloe left the kitchen.

Don shrugged. "Guess I shouldn't use 'dapper' any time in the near future."

Betty Jo turned back to the sink to hide the smile on her face.

After church, Don took the family out to eat at the Steak House. The children liked to eat there because it had a soft serve ice cream machine where they could make their own ice cream cones. Betty Jo was surprised when Chloe didn't protest when they went for their second cones. Maybe Brother Richard's sermon on tolerance that day had done some good.

Patting his stomach, Don pushed his chair back from the table. "I'm as full as a tick."

Betty Jo chuckled. "It's probably that fourth piece of fried chicken that did the trick."

Chloe laughed. "Or it could have been the third helping of collard greens. I'll never understand why anyone would get even one helping of them."

"It's a Southern thing." Betty Jo glanced at her watch. "We need to get going. I have to be at the Columns by one to help get everything set up."

Chloe put her hand on Betty Jo's arm. "Oh, please let me help you."

Betty Jo hadn't expected Chloe's offer of help. Her first thought was to turn her down, but when she caught the pleading in her eyes, she changed her mind. "I could use your help. Thanks."

Don looked at the children. "That means we can get some work done on the go-cart."

All three cheered with excitement.

Chloe snapped her fingers and pointed at the children. "You don't do anything out in that shop until you change out of your Sunday clothes. Do you understand me?"

Betty Jo and Chloe pulled up to the Columns exactly at one o'clock. Betty Jo wasn't surprised to see Dixie's car was already parked in the parking lot. Betty Jo was getting her notebook out of the back seat when Nona pulled in beside them.

Nona quickly got out of her car. "Can you explain to me why we decided to have this thing the day after Daddy's memorial?"

Betty Jo chuckled. "I've been wondering the exact same thing."

The three of them walked up the sidewalk and in through the front door of the Columns together. As soon as they stepped over the threshold, they stopped, astounded by the sight before them. The foyer was adorned with white and pale pink ribbons draped from one side of the ceiling to the other, meeting in the middle at a sparkling crystal chandelier. The table beneath the chandelier was covered with white silk flowing down to the polished travertine floor. In the center of the table was an enormous silver vase overflowing with white and pale pink tulips the exact color of the ribbons overhead. Beyond the foyer was a magnificent curved staircase with its banisters covered in what looked to be thousands of miniature twinkling white lights.

"Can you believe how amazing this looks?"

They all turned to see Dixie coming toward them.

Betty Jo was the first to speak. "It is beyond amazing. I never dreamed it would be so . . ."

"Dazzling!" Chloe finished her sentence.

Betty Jo smiled at her daughter-in-law. "Exactly the word I was looking for."

Dixie gestured for the three of them to follow her. "Come see the room where we'll have the ceremony."

The room Dixie led them to held six round tables covered with white tablecloths. A silver vase with a smaller version of the bouquet in the foyer was placed in the center of each table. There was a small table to the side which held a silver punch bowl and cups. A larger table was set up for serving the cake and finger foods. At the front of the room was a podium and behind it a small table to hold the flowers for the ceremony.

Betty Jo made her way to the podium. "I'll put the notebook with our script up here. Let's go ahead and get the cake out here for the middle of that table. We can have the staff bring the other goodies out and fill up the punch bowl right before the end of the ceremony. Where are the flowers for the ceremony?"

"I put them in the cooler in the back room so they'd stay fresh. I'll get them right before we start," Dixie answered. "I put the Bible on the shelf under the podium."

Chloe glanced around the room. "It looks to me like y'all have everything under control."

Dixie turned to Nona. "What about the guest book? We need to have that out for everyone to sign."

Nona slapped her cheeks with both hands. "Yikes! I forgot all about it."

Dixie arched her eyebrows. "You did bring it, didn't you?"

Hurrying out of the room, Nona called back. "Yes, don't worry. Be back in a minute."

Nona was reaching her hand out to pull open the front door when the door suddenly opened, knocking her back. As she stumbled backwards, Jenny caught her by the hand, stopping her fall. "Oh, Miss Nona, I'm so sorry! I didn't know you were at the door. Are you okay?"

Nona blushed as she released Jenny's hand. "It's all my fault. I'm okay. I shouldn't have been in such a hurry."

Dressed in a black and white checked dress, Layne strolled in the door followed by an entourage which included her mother Miss Louise, her daughter Blair, and her two young granddaughters Madison and Rachel. "What'd we miss?"

Nona hugged Layne. "You missed Jenny saving me from falling flat on my behind."

Blair gave Nona's arm a squeeze as she passed by. "That would have been a sight none of us would want to see."

"Y'all go on in. We're in the room to the left of the staircase. I'll be right back. I have to get something out of the car." Nona opened the door. Before rushing out, she turned back to add, "By the way, y'all look beautiful. Jenny, you look fabulous in your pink dress. It matches the ribbons and flowers. Someone should take a picture."

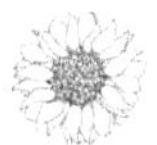

By five minutes before two o'clock most of the guests had arrived. Clearly, Jenny was the center of attention—as it should be—with most of the guests clustered around her. Nona, Dixie, and Betty Jo stood at the entrance to the room, greeting the guests as they arrived.

Dixie glanced down at her watch. "It's time to get started. I'll get the flowers out of the cooler." She hurried toward the kitchen where the flowers were being kept.

Betty Jo watched as Dixie returned with the flowers and carefully placed each one on the table in their order of presentation. When Dixie gave them a nod, Nona turned to Betty Jo. "You're up first. You ready? "

Betty Jo took in a deep breath and slowly blew it out. "As ready as I'll ever be."

As Betty Jo walked to the front of the room, people began to take their seats. When she passed by Jenny's table, she took Jenny by the arm and led her to sit in the chair to the right of the podium. When she stepped up to the podium, the room went silent.

Betty Jo smiled out at the guests. "Dear family and friends, we want to thank you for coming. Today we're resurrecting an old Southern tradition by honoring our Jenny with a White Bible Ceremony." She turned toward

Jenny, who was looking up at her with bright eyes. "Jenny, our hearts overflow with joy that you and Aaron have chosen to be joined together as wife and husband. We congratulate you on this decision and wish y'all a life filled with the happiness you both deserve."

Everyone in the room clapped. As a blush of pink began to creep up her face, Jenny lowered her head. Betty Jo waited until the room was once again quiet.

"Jenny, today we will be giving you two important things which we hope will help you and Aaron form a strong marriage bond in Christ. First, flower by flower, we will build a bouquet. Each flower has special meaning to the person who will be presenting it to you. Second, we will be giving you a Bible, which holds all of the answers to life's problems." She nodded to Layne.

Layne stood, walked to the small table behind the podium, picked up the white tulip from the table, and walked over to stand in front of Jenny. "I give you this white tulip to represent forgiveness along with this scripture from Ephesians 4:32. 'Be kind to one another, tenderhearted, forgiving each other, just as God in Christ also has forgiven you.'"

She handed the flower to Jenny. "I know you remember when Mark was in the hospital fighting for his life, I placed the blame for his accident on someone I'd always counted as one of my dear friends. I was filled with anger and bitterness toward this person even after I learned the truth about what had caused the accident. I didn't think I could ever forgive. Then I received a bouquet of white tulips from my friend and learned they represented forgiveness. As I held that bouquet in my hand, I knew I had a choice to make—live with bitterness, or forgive." Layne looked up at Betty Jo, who was standing behind the podium. "I chose to forgive, and I got back my dear friend." Wiping away a tear, she looked down at Jenny and noticed the tears in her eyes. "Remember this white tulip and always chose forgiveness."

Jenny stood and wrapped her arms around her future mother-in-law. "Thank you. I will remember."

Nona was next. She walked to the small table, picked up the single red rose, and walked over to stand in front of Jenny just as Layne had. "I give you this red rosebud which represents hope. The scripture that goes with this rose is from Romans 15:13. 'May the God of hope fill you with all joy and peace as you trust in him, so that you may overflow with hope by the power of the Holy Spirit.'"

She handed the rosebud to Jenny. "There was a time in my life when I was lost. I felt hopeless, but then I received a single red rosebud. My father told me that it represented hope. That day I realized I wasn't lost or hopeless. Through God's love, I found my hope for the future. I want you to remember this red rosebud if there ever comes a day when you're feeling lost and hopeless. Find in it God's love and His hope for you."

Jenny reached out for Nona's hand. "Thank you. I will remember."

As Nona walked away, Dixie stepped over to the table, picked up the blue iris, and walked over to stand in front of Jenny just as her friends before her had done. "I give you this blue iris, which represents peace. The scripture that goes with this iris is from John 14:27. 'Peace I leave with you, my peace I give you. I do not give to you as the world gives. Do not let your hearts be troubled and do not be afraid.'"

She handed the blue iris to Jenny. "One day you may find that your world has been turned upside down. You may find you don't know which way to turn. Your heart may be so broken or troubled that you won't even know how you're going to make it through the day. That's when I want you to remember this blue iris, which represents peace, God's peace. His peace will calm your fears and bring you the clarity you desire. It's there for you. God gives it freely. All you have to do is ask."

She leaned over and kissed Jenny on both cheeks. Jenny looked up into her eyes. "Thank you, Miss Dixie. I will remember."

As Dixie walked away, Betty Jo raised her hand. A woman from each table stood and took a flower from the floral arrangements on the table. "Jenny, you hold three flowers in your hand symbolizing forgiveness, hope, and peace. However, it takes more than three flowers to make a bouquet complete. Please accept these flowers from your friends and family as a sign of their love and support."

Betty Jo stood back and watched as Jenny accepted the flowers . When she was holding a full bouquet, Betty Jo patted her on the back, took her hand, and led her to the podium. She signaled to Nona and Dixie to join her. "There's more, Jenny. We're not finished."

Dixie took the white Bible tied with a pale pink ribbon and a sprig of baby's breath from behind the podium. "Jenny, we present you with this Bible for you to turn to God's word each day as you look for divine guidance from your Heavenly Father. He will provide you with everything you need for a successful marriage."

Dixie placed the Bible in Nona's hands. Nona said, "Read your Bible every day, in good times and in bad, in times of sorrow, in times of joy, in times of failure, in times of success, in times of illness, in times of health, as your children are born, as you raise your children, and when your children leave your home as adults."

Nona passed the Bible to Betty Jo, who said, "Read your Bible with Aaron and pray together, expecting the Lord to bless you greatly." She handed the Bible to Jenny. "Jenny, we present this white Bible to you with our love, our hopes, and our prayers."

Jenny took the Bible and held it close to her chest. "I promise to cherish this Bible and read it every day." Her voice cracked as she added, "Thank you."

The guests stood as one and began to clap. Betty Jo, Nona, and Dixie smiled. Their first White Bible Ceremony was a success. Mrs. Nancy Jones would be proud.

After settling the bill with Michael, the Columns manager, Betty Jo took a seat on the bottom step of the stairway and watched as Lily and Chloe helped the staff pack up what was left of the finger foods. Even though Betty Jo couldn't take another bite, she was confident her grandchildren would devour the leftovers in a matter of minutes. Nona and Dixie offered their assistance to Jenny and Layne to take the gifts out to the car.

Dixie came in the door with her hands on her back. "Whew! Some of that stuff was heavy."

Nona followed. "I agree. I think some people gave Jenny bricks as gifts."

Betty Jo patted the step she was sitting on. "Bless your hearts! Y'all come on over here and rest your weary old bones."

Dixie sat down next to her while Nona sat on the next step above. Betty Jo clapped her hands together. "I think we all need a big pat on the back. That was truly a success."

Nona smiled over at Betty Jo. "It really was. I couldn't be happier with the way everything turned out."

Dixie nudged Betty Jo with her shoulder. "You'll have to admit my idea of giving this White Bible Ceremony was a good one."

Staring straight ahead, Betty Jo said, "I don't know that I'd say it was a good idea."

Dixie frowned.

Betty Jo teasingly nudged her back. "I'd say it was a great one. If that doesn't motivate Jenny to set a date for this wedding, nothing will."

Dixie chuckled. "I know that's what Layne is hoping."

With their storage boxes and bags stuffed with leftovers, Chloe and Lily joined the three on the stairway. Lily held out a box with petit fours. "Anybody want one?"

Dixie shook her head as she turned away. "I can't even look at food. I ate something every time I passed that table loaded down with food."

Nona groaned. "I know what you mean. Between all the barbecue I scarfed down yesterday and the snacky things I ate today, I may not need to eat for days!"

Lily sighed. "I wish it worked that way, where you could fill up one day and not have to eat for days. I find my problem is that I eat until I could bust one day, and then wake up starving the next!"

They all laughed.

Chloe cleared her throat. "On a more serious note, I have to tell you ladies that your White Bible Ceremony was one of the most eloquent, meaningful showers I've ever attended. Those Bible verses with the flowers and what y'all said about each one truly touched my heart."

Lily put her hand on her shoulder. "I agree with Chloe. It was truly special. I want y'all to do the exact same ceremony one day for Kendall."

Chloe added, "And Kelli." She lowered her head. "Throughout the ceremony I kept thinking about Ethan, our lives together, and how much I miss him. Sometimes I get so scared I won't see him again that I can't breathe." She raised her tear-filled eyes to Betty Jo. "What if. . ."

Hearing the sadness in Chloe's voice broke Betty Jo's heart. Before Chloe could finish her sentence, she reached out and pulled her close. "Oh, Chloe, he's going to come back to us. I just know he will. We need to be patient and trust God to bring him home."

Heart-wrenching sobs began to pour out of Chloe. Nona, Dixie, and Lily moved closer to put their arms around her and Betty Jo.

As Betty Jo cried with Chloe, she repeated the same words over and over as she rocked her back and forth. "Shh. It's going to be okay." She wasn't sure if she was comforting Chloe or reassuring herself.

After several minutes, Chloe's crying stopped. It was several more minutes before she leaned away from Betty Jo. Her azure-blue eyes brightened. "Thank you."

Betty Jo touched her cheek to wipe away a tear. "You know you don't have to keep your worries and fears to yourself. I'm here for you whenever you need to talk."

Cloe reached up for her hand. "It's hard for me to share my feelings, not just with you, but with most people. I'm sorry about the misunderstanding yesterday. It's just that I can talk to Nathan. I didn't realize how much time I was spending with him and how it might look to you."

Betty Jo sighed with relief. "I promise to be more understanding."

Lily stood up and offered her hand to help Chloe stand. "Come on, I'll take you home. You know Dad must be ready for us to take the kids off his hands so he can have some peace and quiet."

Chloe squeezed her hand. "I owe you an apology too."

"We can talk about it in the car." Lily released Chloe's hand and leaned over to pick up the leftovers she'd set down earlier.

When Chloe and Lily were safely out of earshot, Nona asked, "What was yesterday's misunderstanding all about?

Betty Jo crossed her arms. "When we got home from Mr. James's memorial last night, Chloe wasn't home. We didn't know where she was. We tried calling, but it went to voice mail each time. We were worried that something had happened to her or that maybe she'd heard something about Ethan and didn't want to tell us. It turned out she was with Nathan the whole time."

Nona leaned down closer. "With Nathan? Where?"

Betty Jo looked at Nona. "She said they were at the office working on a case and lost track of the time."

Nona leaned back and repeated. "At the office? Why would they go to the office on a Saturday night? That doesn't make sense."

"Exactly what I thought! I began to think something inappropriate might be going on between the two of them."

Nona cocked her head. "Oh, Betty Jo, I don't think Nathan would take advantage of Chloe in her situation. I can't imagine anything inappropriate could be going on."

"After what just happened, I tend to think you're right. That was the first time since the day Chloe learned Ethan was missing in action that she's mentioned her fears to me. I guess she hasn't felt comfortable enough with me to share her feelings and went looking for a sympathetic ear, which she found in Nathan. I feel bad about assuming the worst about her."

Dixie patted Betty Jo's knee. "Well, don't be too hard on yourself. It hasn't been an easy time for you. Plus, she didn't even try to be open with you. The good thing is maybe that's going to change."

Nona clapped her hands together. "I think it's time we headed home too. I'm beat!"

Betty Jo stood. "I'm right behind you."

Chapter Nineteen

Monday morning dawned bright and beautiful. Betty Jo was awake, showered, and dressed before anyone in the house was up. She headed to the kitchen to pop open a can of cinnamon rolls for breakfast. She knew how much fun Dixie would have made of her for not making them from scratch, but that was Dixie's thing, not hers. Her family would enjoy fresh baked even though they weren't homemade. In fact, she wasn't sure if her family had ever had homemade cinnamon rolls. She made a pot of coffee and put the teakettle on the stove. She'd make hot chocolate for the children.

She was surprised by how much energy she had after the long, emotionally charged weekend. She had to admit, she felt optimistic that things were going to be better between her and Chloe. Maybe the two of them could go shopping together today. They could even try to talk Lily into playing hooky from work so she could go along with them. They could make it a girl's day.

She heard noises coming from upstairs alerting her to the children waking up and getting ready for school. The timing was perfect. The cinnamon rolls should come out of the oven as the children were sitting down for breakfast.

Don came up behind her and put his arms around her. "What's that awesome aroma? Don't tell me you're baking cinnamon rolls for us this morning."

She chuckled. "Okay, I won't tell you."

He spun her around to kiss her. "You know you're spoiling us?"

She kissed him back. "That's my goal!"

Kelli came walking in the kitchen holding a yellow bow in her hand. "Gigi, can you put this in my hair? Every time I try, it makes me look stupid."

Following his sister into the room, Matthew sat down at the table and began filling his bowl with cereal. "That's because you are stupid."

Kelli stomped her foot. "That's not nice."

Don rapped Matthew's chair with his newspaper as he took his place at the table. "Matthew, apologize to your sister."

Matthew mumbled, "Sorry."

Don frowned at his grandson.

Matthew turned toward his sister. "I'm sorry, Kelli." Turning back to his grandfather, he asked, "Was that better?"

"Much."

Betty Jo finished putting Kelli's bow in her hair. If she didn't know for certain that over twenty years had passed, she would have thought Ethan and Lily were sitting at her table. She guessed the relationship between sisters and brothers hadn't changed much in those twenty years. She was taking the cinnamon rolls out of the oven when Chloe came in the kitchen holding Chase by the hand.

"Good morning, everyone," Chloe called out in a cheery voice as she helped Chase sit at the kitchen table.

Betty Jo almost dropped the basket filled with warm cinnamon rolls she was carrying to the table when she caught sight of Chloe dressed in a black suit trimmed with white piping and starched white blouse, complete with black heels. It was obvious Chloe was dressed for work. After their conversation at the Columns, she'd assumed she was finished working with Nathan.

Chloe reached out to take the basket from Betty Jo's hands. "Let me help you with that." She set the basket on the table. "These smell delicious. Kids, don't be greedy, just take one."

Dumbfounded, Betty Jo stared at her. "After what you said yesterday, I thought you were through working with Nathan. I was hoping maybe we could go shopping today, you know, together."

Chloe covered her mouth with her hand as she chuckled. "Oh, good gracious, no way. We go to trial today. After all the work I've done on this case, I deserve to be sitting with Nathan in the front of the courtroom."

Hoping to hide her disappointment, Betty Jo turned away and busied herself at the kitchen counter. "Oh, okay. That's fine."

Taking a cinnamon roll from the basket, Chloe sat down at the table. "Maybe we could plan it for some other day, but you must know I do most of my shopping online these days. Going from store to store is such a hassle. Shopping's just not that much fun to me."

"Mama, you're going to a courtroom today?"

Betty Jo was glad Kelli's question took the focus away from the shopping trip she'd imagined would be a bonding experience for them. She grabbed two cinnamon rolls out of the basket as she sat down at the table opposite Chloe. Half-listening to Chloe's explanation of why she was going to be in a courtroom to Kelli, Betty Jo began to consider the reality that it might not be in the cards for the two of them to bond, ever.

After Mark left for work, Layne decided that since it was another beautiful day, she'd start it off with a walk. It seemed she'd eaten all weekend, starting with the barbecue along with all the fixin's on Saturday at Mr. James's memorial and ending with a buffet of finger foods and cake on Sunday. She hoped she could walk off some of those calories before she weighed in at the Skinny Dippers meeting tomorrow. As she leaned over to tie her walking shoes, she realized it'd been more than a few days since she'd put them on. Oh, well. Better late than never.

Before heading out the door, she zipped up her jacket, put in her earbuds, and started her audiobook on her cell phone. Her regular walking route took her down her driveway, two blocks to the stop sign, turn left, and three times around an older neighborhood that had very little traffic. She then retraced her path back home. She was on her second time around the neighborhood when she recognized Aaron's patrol car coming towards her. He slowed, pulled over next to her, stopped his car, and lowered his window.

She took out her earbuds and leaned in the open window. "Hey, you, what's up?"

"Good things! How about you get in so we can talk?"

She narrowed her eyes, "What's going on?"

His mouth curled up in a smile. "Get in, and I'll tell you." He leaned over and opened the passenger side door.

Frowning at him as she walked around his car, she couldn't imagine what he had to tell her. Aware of the life-changing events happening to her friends, she hoped what he had to say truly was good news. She sat down in the passenger seat and closed the door. "Okay, hit me with it."

Aaron turned in his seat to look straight at his mother. "I'm not sure what all happened at that fancy thing your friends had for Jenny yesterday, but after you dropped her off at her house, she got in her car and came straight to mine. She was all fired up, telling me about flowers and Bible verses and a white Bible. I haven't heard her that excited about anything in a long time."

Layne smiled at her son. "That's great, Aaron. I'll have to let Nona, Dixie, and Betty Jo know how excited she was."

"That's not all you'll need to let them know, Mom."

Layne raised an eyebrow. "It's not?"

"You'll also need to let them know that there's going to be a wedding next Saturday!"

Wide-eyed, Layne put both hands to her chest. "Your wedding?"

Aaron nodded. Layne reached over the console and wrapped her arms around her son. "That's the best thing I've heard in a very long time! Congratulations, Son!"

After a minute, Aaron pulled away from her hug. Holding his mother by her shoulders so he could see her face, he explained, "Jenny and I are so excited. We spent half the night talking about the uncertainty of life with all that's happened lately with Mr. James dying and Ethan missing in action. However, one thing we are certain about is our love for one another. We decided we don't want to wait any longer to be married. We want to be married as soon as possible, and since we're both off next weekend, we decided to do it Saturday."

Layne wiped away the tears of joy rolling down her cheeks. "I think that's one of the best decisions you two have made in a long time. Does your dad know?"

"I hope you're not mad, but I told him first thing this morning. He's the one who told me where to find you."

Layne playfully hit his arm. "Don't be silly. Why would I be mad about that?" She took her cell phone from her pants pocket.

"Who are you calling?"

"Jenny, of course."

"I don't think she'll answer. She's working."

"Then I'll leave her a message."

"You've reached the voice mail of Jenny Levins. Please leave your number and brief message. I'll return your call as soon as I can. Thank you."

Layne waited for the beep. "Jenny Levins, you have made your future mother-in-law the happiest person in Kerry, Georgia. Please come by the house as soon as you get off work. We've got some major planning to do if we're going to pull off a wedding in only five days. Love you!"

Aaron ran his hands through his hair. "Mom, please don't make this into a big deal. We want a simple, small wedding in the chapel at the church with only a few guests. Jenny's sister Emma is going to fly out on Friday."

"But, Son, a wedding is a big deal." Layne sat back against her seat and sighed. "However, I can do simple."

Aaron leaned over to kiss his mother on the cheek. "Thanks, Mom." He turned away, put his hands on his steering wheel, and stared straight ahead. "Now, get out of my patrol car. If the sheriff saw me sitting here talking with a civilian, I might lose my job, and as a man about to take on a wife, I can't afford to do that."

"Ha, Ha. Very funny!"

They both laughed as she got out of the car. As she watched her son drive away, Layne couldn't remember the last time she'd felt this happy.

Thank you, God, for the joy of unexpected blessings.

Betty Jo woke up with a headache. It'd started Monday morning with Chloe's announcement she was going to court with Nathan instead of shopping with her. When Chloe hadn't come home before her children went to bed, it had gotten worse. She'd hoped two aspirins and a good night's rest would be the cure, but it persisted through breakfast on Tuesday morning. After Chloe and the children left and Don was on his way into town to get parts for his go-cart project, she considered crawling back into bed until she looked down at her phone. On the home screen was a group text to her, Nona, and Dixie from Layne.

Have news. C U at SD.

It took her a few seconds to understand that "SD" stood for Skinny Dippers. She hadn't even remembered that it was Tuesday, let alone a Skinny Dippers meeting day. She wondered what Layne's news might be. She hadn't qualified her news as good or bad. If it was bad news, she'd rather not know. In the past few weeks, she'd had her fill of bad news. But, if it was good news, that was another story. She could use some of that. Glancing up at the kitchen clock, she calculated she had plenty of time to shower, dress, and drive to the Skinny Dippers meeting at the Dream Bean.

She was pleased when she found a diagonal parking place on the side street next to the coffeeshop. She avoided parallel parking like the plague. She looked down the block and watched with envy as Nona expertly parallel parked her car in a very tiny space. "How do you do that?" she called out to her.

Nona laughed. "Practice. My daddy made me do it over and over until I could just about do it blindfolded."

Betty Jo shook her head. "You were lucky to have a father that would take the time to do that. Mine never helped me with anything. He basically threw some car keys at me and said 'Drive'!"

They entered the coffeeshop and walked up the stairs together to the meeting room where they saw Layne and Dixie were already seated.

Betty Jo and Nona joined their friends, and Betty Jo glanced around the room. "Where's our wonderful motivational leader today? Don't tell me Doreen's late."

Dixie leaned in close to Betty Jo. "Oh, I guess you haven't heard. Doreen ran off with a traveling salesman she met three weeks ago."

Betty Jo slapped her on the knee. "You just made that up, didn't you?"

Dixie put her hand over her heart. "I swear it's true."

Nona's eyes lit up as she looked at Betty Jo. "Dixie might be telling the truth. After all, she did lose a ton of weight and was looking pretty good."

Layne nodded in agreement. "Good enough to attract someone traveling through Kerry."

"Ladies, may I have your attention, please?"

They looked to the front of the room to see Sharon Ford, Kerry's best real estate agent, standing there. "Your attention, please. It seems Doreen has quit without giving notice. We don't know where she put our cards with recorded weights or even where she put the scales. Therefore, today's meeting is canceled."

There was mumbling all over the room.

Betty Jo chuckled. "It looks like you were right after all, Dixie." Taking Dixie by the hand, she began pulling her to her feet. "Come on. Let's go on downstairs. We all need coffee and a muffin. Plus, I can't wait to hear what news Layne has to tell us."

They were soon in place at their regular booth. As soon as smiling Anna Clare had taken their orders, they were looking to Layne to give them her news.

Beaming with excitement, Layne put both hands in the middle of the table. "Dixie, your idea worked. Aaron and Jenny have decided to get married, not in Bowers and not just sometime in the future, but right here in Kerry at the chapel this coming Saturday!"

Dixie squealed. "I was so hoping that was your news."

Nona grinned. "Congratulations! That's great news."

Betty Jo's eyes glistened with tears. "It really is great news, Layne. Congratulations."

Layne noticed the tears in Betty Jo's eyes. "Don't be sad, Betty Jo. This is a happy event, and we need to celebrate."

Betty Jo wiped at her eyes. "You're right. This is happy news. Sorry, I shouldn't be crying. "

Layne put her arm around Betty Jo. "No, I'm the one who's sorry. Here I am telling you not to be sad. I should be more sensitive to what you're going through, wondering where and how Ethan is every minute of every day."

Hearing the tenderness in Layne's voice, Betty Jo couldn't hold back the tears. They began to flood down her face.

It took a few minutes for her tears to stop. Nona handed her several napkins to wipe her face and blow her nose. "I don't know how you've held it together so well for so long."

Betty Jo lifted her face to offer a thin smile. "To tell you the truth, I don't either. I do trust that God will bring him home, but occasionally, I waver in that trust and. . ." She pointed to her face. "You see what happens."

The women all chuckled. Before anyone could say anything else, Anna Clare was at their booth with their orders.

Betty Jo took a sip of her coffee before turning to Layne. "I am happy for Jenny and Aaron. I think it's great news they've decided to get married this Saturday and right here in Kerry. I know Miss Louise has to be thrilled."

Layne began to choke on the muffin she'd just bitten into. "Good grief! I hadn't even thought to tell Mama!"

Betty Jo patted her on the back. "It's okay. It doesn't matter when she hears it, it'll still be good news to her."

Layne gave her a doubtful look as she crossed her fingers. "Here's hoping she doesn't hear it from anyone else before I have a chance to tell her."

"We haven't had a chance to talk about your good news, Nona. How are you handling the idea of being a grandmother?" Dixie asked.

Nona took in a deep breath and slowly blew it out before answering. "It all feels surreal to me." She went on to explain, "Y'all know how much it hurt me when Grace wouldn't talk to me for almost three years. I knew she blamed me for the divorce, but when she didn't even reach out to me through that whole ordeal with Amy, she truly broke my heart. Then she shows up at Daddy's memorial and announces that she's going to have a baby and wants me to be a part of the baby's life, which does makes me happy. Yet, I feel I can't allow myself to be as excited as I want to be, because I can't trust her. I'm afraid if I let my guard down and fall in love with my grandchild, she might just rip the baby out of my life on a whim."

Shaking her head, she looked around the booth at her friends. "I've handled cases for grandparents who were suing their own children for visitation rights to their grandchildren. I'm afraid I might end up being one of those grandparents."

Dixie put her arm around Nona. "Oh, Nona, I'm so sorry. I never even thought about something like that happening."

Betty Jo smiled reassuringly at Nona. "I'll be praying that never happens. I can't imagine why any daughter in their right mind would rob their child of the pure, unwavering love of a grandparent."

Nona lifted an eyebrow. "Let's just hope that Grace stays in her right mind."

Dixie drummed her fingers on the table. "I haven't wanted to say anything, because I don't want to make a big deal out of it like I did the last time with getting my hopes up and all." She paused, folding her hands in front of her. "It looks like Jason is going to come home this weekend for a visit."

Betty Jo clapped her hands together. "Oh, Dixie, that's great news."

Dixie put both hands out. "It is, but I'm going to play it down, keep it low-key."

Nona nodded. "I think that's the smart way to go with this first visit home."

Layne took one of Dixie's outstretched hands. "What is that old saying? 'Slow and steady. steady and slow, that's the only way to go.'"

"That's my plan exactly."

Chapter Twenty

Nona went straight to the office after leaving the Dream Bean Coffee Shop. She was anxious to find out if the civil lawsuit she'd handed over to Nathan when her father's mental stability had declined was finished. If all went as expected, the jury would find in their client's favor once the vast amount of the evidence against the defendant had been presented.

As soon as Lily saw Nona come through the front door, she was out from behind her desk to greet her. "Good morning, Ms. Foxx."

Nona looked at her anxiously. "Any news?"

"No, ma'am. They're still in court. Can I get you some coffee?"

Nona took off her coat and handed it to Lily. "No, thanks. I've had plenty this morning. Any messages for me?"

Lily leaned over her desk and picked up a sticky note. "Yes, ma'am. You had one call from Mr. Riley. He asked for you to call him back when you have a minute. He said it's nothing urgent."

As Nona headed to her office, she called back to Lily, "Please get Riley on the phone. There's no time like the present to take care of a non-urgent phone call." She paused as she passed the office that had once been her father's. She hadn't given any thought as to what she would do with his office, knowing he would never return. She stepped inside and glanced around the room. Even though he'd retired several years ago, she'd kept it as he'd left it, out of respect. Her eyes stopped on his worn leather chair pulled up to his mahogany desk. She shuddered. It was eerie how she could almost feel his spirit in this room.

"I've got Mr. Riley on the phone. Do you want me to transfer it to Mr. James's office?" Lily asked from the doorway.

She hurried past Lily, closing the door on her father's office as she left. "No, I'll take it in my office."

Her phone rang as she sat down at her desk. "Hello, Riley. How are you this morning?"

Riley ignored her question. "Homewood called earlier asking when we would be collecting Father's things. That's the second time they've called about this."

Nona sighed, realizing this was one more thing needing to be dealt with that she hadn't taken the time to think about. "We do need to take care of that ASAP. I'm sure they need us to get everything out of his room so they can move another person in."

"I'm sure they do. When can you get to it?"

Riley's words screamed through her mind. *When can you get to it?* She should be asking him when he could get to it. Her brother's lack of initiative and responsibility concerning their father's death was exasperating. He expected her to handle everything while he stayed in the background and watched. What irritated her most was how she'd fallen right in with his expectations. But now she'd had enough.

She cleared her throat, hoping to keep the annoyance she was feeling toward her brother out of her voice. "Riley, you need to handle getting Daddy's things from Homewood. With all that's going on here, there's no way I can do it."

Nona could hear the surprise in her brother's voice. "Oh, okay. I can take care of that. I just thought you'd want to handle it like everything else, but I can if you really want me too."

"I really want you too, Riley. Thanks." She ended the call and sat back in her chair wondering why she hadn't handed more things over to him before now.

She was startled by the ring of her office phone almost the instant she'd hung up from talking to Riley. Sure it was Riley calling her back with some excuse about why he couldn't take care of the problem at Homewood, she shouted into the phone, "Yes, what it is now?"

For a long moment there was only silence in her ear. She was about to hang up when she heard Lily's soft voice. "Ms. Foxx, I thought you would want to know Nathan is back from the courthouse."

"Thank you, Lily. I'll be right out."

As soon as she opened her door, she heard sounds of excitement floating down the hall. In that moment, she knew that Foxx & Foxx Law Firm had won another case. She hurried down the hall toward the voices. She found Nathan sitting at his desk with Lily and Chloe behind him looking over his shoulder.

All three looked up as she walked in the room. Nathan waved her in. "Nona, come check this out!"

Chloe stepped to the side and Nona took her place behind Nathan. She looked at the documentation he was pointing out. Her breath caught in her throat when she saw the jury's award to their client was six hundred thousand dollars. She picked the paper up for a better look to make sure her eyes weren't deceiving her.

Wide-eyed, she looked from the paper to Nathan and then back to the paper. "Nathan, this is whole heck of a lot more than we anticipated."

Nathan nodded. "I'm telling you, that jury loved us. From the very minute they took their seats, I felt something good was coming our way."

Nona had never heard Nathan's voice filled with so much excitement. She patted him on the back. "Congratulations."

Nathan looked to Chloe. "You need to congratulate Chloe as well. She was a true asset in preparing for trial."

He suddenly stood up, pulled Chloe into his arms, and spun her around. For a split second, it looked to Nona as if her was going to kiss her When she caught a glimpse of Lily's face, she could tell it looked like that to her as well.

Chloe giggled when Nathan released her. Her eyes sparkled as she looked up at him. "Oh, Nathan, I was happy to do what I could to help."

Nathan beamed down at Chloe. "You were a big help."

As Chloe straightened her hair and smoothed out her suit, Nathan gazed at her with what looked to Nona like affection.

Nona cleared her throat and stepped between them. "Glad you could help us out on this case, Chloe." She took Chloe's arm in hers and began leading her away from Nathan and out of his office. "We don't want to keep you. I'm sure you want to get home to see how Don and your kids are doing with the go-cart project."

Nathan hurried to his office door, putting out both hands in front of him to stop their leaving. "Wait, I thought we'd celebrate with a fancy lunch."

Chloe patted Nona's hand. "I really don't need to get home right away. You know, the children aren't even out of school yet."

Lily, who'd been standing in the back of the room, rushed to Nona's side. "I think Mr. Weaver is right. We should make it a true celebratory lunch. I'll call Heather and Mr. Montgomery to come join us."

Nona started to protest, but reconsidered when she understood what Lily was trying to do. Calling Heather, Nathan's wife, to join them, was a fine idea. Having Monty come too was an added bonus. "I like that idea, Lily. Go ahead and give both a call."

Nathan shook his head. "You won't be able to get in touch with Heather. She and Grayson have gone to Valley, Alabama to visit her mother for a few days. So you'll just need to call Mr. Montgomery to come join us. How's the Rustic Bistro sound to y'all?"

Lily gave a sideways glance to Nona, who nodded her approval. "Okay, Mr. Weaver. I'll call Mr. Montgomery and then call ahead to the Rustic Bistro to make reservations."

Betty Jo was starting the washer with her second load of laundry for the day when she heard Don come in the back door.

"Betty Jo, where are you?"

"In the laundry room."

She began folding the sheets she'd just taken out of the dryer as she waited for him to come to her. She smiled at him when he walked in.

"You're just in time to help. You know what a lousy job I do folding sheets. I never understand how to fold the fitted one."

Don laughed as he picked up the corner of a fitted sheet. "That's because you just wad them into a big mess. You don't want to take the time to do it right. Here, just give it to me. I'll do it."

She let go of her end of the sheet and picked up a pillowcase. "Where have you been all morning?"

"I had to pick up some parts I ordered for the go-cart from Barney's Auto. Then I ran a couple of errands I've been putting off like getting our license plates renewed."

Betty Jo set the folded pillowcase aside and picked up the matching one. "It's that time already? Seems like you just did that."

"It comes around the same time every year." Don pulled another fitted sheet from the pile. "I found out a couple of things you might find interesting while I was at the courthouse."

"Oh?"

"First of all, I was there when everyone was buzzing with the news that Nathan won that case he and Chloe have been working on these past few weeks. I heard it was a big win for them."

Betty Jo had moved on to matching socks together. "That's great news. Maybe now Chloe will be home more often. What else did you find out?"

"You remember how we thought it was strange how Heather didn't come to Mr. James's memorial with Nathan?"

Betty Jo nodded absentmindedly as she continued matching socks.

"Well, the talk around the courthouse is that she packed up and left him."

Betty Jo dropped her hands to her side and stared at her husband. "You're saying that Heather has left Nathan."

"That's what the talk is. She's taken Grayson with her to live with her mother in Valley, Alabama."

"I can't believe it. I was with Layne most of the morning. She didn't say a thing about Heather leaving." Eyes wide, Betty Jo put both hands over her mouth. "Oh, Don, I wonder if she even knows."

Betty Jo's cell phone rang. She looked down at the screen to see it was Nona calling. She shook her head to clear her mind before answering. "Hi,

Nona.”

“Betty Jo, I know this is going to sound crazy, but I need for you to call Layne to ask her to go to lunch with you. Then the two of you need to get down to the Rustic Bistro as soon as you can.”

“Call Layne to go to lunch? What’s going on?”

“I don’t have time to explain it all right now, but I need for you two to pretend you just happened to stop by the Bistro for lunch and then accidentally run into us.”

“Us? Who are you with?”

“You’ll see when you get there. You need to drop what you’re doing and call Layne now.”

“Okay, I’ll do what you ask, but you’re right about it sounding crazy.”

“You’ll thank me when you understand why I asked you to come.” Nona ended the call.

Don put down the sheet he was folding and asked, “Is everything okay? What’s going on?”

She took the phone away from her ear and stared at the screen. “I’m not sure.” She frowned. “Nona wants me to call Layne and take her to lunch at the Rustic Bistro.”

Don went back to folding. “That doesn’t sound so bad to me.”

“Not bad, but weird.”

She speed-dialed Layne’s number. Layne answered on the third ring. “Hey, Betty Jo.”

“I know this is going to sound crazy and a little weird, but I just got a call from Nona. She wants both of us to go to lunch at the Rustic Bistro right now. She wouldn’t tell me why, but she said we’d understand when we got there.”

“Sounds like we better do what she’s asked. See you in ten.” Layne ended the call.

Betty Jo stood for a moment in astonishment of how Layne had accepted her request without hesitation or questioning.

Fifteen minutes later, Betty Jo and Layne were walking into the Rustic Bistro. Betty Jo was still confused by Nona’s strange request, but trusted that she had a good reason for wanting them there. When they were led into the restaurant by a waiter, the reason became clear. Betty Jo noticed

Nona was sitting at the end of a table with Monty sitting next to her and Lily next to him. Across the table from them were Nathan and Chloe. Nathan's arm was resting casually across the back of Chloe's chair. Their heads were leaned in close to one another as if they were two lovers sharing a secret.

Nona jumped up from the table the minute she spotted Betty Jo and Layne. "Hello, you two! What a coincidence to see you here." She leaned over as if to give Betty Jo a kiss on the cheek, but instead whispered in her ear, "You see why I asked you here."

Betty Jo said, "I can't believe y'all are here. Layne and I were hungry for some of their chicken salad with homemade chips."

Monty stood. "Won't y'all join us? I'll put a chair at the end of the table. Betty Jo, you can take my seat. I think there's room for a chair between Chloe and Nathan." Monty motioned for Nathan to get up. "How about you grab that chair over there against the wall for yourself, and your mother can take your seat."

After everyone was seated, Nona announced. "We're celebrating Nathan's big win for Foxx & Foxx."

Layne leaned over to hug Nathan. "That's great, Nathan! I'm so proud of you, but I would've thought you'd want Heather here with you to celebrate." Smiling, she turned to Chloe. "Have you met Nathan's beautiful wife Heather, of almost ten years, and their precious son Grayson?"

Chloe returned her smile. "Yes, I believe I have met her. I believe their son is in the same class with my son."

Turning back to Nathan, Layne asked, "You did invite Heather to join you, didn't you?"

Betty Jo could see Nathan stiffen at his mother's question. "Heather's in Alabama visiting her mother."

"Really? She didn't say anything to me about leaving for a visit. Where's Grayson then?"

"Oh, he's with Heather." He took a drink of water.

Betty Jo watched as the muscle in Nathan's lower jaw began to twitch. Could that twitch mean Nathan was not being truthful? If she had to guess, she'd guess Nathan was hiding something. Was something going on between him and Chloe? Is that why Heather was in Alabama and why Nona had insisted they show up for lunch?

Layne smiled. "I'm sorry she couldn't be here, but I'm glad I happened to stop by and can help you celebrate." She picked up her glass and held it out. "A toast to Nathan's success."

All raised their glasses, toasting Nathan. "Here! Here!"

It was obvious to Betty Jo that Nathan didn't seem as happy as he'd been when they first entered the restaurant. She could only imagine it was because he was now sitting next to his mother and not Chloe. However, it seemed that Chloe was as happy as ever. Maybe the attraction she witnessed between the two of them when she arrived was actually one sided—Nathan's side. She wondered if Chloe was pretending to be clueless or truly unaware of Nathan's obvious attraction to her. She hoped it was the latter. A shudder ran down her spine. It'd be a devastating blow for Ethan to come home to find his wife was attracted to another man. She couldn't let that happen.

Betty Jo put a smile on her face and joined in with the conversations going on around the table, but the worry about Chloe's feelings for Nathan were heavy on her heart. She picked at her chicken salad and the homemade chips on her plate. She noticed Layne hadn't touched her lunch either. She imagined Layne was as concerned as she was about Nathan and Chloe's relationship. She wondered if on the way to the restaurant she should have told Layne about the rumor going around the courthouse about Heather leaving Nathan. It hadn't felt right to her to spread gossip which may or may not be true. She hoped Nathan would tell his mother the truth about what was going on with his wife before she left for Alabama.

Nona tapped her knife against her glass to get everyone's attention. "In honor of Nathan's win today, I'm giving Nathan, Chloe, and Lily the rest of the week off. Y'all have earned it."

Lily's face lit up as she looked at Nona. "Thank you! I can sure use some time off."

With a bright smile on her face, Chloe reached across the table for Betty Jo's hand. "This means now I have the time for us to go on that shopping trip together."

As Betty Jo took Chloe's hand in hers, she realized she worried too much. "Yes, it does!"

When lunch was finished and everyone began to leave the restaurant, Layne pulled Nathan to the side. "Tell me the truth, Nathan. Is something going on with you and Heather that I should know about?"

Nathan was confused by his mother's question. He'd thought his explanation about why Heather wasn't there to help celebrate his win would be enough to appease her concerns. He wasn't ready to tell her anything more. "No, Mom, nothing else is going on. It's been a while since Heather's seen her mother. I encouraged her to go since I've been working overtime preparing for this case. So, she and Grayson went."

"She and Grayson will be here for Aaron's wedding this weekend, right?"

Nathan gave her a blank stare.

"You have told Heather about Aaron's wedding this weekend, haven't you?"

Nathan shook his head and leaned over to give his mother a kiss on the cheek. "Not, yet, but I'll call her as soon as I get home."

As he walked to his car, Layne called to him, "Don't forget, Nathan. Aaron wants the whole family there."

Without turning around, Nathan waved his acknowledgment and got into his car.

As soon as Layne shut her car door, she turned in her seat to Betty Jo. "Do you think Nona asked us to lunch because of the way Nathan was acting with Chloe?"

Betty Jo stared straight ahead, trying to decide if she was going to be honest or deflect her friend's question. She chose honesty. "Yes, I do. I also believe their working together was not a good thing for either one of them."

Layne bit her lip. "I think you may be right." She turned back in her seat and fastened her seat belt.

Betty Jo started the car. "I for one am glad that case is finished. They need to take a break from one another."

"Has Lily mentioned anything to you about how Nathan and Chloe are getting. . .well, too close to one another?"

Betty Jo kept her eyes straight ahead on the road. She wasn't sure how she should answer Layne's question. She didn't want to lie, but she didn't think it would be right to share her suspicions when she didn't have any facts. "Too close? She hasn't really said that."

Layne was silent until Betty Jo pulled up to her house. "Thanks, Betty Jo." She opened her car door to get out, but suddenly turned back. "I'm worried that Chloe's the reason Heather is in Alabama visiting her mother."

Betty Jo raised one eyebrow and looked directly at Layne. "You think Chloe's the reason, not Nathan?"

"What I mean is the way Chloe has been flirting with Nathan."

Oh, no, she didn't just accuse Chloe of being the flirt. Betty Jo took a deep, calming breath, then forced a smile on her face. "I think you've got it backwards. I believe Nathan has been coming onto Chloe because her husband isn't here. He believes she's vulnerable, and Heather had enough of it and left him."

Layne frowned. "No one said anything about Heather leaving Nathan?"

Betty Jo realized she'd said too much. This needed to end. She reached out her hand to Layne. "I'm sorry, Layne. I don't know if that's true. I was upset and lashed out. I shouldn't have said that. Forgive me?"

Layne took her hand. "Of course, I forgive you. I'm sorry too. I guess with all that's going on right now with the wedding and stuff, I overreacted."

"Let's put this behind us."

"Sounds good to me."

Layne closed the door and gave a wave as she walked into her house. Betty Jo waved back as she pulled out of her driveway. She was glad all was forgiven. She had enough to worry about without worrying if Layne was upset with her.

Chapter Twenty-One

Lily, Chloe, and Betty Jo left bright and early Friday morning for their shopping trip to Atlanta. They considered going to Savannah, but Lily knew the Atlanta stores better, so that made their decision. Betty Jo was excited that Lily was taking them to lunch at her favorite restaurant. She needed a change from the usual Kerry eateries and was looking forward to something different. Kelli, Matthew, and Chase made her promise she would bring them home something special. Don was taking and picking up the children from school. They had big plans on finishing up their go-cart project. Betty Jo had her doubts if it would ever be "finished up."

The women decided Aaron's and Jenny's wedding gave them the perfect opportunity to buy new outfits to wear. With their cute, young figures, Lily and Chloe had several choices. With Betty Jo's older and rounder figure, she didn't have the luxury of choice. After going through several shops and trying on multiple ensembles, she finally found one that looked and felt good on her. All three were satisfied with their choices.

Chloe and Lily's last stop was to a children's clothing shop. They each bought several sets of clothes for their children. While they were busy shopping, Betty Jo headed to the toy store and loaded her cart down with books, puzzles, games, modeling clay, crayons, colored pencils, Star Wars play sets, Batman play sets, and Barbie and Ken dolls.

As Betty Jo climbed in the back seat of Lily's car for the ride home, she had to admit that it'd been a good day. She would go as far as to say that it was even a bonding day for all three of them. She hoped many more would follow.

As Lily pulled onto the interstate, she caught sight of her mother in her rearview mirror. "What are you grinning about, Mom?"

Betty Jo put her hands to her mouth. "Oh, my, was I grinning? I was just thinking about what a great day I had with the two of you."

Chloe nodded in agreement. "Me too. It was a fun shopping trip."

Lily chuckled. "Well, I agree, and that makes it unanimous. I had a wonderful time. I've always loved shopping with you, Mom. You may not know this, but you can be fun when you want to be."

"Oh, really? That's good to know. I'll try to want to be fun more often."

They all laughed the easy laugh of friends.

Betty Jo heard the music of a cell phone, but it took her a minute to realize it was hers. She dug through her purse, found her phone, and hurried to answer it without taking the time to see who was calling. "Hello."

"Betty Jo, where are you?" Don's voice came through her phone low and serious.

She was immediately alarmed. Frightening images of harm falling on Ethan or the children flashed through her mind. She kept her voice soft hoping Chloe and Lily wouldn't hear her fear. "Don, what's wrong?"

He asked again. "Where are you?"

"We just left Atlanta. We're on I-75 heading home. Why?"

"I just wanted to make sure you were on your way home."

She could tell he was holding something back from her. "Don, tell me what's going on."

"I'm doing my best to keep the kids from finding out what's happening. Those two officers from the Air Force are here. They won't tell me anything. They want to talk to Chloe. Y'all need to get here as soon as you can." He ended the call.

Betty Jo slowly took the phone from her ear.

Staring intently at her through the rearview mirror, Lily asked, "Is everything okay?"

Betty Jo forced a smile. "Yes, that was just your dad checking on us."

Without turning around, Chloe added, "I'll bet he wants to know when we'll be home. I'm sure he's had enough of being in charge of the kids."

"That's exactly what he wanted, to know when we'd be home."

"I'm doing my best to get us there as soon I can."

Don's words kept going through Betty Jo's mind. *Two Air Force Officers are here. Won't tell me anything.* Were they bringing good news, or news that would destroy her family? *Dear Lord, please let it be good news.*

Betty Jo debated about whether she should share that there was news awaiting them when they arrived home or allow Chloe and Lily a worry-free trip home. After considering how she would feel if someone kept such news from her, she knew what she had to do.

Chloe and Lily were chatting about their purchases.

Betty Jo cleared her throat. "Could I interrupt y'all?"

The two stopped talking, giving Betty Jo their attention.

Chloe turned around in her seat. "Sure, what's up?"

"Well, I wasn't totally honest with y'all about why Don called."

Chloe frowned. "There's nothing wrong with the kids, is there?"

Betty Jo leaned forward to put a comforting hand on Chloe's shoulder. "The children are fine. I didn't tell you that Lieutenant Colonel Wilkerson and Captain Reeves are at our house wanting to talk to you, Chloe. Sorry, I should have told you right away, but I didn't want to upset either of you."

"Mom! That's not something you keep as a secret!"

"I know, and I'm sorry I didn't say something right away. Don is doing his best to keep the children busy and away from the officers."

Chloe turned and stared out her window as she spoke in a soft, detached voice. "So, you think they've come to bring us bad news?"

"No, not at all. I have to believe they've come to bring you the good news that Ethan's been found."

Chloe reached up to pat Betty Jo's hand. "Let's pray you're right."

"That's what I've been doing since I got the call."

All three were lost in their thoughts and didn't speak the rest of the way home.

It was just starting to rain as Lily pulled into her parents' driveway. She parked behind the black military SUV. Without saying a word, the women unbuckled their seat belts, stepped out of the car, and began walking toward the house. Betty Jo recognized Lieutenant Colonel Wilkerson and Captain Reeves as they walked out of the shadows of the front porch each holding an umbrella shielding them from the rain. She searched their faces for a sign of what news they'd come to deliver, but neither face offered a hint. Grasping hands, the three women moved closer to one another, ignoring the rain that was beginning to soak through their clothes.

The officers moved their umbrellas over the three offering some shelter from the rain that was falling harder. They all jumped at the sound of thunder followed by a flash of lightning.

Betty Jo raised her voice above the sound of the rain pounding down on the umbrellas. "I don't think it's safe to stay out here. Let's go inside."

All five hurried to the house. Betty Jo looked around for Don, but when she didn't see him decided he must be still be keeping the children busy in the shop. They went into the house through the garage. Betty Jo, Chloe, and Lily hung their soaked jackets on hooks outside the kitchen door. Betty Jo opened the door and they all followed her inside. "Sorry y'all had to wait for us. Can I get you a cup of coffee to warm you up?"

Both officers took off their hats but remained standing at the door, not wanting to track water into the house. Captain Reeves spoke. "No, ma'am, but we wouldn't mind the use of a towel."

Lily hurried to the laundry room, grabbed two towels off the shelf, and handed one to each officer. Six anxious eyes watched as they dried off.

Chloe sat down at the kitchen table and motioned to the officers. "Please, sit. I assume you've come to bring us some news about my husband."

Captain Reeves sat while Lieutenant Colonel Wilkerson remained standing. "Yes, ma'am, we have." He glanced around the table at Betty Jo and Lily.

Chloe smiled grimly. "It's all right if they hear whatever it is you have to tell me."

Lieutenant Colonel Wilkerson joined Captain Reeves at the table. "Yes, ma'am. I'm pleased to bring you the information that Lieutenant Colonel Breedlow is no longer classified as MIA. He is en route to Langley Air Force Base at this very minute."

For several moments, no one moved or spoke as the news filtered through their minds.

Chloe folded her hands in front of her as she began to softly cry. "Thank you, Lord. I was afraid you were going to tell us he was dead."

Betty Jo and Lily rushed to Chloe's side, embracing her and crying tears of relief.

When Betty Jo was once again in control of her emotions enough to speak, she asked, "Has Ethan been. . . injured?"

She watched in astonishment as the usually serious face of Captain Reeves broke into a smile. "The report we've been given indicates the lieutenant colonel shows signs of being malnourished, but has sustained only minor injuries."

Betty Jo, Chloe, and Lily looked at one another and burst out with nervous laughter.

Betty Jo wiped away the tears running down her cheeks. "Can you tell us what happened? Where he's been?"

Captain Reeves looked at Lieutenant Colonel Wilkerson, who gave a slight nod of his head. "We can't give you the location of where he went missing or where he was found, but we can tell you that he was traveling with a convoy in a Humvee. Due to faulty navigational equipment, the convoy made a wrong turn into an unfamiliar territory. After traveling several miles, they were unexpectedly hit by fire from insurgents, forcing the convoy to split into three separate groups."

Captain Reeves paused and looked to Lieutenant Colonel Wilkerson, who picked up the story. "The lives of six American soldiers were claimed, but Lieutenant Colonel Breedlow, along with three other soldiers, escaped. They hid in various locations around the country for the past few weeks until they were able to find refuge among some villagers who were able to get them to safety."

Betty Jo realized she'd been holding her breath the whole time he'd been talking. She let it out. She couldn't begin to imagine what horrors her son had endured these past few weeks. Her heart broke for the six soldiers who had lost their lives and their families who would suffer their loss. She bowed her head and silently prayed, *Dear Lord, thank you for watching over Ethan and for keeping him safe. Be with those families who lost their loved ones. Bless them with comfort and peace. Amen.*

Chloe, who had not spoken since the captain began his story, looked at Captain Reeves. "When can I see him?"

Lieutenant Colonel Wilkerson answered her question. "Lieutenant Colonel Breedlow will arrive at Langley Air Force Base within the hour. We're here to take you back with us."

Chloe put her hand over her heart and asked in a breathless voice, "Now? I can see Ethan today?"

Lieutenant Colonel Wilkerson smiled. "Yes, ma'am. We can leave as soon as you're ready."

With tear-filled eyes, Chloe reached out to Betty Jo and Lily, who took her hands in theirs. "I can hardly believe Ethan's coming home."

Lily patted her hand. "Thank God the nightmare is over."

Betty Jo squeezed Chloe's hand. "You need to get ready. The quicker you get there, the faster we can get Ethan home. Also, I think the children should be told you're going with these officers to get their daddy and bring him home. They don't need to know anything about the ordeal he's been through, just that their daddy's safe and is coming home."

After giving her mother-in-law's suggestion some thought, Chloe nodded in agreement. "I think you're right. The children need to know their daddy's coming home."

Releasing Chloe's hand, Betty Jo turned to Lily. "You should help Chloe pack. I'm going to the shop to tell Don the good news. I know he's anxious to know what's happened."

Betty Jo turned to the officers before heading out the door to find Don. "Y'all are welcome to wait here."

Just as she was turning the doorknob, Chloe grabbed her hand. Betty

Jo looked up to meet her threatening eyes. "I need to be the one to tell the children. Don't say anything to my children about their father." She released her hand and hurried up the stairs.

Betty Jo frowned as she stared after her. Why had Chloe felt she needed to be warned against telling the children? She'd had no intention of telling them. It was their mother's place to share the good news with them, not her. She shrugged, wondering when or if she'd ever understand her daughter-in-law.

As Betty Jo approached Don's shop, she caught the unmistakable high-pitched roar of a go-cart engine coming from inside. *Could Don and the children have actually fixed Ethan's old go-cart?* She quickened her steps. Opening the door left no doubt that the old go-cart had been revived.

She called out her husband's name, but her voice couldn't be heard over the engine. She walked over to find Matthew sitting low in the go-cart's seat with Don, Kelli, and Chase standing over him. She yelled, "Don, don't tell me you're going to let Matthew drive that thing."

A smile danced across Don's lips as he turned to her. "No, he's just revving it up. When we get it outside, I'll be the test driver. They'll need driving lessons before I let any of them drive it." He held out his arms toward the go-cart. "Check it out. We got it running!"

Betty Jo put her fingers in her ears as Matthew revved the engine. She leaned in close to Don's ear. "I need to talk to you alone."

Don nodded and held up one finger. He leaned over Matthew's shoulder and turned the key, shutting down the engine. "Good job, Matthew. Y'all get those rags over there and wipe it down. I'll be over here talking to your Gigi."

Matthew stood from his seat and gave him a thumbs-up. "Will do, Pops."

Betty Jo followed Don to the front of the shop. As soon as she reached his side, she blurted out, "They found Ethan. He's in good shape and on his way to Langley."

Don swayed on his feet. She reached out to hold him steady. He folded his hands as he looked up. "Thank you, Lord." When he looked back at her, she noticed tears in his eyes. "Our boy is coming home, Betty Jo. Our prayers have been answered."

When Don took her into his arms, Betty Jo felt the peace she'd longed for since she'd first learned Ethan was missing.

With Lily's help, it didn't take long for Chloe to get packed. By the time Betty Jo got back to the house, she was coming down the stairs with her suitcase in hand. She stopped her at the bottom of the stairs. "Chloe, I told Don the good news about Ethan. He's bringing the kids inside in just a minute for you to share the good news with them. I wanted to prepare you first. They are an excited bunch. They got Ethan's old go-cart running. I'm sure they're going to want to tell you all about it."

Chloe set down her suitcase. "You're kidding me! I never dreamed they'd ever get that old piece of junk running." She took a deep breath and squared her shoulders. "I'm ready for them."

They turned at the sound of three excited children running in the side door.

"Mama, we got it running!" Matthew called out.

"It's really cool, Mama," Kelli added.

Chloe sat down at the end of the living room couch.

Chase crawled up in his mother's lap. "Wait until you hear how loud it is!"

"Wow! That's just great." Chloe patted the couch cushion. "Kelli and Matthew, come sit here with me. I've got my own great news to tell you."

Kelli and Matthew sat down next to their mother. "What news?" Kelli asked.

"Your daddy's coming home!"

All three children jumped up and began cheering.

"I'm leaving in a few minutes with the two officers who are waiting for me in the kitchen to get your daddy and bring him home."

Kelli stopped mid-jump and asked, "Can I go with you?"

"Not this time, baby. You get to stay here with Gigi and Pops. Then when Daddy and I come home, we'll have a party."

"A big party with cake and ice cream?" Chase asked.

Chloe pulled him in close to her. "Yes, Chase, a big party. We are going to celebrate your daddy's coming home to us."

Chapter Twenty-Two

After the thunderstorm on Friday, Betty Jo was grateful to wake up to find the sun shining in through her bedroom window on this Saturday morning. She realized it was the first time in a very long time she'd slept soundly through the entire night. She rolled over and stretched, expecting to find Don still fast asleep beside her, but found his side of the bed empty. It wasn't like Don to be up and about this early in the morning, especially after the events of the day before. She got out of bed, took her robe from the chair, slipped it on, and began her search for her husband. She glanced over to the bathroom door thinking he might be taking a shower, but the door was wide open with the light off. She hoped she might find him in the kitchen surprising her by fixing breakfast for the family. She passed through the empty living room on her way to the kitchen. When she found the kitchen empty as well, it was becoming clear to her he wasn't inside the house. She looked out the back door, checking to make sure his truck was still parked in the driveway. It was, along with her car, exactly as they'd parked them when they'd arrived home yesterday.

Knowing her husband of over forty years as she did, the next two logical places to check would be his workshop or his greenhouse. He was always finding something in either place to tinker with. After his successful project of fixing up Ethan's old go-cart, he'd be looking for another endeavor to fill his days. She decided rather than traipsing outside through the wet grass looking for him, she'd fix a pot of coffee and start breakfast. She'd wait in the nice warm kitchen for him to come back to the house, and she hoped it would be soon. If he hadn't eaten anything since yesterday, he'd need to eat to keep his blood sugar from falling.

She was putting the final touches on the breakfast casserole when she caught the sound of soft footsteps descending the stairway. After putting the casserole in the oven, she turned to find Chase standing in the kitchen doorway rubbing sleep from his eyes. Her heart overflowed with love for her youngest grandchild. She hurried over to pick him up. He opened his arms to her and rested his sleepy head on her shoulders.

"What are you doing up so early?"

"I wanted to see if my daddy was home yet," he answered without lifting his head.

Still holding Chase, she pulled out a chair from the table and sat down. "It's way too early for your daddy to be home. He and your mommy will be home for supper tomorrow night. I'm going to make your daddy's favorite cake and Pops is going to grill steaks."

Chase pulled away, giving her a serious look. "And Daddy's going to be so happy to see us that he's never going to leave us again, right?"

Betty Jo gently placed her hand against his cheek. "Your daddy is going to be so happy to see you."

Chase put his hand on hers. "And he'll never leave us again, will he, Gigi?"

Betty Jo drew him in close to her. "Oh, Chase, I wish I could tell you that he won't ever leave again, but I can't. I can tell you that if he does have to leave again, he will miss you every single day until he comes back home."

"And I'll miss him until he comes home."

She rocked him back and forth. "That's right, Chase, until he comes home."

"Until who comes home?"

Startled by the voice, Betty Jo jumped. She turned around to find Matthew standing behind her chair. "Matthew, don't sneak up on me like that. You scared me half to death."

"I didn't mean to, Gigi. I just heard talking and thought Daddy might be home."

Betty Jo took Chase from her lap and sat him in the chair as she got up to check on the casserole. "I know both of you are excited about your daddy coming home. I'm excited too, but I told both of you last night that your daddy and mommy won't be back until suppertime tomorrow night. Y'all need to chill out."

Matthew sat down next to Chase. "Okay, Gigi, I'll try, but I'm not making any promises."

"How about y'all go upstairs and wake up Kelli? This casserole will be ready in about fifteen minutes. That gives us enough time for me to get Pops in here for breakfast while you get Kelli."

Matthew folded his arms in front of him. "I'd rather just stay right here and wait for my breakfast."

Betty Jo put her hand to her mouth, stifling a laugh. Her oldest grandson often made her laugh when she shouldn't. "If you want to have breakfast, you'd better get yourselves up those stairs to wake Kelli right now!"

Understanding that his grandmother was serious, Matthew quickly helped Chase off the chair and the two headed up the stairs to wake Kelli.

Going out through the garage door, Betty Jo took one of Don's jackets from the hook and put it on as she took off across the yard to Don's workshop. She was halfway to Don's shop when she heard sirens in the distance. She stopped, listening to see which direction they were heading. She couldn't tell if the siren was from an ambulance, fire truck, or the police car. Whichever it was, the sound was getting closer. It sounded as if they were heading straight for her house. Had something happened to Don? Had he called an ambulance?

She quickened her pace. With her heart pounding, she threw open the workshop door calling out his name, and frantically began to search the building for any sign of her husband. The go-cart was still in the same spot where he'd parked it alongside his beloved 1959 Chevy Apache truck. She searched through the shop looking in and around everything. Satisfied Don was not in his shop, she rushed out the back door to look for him in his greenhouse.

She had taken only a few steps toward the greenhouse when she heard the familiar, comforting sound of whistling. It was one of Don's favorite songs. Slowing her steps, she began to softly sing the words that went along with his tune:

"I've got the joy, joy, joy, joy down in my heart."

The door squeaked as it opened, but Don didn't seem to notice, completely caught up in his work. His back was to her, so she couldn't tell what he was busy doing. Not wanting to startle him, she began to sing a little louder as she walked up to him.

"Where? Down in my heart! Where? Down in my heart! I've got the joy, joy, joy, joy down in my heart to stay."

Still whistling, Don turned around to her. They finished the song together then fell into a laughing embrace.

When they parted, Betty Jo playfully hit him on the arm. "You scared me to half to death!"

Don rubbed his arm where she'd hit him. "Ouch! How did I do that?"

"I didn't know where you were and then I heard sirens and then—"

"You overreacted again, right?"

"Maybe a little." She stepped around him. "What are you doing in here?"

Don picked up his kitchen shears and turned back to his pots of blooming sunflowers. "I woke up early this morning, and when I saw the sun shining in through the window, I thought of my beautiful yellow Sundance Kid sunflowers that were blooming out here in my greenhouse. You know what these sunflowers stand for, don't you?"

Betty Jo took one of the cut sunflowers in her hand, admiring its bright yellow color. "No, I don't think I do." She smiled up at her husband. "Why don't you enlighten me?"

Don held one out at arm's length. "They stand for joy. And that's what I woke up feeling this morning—pure joy. Joy for my son no longer missing, and coming home. Joy for the love of my children and grandchildren. And most importantly, the joy I find every single day in loving you." He placed the sunflower in her hand.

Tears welled up in Betty Jo's eyes. "Oh, Don, that's one of the sweetest things you've ever said to me." Standing up on her tiptoes, she kissed him.

"I'm going to fill these two blue vases with these joyous sunflowers and put them in our home to welcome Ethan. Then I'm going to fill this white vase with sunflowers to share our joy with Aaron and Jenny on their wedding day."

"Oh, Don, that's perfect!"

Together, they began to arrange the sunflowers in the three vases.

"Do you know what Bible verse comes to my mind when I think of joy?"

Don stopped to think. "I'm not sure."

"'Consider it pure joy, my brothers and sisters, whenever you face trials of many kinds, because you know that the testing of your faith produces perseverance.' James 1:2-3."

Don nodded. "That's a good one for all we've been through lately. I think through our faith, we have shown perseverance, and now we have joy down in our hearts to stay."

"I agree." She smiled up at her husband.

As she went back to her arrangement she suddenly remembered. "Oh, my goodness gracious! I've gotta go. My breakfast casserole may be burned to a crisp." She was out the door and hurrying toward the house before Don could respond.

He rushed to the door to call after her. "If it's burned up, I'll take y'all out to breakfast."

The children enjoyed their breakfast out at the Dream Bean Coffee Shop. Instead of being upset about the fiasco with the burned breakfast casserole, Betty Jo decided to brush it off and put it down as a memory her grandchildren could laugh about in the years to come. As soon as they got home, she hurried to get all three children, as well as herself, ready for Aaron's wedding. Kelli was excited about wearing the brand-new dress her mother had bought her in Atlanta especially for today. The boys were less than thrilled to be putting on "Sunday clothes," as they called their new clothes, on a Saturday morning. From the looks Don was giving her, she knew he agreed with his grandsons. He'd much rather be headed to the pond to fish.

The wedding was scheduled to take place at eleven o'clock in the chapel of the church. Betty Jo hoped they wouldn't be late. She began to relax when they were dressed and on their way to the church by ten thirty. She was surprised to see the number of cars in the parking lot. She hurried the children and Don with his white vase filled with sunflowers inside the church and down the steps to the chapel.

Zeke, Blair's husband, was standing at the entrance to the chapel. Betty Jo took notice of how handsome he looked in his gray pinstripe suit. "Good morning, Zeke. You're looking mighty fine on this beautiful Saturday morning."

Zeke blushed, matching the pink rose in his lapel. "Thank you, Miss Betty Jo. You're looking your usual beautiful self."

Betty Jo was feeling beautiful in her new mint-green dress. "Why, thank you, Zeke."

Don handed Zeke the vase of flowers. "I brought these for the wedding."

Zeke took the vase and placed them on a table spilling over with gifts. "Thank you, Mr. Don." He held out his arm for Betty Jo to take and escorted her followed by her family to the pew behind Dixie's family.

Betty Jo glanced around the chapel. The first thing to catch her attention was the number of white tulips, red rosebuds, and blue irises— the flowers presented to Jenny during her White Bible Ceremony— decorating the chapel. The second thing to catch her attention was seeing Jason, looking healthy and handsome, sitting with his family in the pew in front of her family. Both filled her heart with joy and brought tears to her eyes.

As she opened her purse in search of a tissue to wipe her eyes, she felt a tap on her shoulder. She looked back to find Nona, Monty, and Riley seated in the pew behind her. Nona pointed to Jason. Betty Jo nodded. They smiled at one another knowing how happy Dixie was to have Jason sitting beside her.

Betty Jo was relieved when Lily and Kendall joined them in their pew. They arrived only seconds before Miss Louise, smiling from ear to ear in her bright pink dress, came walking down the aisle on Nathan's arm. A few steps behind them came Layne, looking proud and beautiful in her pale pink suit on the arm of the handsome groom. Before leaving his mother in her pew, Aaron leaned over and kissed her on both cheeks. He and Nathan then joined the minister at the front of the chapel and watched as their two precious nieces dressed in long white dresses came down the aisle. Both Rachel and Madison were to throw flowers as they made way for the bride, but in reality, only Rachel threw flowers. Madison waved to everyone then walked to the front of the chapel and curtsied. The guests laughed at the innocence of the moment, but when she started back down the aisle to repeat her performance, Blair whisked her away. Emma, Jenny's sister, looking stunning in a full-length pale pink strapless dress, made her way down the aisle.

When the organ sounded a chord calling all to attention, Layne stood, turning her attention to the back of the chapel and signaling all to stand. Betty Jo gasped when she saw Jenny standing there in a full-length vintage ivory wedding dress. It was the same dress Layne had worn on her wedding day with only a few modifications. Her eyes were sparkling under her ivory beaded lace veil. Her long dark hair cascaded across her shoulders and down her back. In her hands was a simple bouquet of pink roses. One of her arms was through Mark's. They stepped off as the organ began to play "The Bridal Chorus" from Wagner's Lohengrin, the traditional "Here Comes the Bride." When they reached the front of the chapel, Mark handed Jenny off to Aaron, then took his seat next to Layne. All the guests sat.

Watching the pomp and beauty of the wedding ceremony brought tears once again to Betty Jo's eyes. As she dabbed them away, she was thankful she'd uncovered a pack of tissues in her purse. She realized that not all the tears streaming down her cheeks were for the wedding. Some were tears of joy for Ethan being found alive and at this very moment being reunited with his wife. She looked down the pew at Don, Chase, Matthew, Kelli, Kendall, and Lily. Her heart was filled with gratitude to God for the many blessings He had showered on her family.

Her attention was drawn back to the front when she heard the minister announce, "You may kiss the bride." Aaron pulled back Jenny's veil, held her face in his hands, and lovingly kissed her. Jenny slipped her arm through Aaron's as they turned to their guests. The minister proclaimed in a loud voice, "I present to you, Mr. and Mrs. Aaron Patrick Weaver."

Joining the other guests, Betty Jo stood and began clapping as the bride and groom rushed down the aisle.

With concern on her face, Kelli looked up at her grandmother. "Gigi, why are you crying? Are you sad?"

Betty Jo wiped away her tears and leaned down to answer her granddaughter. "No, Kelli, these are tears of joy."

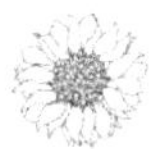

The reception following Jenny and Aaron's wedding was to be at the Columns. Jenny had fallen in love with its Southern charm at the White Bible Ceremony and insisted it was the perfect place for their wedding reception. Since it was a beautiful day and only a few blocks away from the church, most were walking. Don hurried out of the chapel to catch up with the children as they ran ahead. Betty Jo noticed Lily and Jason left the chapel together.

Betty Jo was by far the slowest of the walkers. Looking ahead, she noticed Nona and Dixie standing to the side waiting for her. Reaching them, she gave them a grateful smile. "Sorry I'm such a slowpoke. Thanks for waiting."

Nona chuckled. "No problem. We usually have to wait for the late Betty Jo."

Betty Jo playfully punched her arm. "Ha! Ha! Aren't you the funny one!"

Standing on one foot to adjust her shoe, Dixie grabbed hold of Nona's other arm for balance. "I, for one, was glad to have the chance to stop. I don't know what I was thinking when I put on these high heels. I haven't worn heels in months."

Betty Jo sighed. "Sorry, I can't empathize with you. I don't even remember the last time I wore heels!"

Releasing her grip on Nona's arm, Dixie took a couple of trial steps. "That's better. Let's go, or we'll be the late ones."

As the three resumed their trek to the Columns, Betty Jo looked over at Dixie. "Jason is looking good and much stronger than the last time I saw him. It's good to see him out and about."

Dixie smiled. "He does look good, doesn't he? I didn't ask him to come to the wedding. He decided that all on his own."

Nona nodded. "I'm glad he did."

"I am too." Dixie looked heavenward. "I'm praying it's a sign that he's wanting to join the world once again, but I'm not pushing him. I'm taking this one day at a time."

Betty Jo put her arm through Dixie's. "Good for you."

Dixie leaned in close to Betty Jo. "I know you have to be on cloud nine with Ethan coming home."

"I am. I cannot wait to see him in the flesh. Don and I talked to him last night, but only for a few minutes. I want him right here where I can touch him."

"We're here," Nona announced. "And we're not the last ones."

Kelli and Matthew came running down the steps toward Betty Jo. "Gigi, we've been waiting on you. Pops said we couldn't go inside until you got here."

"Well, I'm here now, so let's go in." Betty Jo took hold of Don's outstretched hand. The two followed their grandchildren inside.

The Columns was decorated much like it had been for the White Bible Ceremony with the white and pale pink ribbons draped across the ceiling. One thing that was different was the table beneath the crystal chandelier. Instead of holding an enormous silver vase filled with flowers, it held the white Bible they had presented to Jenny. Beside the Bible were pink highlighters and pens. In a silver frame standing on the other side of the Bible were directions the guests were to follow.

Please highlight your favorite scripture and sign your name next to it.

Don looked at Betty Jo. "I don't think I've ever seen anything like this at a wedding reception."

She shook her head. "Me either, but I like the idea." She took one of the highlighters from the table. "I know exactly what verse I'm going to highlight." She turned to James 1 and marked verses two and three.

When she glanced up at Don, he was smiling. "That's exactly the passage I was thinking of myself. Go ahead and sign both of our names to it. I'm sure they will have trials in their lives and find the joy in their perseverance."

Chase pulled on Betty Jo's sleeve. "Gigi, I'm hungry. Can we go home?"

Betty Jo finished signing their names to the verses, then took Chase by the hand. "We just got here. I promise you they're going to have plenty to eat. You won't be hungry for long."

She was right about having plenty to eat, and the best part according to the children, was the pizza table. Once the children found that, she didn't hear any more complaints about wanting to go home.

The Fearsome Foursome, along with their husbands and Monty, Riley, and Miss Louise, sat at one large round table eating, laughing, talking, and sharing stories. Betty Jo couldn't remember the last time they'd all been together when there wasn't some crisis they were having to deal with. So much had happened in their lives over these past few years. She knew most likely more crises would come their way, but for now, it was nice to simply enjoy one another's company.

Betty Jo was half-listening to Don tell a story she'd already heard more than a few times. She leaned closer to Layne. "That was truly a beautiful wedding. Jenny and Aaron looked so happy and in love the whole time."

"I thought the same thing. The day Jenny came into our lives was a Godsend. She just fit right into our family."

"What a blessing. I keep thinking Chloe will fit into our family, but . . ."

Layne frowned. "I know what you mean. With one son, I feel like his wife is my daughter, but with the other son, I don't know how I feel about his wife."

Betty Jo arched one brow. "You're talking about Heather, right?"

Layne nodded. "I'm not sure how much longer she's going to be a part of our family. Things don't seem right between Nathan and her. You noticed she didn't show up for the wedding?"

"I did notice that. You know, I went through a child's divorce with Lily. I was worried about what it would do to Kendall, but it's turned out for the best for all three of them." Betty Jo glanced over to the table where Lily and Jason were sitting. "You just never know. Life can surprise you sometimes."

Layne noticed where Betty Jo was looking. "How very true."

Betty Jo's attention was brought back to Don when the men at the table began to laugh. She smiled. He always did get a laugh from telling that story.

Everyone at the table gave Monty their attention when he suddenly stood up and tapped his glass with his knife. "I would appreciate it if y'all would kindly give me your attention."

Betty Jo noticed that the whole room had grown quiet, even the children's pizza area. Monty waved his hand toward Nona. "As many of you know, I have been dating this beautiful, intelligent, close-to-perfect woman to my left for some time."

A pink blush colored Nona's cheeks as she gave a slight shrug of her shoulders. "I don't know about close-to-perfect."

The guests chuckled.

Monty grinned. "True. She's not close-to-perfect. She is perfect. . ." He paused as he looked down at Nona, the smile gone from his face, only love shining through his eyes. "For me."

In one swift move, he pushed back his chair, got down on one knee in front of her, took a small jewelry box from his suit's breast pocket, opened it, and held out a three-row diamond and emerald engagement ring to Nona. "Will you spend the rest of your life with me? Marry me, Nona, please."

Nona gasped. Her hands went up to her mouth. Her face lit up as she reached out to put her arms around his neck. "Yes, Michael Montgomery, I will spend the rest of my life with you. I will marry you."

They kissed for a long time, ignoring the cheers that erupted around them.

231

Chapter Twenty-Three

*A*fter Jenny and Aaron cut the cake, threw the bridal bouquet—which Lily caught—and left for their honeymoon, Betty Jo and Don rounded up the children and headed for home.

No one spoke for several miles. Betty Jo sat silently as she contemplated the events of the day. She couldn't be any more thrilled for Nona. She'd liked Monty from the start. She was confident the two of them would be happy together. After proposing, Monty told the group that he'd asked Mr. James for Nona's hand only days before he'd passed away. Mr. James had been in his clear mind on that day. He'd told Monty that Nona had a mind of her own and he couldn't answer for her, but he'd be proud to have him as part of their family.

"Well, I have to say that was one of the best wedding receptions I've ever attended."

Don's words brought Betty Jo back to the present. "It was an eventful day for sure." She turned around to check on the children in the backseat. She found them leaning against one another, fast asleep. "Looks like we'll be carrying three youngins upstairs to bed for a nap."

"They sure were good at the reception. Hardly heard a word out of them."

"That's because they were in a pizza coma."

Don nodded in agreement, but his attention was on the black SUV he spotted parked in their driveway. "What in the world is that car doing here again?"

Betty Jo felt her body stiffen with fear. *Were the two officers back to let them know something had gone terribly wrong with Ethan's return?*

Don stared straight ahead. "Well, I'll be darned."

Betty Jo followed Don's gaze. Stepping off the front porch, waving both hands as he walked toward them was Ethan, their son who was lost and now was found. She got out of the car. More than anything, she wished her legs could run. Instead, she stood and held her arms out to him just like she'd done when he was a toddler and she was paralyzed. An understanding smile crossed his face. He ran into her arms, lifting her off her feet as he swung her around.

Betty Jo held him close. "Thank, God, you're home. You had us worried."

Still holding his mother, Ethan said, "I didn't worry, Mom, because I knew you were praying for me. I felt God watching over me every minute."

She held onto the back of his head as she looked into his eyes. "I trusted Him to watch over you and bring you home."

Suddenly, the back door of the car flew open as three children came pouring out.

"Daddy! You're home!"

Ethan pulled all three children into his arms, showering them with kisses. As Betty Jo watched, she couldn't remember when she'd felt God's blessings more than at this very moment in time. She looked heavenward. "Thank you, God!"

-Three Weeks Later-

Betty Jo was in the laundry room at the back of the house, folding another basket of laundry she'd just taken out of the dryer when she heard Ethan call out from the kitchen, "Mom, have you seen the keys to my truck? I'm sure I hung them up on the hook in the kitchen."

Shaking her head, she recalled one of her mother's sayings that she never understood until now. *The more things change, the more they stay the same.* There was no doubt that things had changed since Ethan had lived at home as a teenager, but his problem of misplacing his keys had stayed the same. She knew she'd mostly likely find them in the catch-all basket by the garage door, just as she had years ago when he'd misplaced them.

She called back. "Did you check the basket by the garage door?"

There was silence for a few minutes while he searched. "Got 'em. Thanks, Mom."

She turned back to her folding. She looked at the pile of laundry still waiting to go in the washer. It seemed as if it was never ending, but she knew it was going to end very soon. Ethan and his family would be moving to St. Mary's by the end of the month, and their laundry would be going with them.

She had mixed feelings about their leaving. On the one hand, she'd loved having her grandchildren living here and getting to know them for the precious, fun-loving children they were. On the other hand, with all the extra work involved in taking care of three young children, she rarely had time to herself and to do other activities she enjoyed. She felt guilty when she thought of the peace and quiet she and Don would have once again after they moved out. The good in all of this was that they would be only a few hours away. They could visit often instead of twice a year like it had been when Ethan was working at the Pentagon.

"More laundry?"

Startled by Don's voice, Betty Jo jumped.

He stepped into the room. "Sorry, I didn't mean to scare you. I wanted to tell you that I have to run to town for a couple of things. Wanted to check with you to see if you needed anything."

Don's new project was fixing up a 1944 World War II US Army Jeep. From the shape it was in, Betty Jo was sure it'd be his project for quite some time. "We could use a gallon of milk."

"Another gallon? Didn't I just buy one the other day?"

"Yes, and it's almost gone. I have Skinny Dippers this morning, so I won't be home when you get back. Don't just set the milk on the counter. Please put it in the fridge."

Don pursed his lips. "I only did that once, and that was because I was in a hurry."

"Well, don't be in a hurry today."

"Okay." Don kissed her on his way out of the laundry room.

She checked her watch. If she hurried, she could finish folding the basket of laundry and still get to her meeting on time.

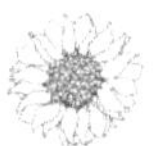

Betty Jo got a parking place right in front of the Dream Bean Coffee Shop. That rarely happened. She usually had to drive around the block at least once before she found a place to park. She looked around to see if Layne, Dixie, or Nona had already arrived. She didn't see their cars. As she climbed the stairs up to the Skinny Dippers meeting, she wondered who'd been hired to take Doreen's place. They hadn't had a meeting for the past two weeks, but were told last week that someone had been hired to be in charge of the meetings.

When she pulled the meeting room door open, she was surprised to find the room empty. She had a panic moment as she wondered if she'd come on the wrong day. She pulled her cell phone out of the side pocket of her purse to check the day and date. It was Tuesday, but looking at the time, she realized she was fifteen minutes early. She looked down at her watch to see that it was running fifteen minutes fast. That's when she remembered she'd purposefully set her watch fifteen minutes fast so she wouldn't be late picking the kids up from school yesterday. She slapped her head with the heel of her hand and took a seat in the empty room.

She took her watch off her arm and was correcting the time when she heard the swish of the door opening. Coming through the doorway was a short, stocky woman with inch-long spiked, shockingly white hair. She had piercings in one eyebrow and nostril. She wore black leggings that accentuated the rolls and dimples in her rather round bottom and a long purple T-shirt with "Why Fit In When You Were Born To STAND OUT!" across the front. Sure the woman was lost, Betty Jo asked, "May I help you?"

The woman looked at Betty Jo with a bright smile. "Is this the room where the Skinny Dippers meet?"

The woman's soft, slow, liquid drawl wasn't the voice Betty Jo expected. "Yes, it is."

Holding out her hand, the woman strolled over to where Betty Jo sat. "I'm your new Skinny Dippers leader, Brenda Harris."

Brenda didn't look like any leader they'd ever had. Betty Jo hoped her face didn't show her surprise. She stood to shake Brenda's outstretched hand. "Nice to meet you. I'm Betty Jo Breedlow."

Brenda put her other hand on top of Betty Jo's as she looked directly into her eyes. "It's my pleasure to meet you, Betty Jo."

Betty Jo could feel Brenda's sincerity as their eyes met. She noticed her clear blue eyes sparkle when she spoke. She decided in that moment she was going to like their new leader.

As the room began to fill up, Betty Jo searched for her friends. She couldn't wait to see their reactions when they met their new leader. Most likely their first impression of Brenda would be exactly as hers had been. Of all the days for all three of them to be late, it looked like it was going to be this day. Brenda called the meeting to order. Betty Jo moved to the back of the room, saving three seats. She couldn't wait for them to get there.

She'd just sat down when Nona, Layne, and Dixie came through the door together. Betty Jo waved to them. They hurried to take the seats she'd saved.

Nona looked around the room. "This place is packed. No wonder we couldn't find a parking place."

Keeping her voice soft, Dixie leaned close to Betty Jo. "How's the new leader?"

She smiled and pointed to the front of the room where Brenda stood ready to address the group. Out of the corner of her eye, she watched her friends for their reaction.

Brenda spread out her arms. "Welcome to Skinny Dippers! I'm Brenda Harris, your new leader."

Nona's jaw dropped. Layne's hands went to her mouth. Dixie's eyes grew wide. The three turned and stared openmouthed at Betty Jo.

Betty Jo leaned in close so all three could hear her. "Don't be so quick to judge her. Just listen. I promise you're going to be pleasantly surprised." She leaned back, giving her full attention to their new leader.

"I know some of you are wondering why I was chosen to lead your group. I may not look like the one to lead the weight-loss charge, but I'm going to do my best to motivate and encourage each one of you." By the end of the meeting, all four friends were convinced Brenda was going to be a great Skinny Dippers leader.

When the meeting was over, the friends headed down the back stairs to the coffeeshop. As soon as they were seated in their usual booth, Nona turned to Betty Jo. "Okay, you were right. I was pleasantly surprised."

Dixie nodded in agreement. "I think we finally have a winner."

Layne ran her fingers through her hair. "Do y'all realize how many years we've been going to these Skinny Dippers meetings and how many leaders we've had?"

Dixie began to count on her fingers. "Seven years?"

Layne rolled her eyes. "Almost nine years!" She let that number sink in. "And how much weight have y'all lost in those nine years?"

Betty Jo chuckled and put her hands palms up on the table. "Not sure how much, if any, I've lost, but I can tell you that I love it when Tuesdays come around so I can go to my Skinny Dippers meeting and be with y'all."

Dixie put her hands over Betty Jo's. "Being with y'all, sitting here in this booth together, and sharing what's going on in our lives is the highlight of my week."

Nona spread her arms wide. "If only these walls could talk, what a tale they would tell."

They all laughed.

"Y'all are in a good mood this morning," Anna Clare said, pulling out her pad and taking the pencil from behind her ear. "What can I get for y'all this morning? The usual, or are you going to be adventurous today?"

Betty Jo rested her elbows on the table and made a steeple with her fingers. "What would you suggest we have that would be 'adventurous'?"

Anna Clare tapped her pencil on her pad. "Hmm. How about Quinoa Breakfast Bowl or an Avocado Egg Toast or—"

Betty Jo held up her hands. "Enough, Anna Clare, I'll stick with my usual blueberry muffin and coffee."

"Same here."

"The usual for me."

"And me."

Anna Clare wagged her finger at the four of them. "Y'all are not at all brave."

Nona gave a dismissive wave of her hand. "I disagree with her. I think we're some of the bravest women I know."

"You are so right, Nona." Layne pounded the table. "I can't think of one time any of has backed down from a life challenge. And, you must admit, we've had our share of life's challenges these past few years."

Dixie blew out her cheeks. "You're right about that. I had this crazy notion that when my children were all grown and I retired, life would be smooth sailing. Boy, was I wrong!"

Betty Jo scoffed. "'Smooth sailing'? Ha! It's more like trying to keep your head above water in rough seas, praying you won't drown."

They were silent for a minute as they considered Betty Jo's statement.

"I know our faith in God anchors our lives." Betty Jo reached out both of her hands to the middle of the table. "And I know one other thing for sure." She paused as she looked around the booth at her friends. "I know I would have drowned in those rough seas if it weren't for each one of you, my friends. Your loving support and friendship have been my lifesavers."

Layne, Nona, and Dixie reached in to take hold of Betty Jo's hands. Their faces shone bright with forgiveness, with hope, with peace, and with joy. They were The Fearsome Foursome.

The End

About the Author

Carol has always been a devoted reader of Women's Fiction. However, as she grew older and wiser, she noticed the characters in her books were not aging along with her. It appeared as if most of the main characters the authors were creating were never older than forty. If there was, by chance, the mention of a character in the ripe old age of fifty or more, they were either there to support or hinder the younger main character.

When Carol retired after thirty years of teaching, she decided it was time to follow her life-long dream of writing a novel. Drawing on her disappointing reading experiences of forty-year-old main characters, she was determined to write a Women's Fiction book series about women who had aged past forty. Her idea grew into the Kerry Book Series.

Carol's Kerry Book Series features four retired, vibrant, Southern women–Layne, Nona, Dixie, Betty Jo– who have been friends for more years than they can remember. Their friendship, along with their faith in God, gives them the strength and courage they need to make it through life's trials.

Carol released her first book in the series, *Forgiveness.* She then followed with her second book, *Hope* (Nona). *Peace* (Dixie), was Carol's third book in the series. *Joy* (Betty Jo), completes the series.

Acknowledgments

As I end my Kerry Book Series with this final book *Joy,* there are several people I want to thank. I thank the love of my life my husband, David. You helped me to believe that I can do anything I set my mind to and you've helped me achieve what I once thought was impossible. I couldn't have written these four books without you. I thank Kris, my daughter, for her honesty, even when I didn't want to hear it. Thank you to my sister Kathy for believing in me from the very beginning and brightening my dark days. Thanks goes to my sister Barbara for cheering me on.

I am eternally grateful to the best friends in the world—— Linda, Julie, and Olivia—for not laughing when I said I was going to write a book series. My thanks and appreciation to Dawn, my niece, and J. D., my nephew, for their expertise. Thank you to Ellen Tarver, my editor, for helping me fine-tune my craft.

Thank you to everyone who has taken time out of their day to read my books. Thank you to those who purchased my book and helped calm my fear that I wouldn't sell any. Thank you to those who have recommended my books to their friends and continue to spread the word. Thank you to everyone who showed up for my very first book signing to show your support and to Lydia and Pat for hosting it. Thank you to everyone who has reviewed my book - there is no greater gift to an author. Thank you to everyone who has sent me honest and kind words - it means more than you know.

And, the most important thank you...THANK YOU to God for His many blessings and for His gifts of forgiveness, hope, peace, and joy.

May God bless each and every one of you!

Carol